Praise for
FURNACE

'Alexander Gordon Smith employs tight, gutsy language to tell Alex's story . . . This is a punch-between-the-eyes kind of read, punishing in every sense, Gothic in its horrors, darkly claustrophobic . . . Readers may find the wait between volumes a long stretch.' *Financial Times*

'An adrenaline-packed thriller for teens that grumpy boys will gulp down as escapism.' Amanda Craig, *The Times*

'[*Furnace*] will be addictive and gripping for teenage readers who like their villains really, really bad and the fear factor ramped up high. The start of an adventure series – but not for sensitive souls.' *Daily Mail*

'Smith is a fantastic writer; the prose is sharp and focused, with descriptions that bring this alternate reality to life.' *Bookbag*

'You'd be a fool to miss out on this tense, exciting and terrifying read.' *Flipside Magazine*

Other praise for Alexander Gordon Smith:

'*The* such an
enterta mouthed
with e cters and

Death s

wishing you were just a little bit more like them your-self . . . this one rattles, rocks and rolls.' John Boyne, author of *The Boy in the Striped Pyjamas*

'*The Inventors* is a rip-roaringly exciting tale.' *Independent on Sunday*

'*The Inventors* is a captivating story that should not be missed.' G. P. Taylor, author of *Shadowmancer*

FURNACE: DEATH SENTENCE

Alexander Gordon Smith, 30, is the author of *Furnace: Lockdown* and *Furnace: Solitary*, as well as *The Inventors*, which was shortlisted for the 2005 Wow Factor competition, and *The Inventors and the City of Stolen Souls*. He has also written a number of non-fiction books, as well as hundreds of articles for various magazines. He is the founder of Egg Box Publishing, an independent press that promotes talented new writers and poets, and is the co-owner of Fear Driven Films, a production company shooting its first feature in 2009. He lives in Norwich.

Find out more at:
www.alexandergordonsmith.com

BENEATH HEAVEN IS HELL
BENEATH HELL IS

FURNACE

DEATH SENTENCE

ALEXANDER GORDON SMITH

F.
188L1

ff

faber and faber

To Matthew, my brother,
so close, so far away.
I hope that one day
I can share these stories with you.

First published in 2009
by Faber and Faber Limited
Bloomsbury House, 74–77 Great Russell Street,
London, WC1B 3DA

Typeset by Faber and Faber Limited
Printed in the UK by CPI Bookmarque, Croydon

A CIP record for this book
is available from the British Library

ISBN 978–0–571–24561–1

2 4 6 8 10 9 7 5 3 1

DEAD

I died in that room.

I died there amongst the corpses in the darkness at the bottom of the world. I died with the fires of the incinerator still burning on my flesh, like hell itself had its fingers in me. I died with the warden's howls of laughter ringing in my ears.

But it wasn't a merciful death. My heart didn't stop beating. My lungs didn't stop clawing at the hot air. The white-hot pain didn't leave my muscles, my skin, my bones. And I didn't drift into oblivion the way I'd always dreamed death would be. No, I was in Furnace Penitentiary. And here even death doesn't dare show its face. The Grim Reaper had abandoned me like everyone else, leaving me alone with my nightmares.

They say your life flashes before your eyes when you die. Well, that's only half true. You don't see the happy times, the laughter. You only see your failures. Lying there with the thunder of the blacksuits raging above my head and the smell of burning flesh in my throat, I saw the endless mistakes of my life laid bare.

1

I saw my crimes, the night my old friend Toby and I had broken into our last house. I saw the blacksuits, Moleface pulling the trigger that reduced Toby to a stain on the carpet. I saw my trial for his murder, the way the world turned against me with the crash of a gavel. I saw my first day in Furnace, buried forever beneath the ground.

I pictured Donovan, and Zee, our plan to escape. I saw us smuggling gas-filled gloves from the kitchen into the chipping room and blowing out the floor. I saw our punishment for trying to escape – trapped in the guts of the prison with the rats hungry for our blood, and the lightless coffin of solitary confinement.

I was forced to relive the horror of what they'd done to Donovan. Stripped of everything human, packed with muscle and gristle and something bad that dripped darkness into his veins. Then the horror of what *I* had done to him. Pressing a pillow to his face until he was no longer a monster, until he was no longer anything. I saw it all, the worst bits of my life paraded in front of me by my own stuttering heartbeat.

I tried to remember something good. Something hopeful. I mean, we'd almost made it after that. Me and Zee and the kid called Simon. We'd almost climbed our way to freedom up the incinerator chimney. I still had that splinter of daylight in my mind. I had seen the sun, and it had seen me, and maybe that was enough. Maybe I could die now knowing I'd broken Furnace, knowing that I had breathed fresh air once again.

Except the death Furnace had in store for me wasn't

a genuine one. The blacksuits had lit the incinerator when we were halfway up, and they had pulled us from the flames with hunger in their silver eyes. And I knew what was coming.

My my, look what the rats dragged in. Get them into surgery, prep the wheezers. We can still use them.

The echo of the warden's voice, one of the last things I would ever hear. Because I died in that room. Like all the other lost boys of Furnace I would soon be reborn, but I wouldn't be me. I would become a blacksuit, my heart as dark as my jacket. Or I'd become a rat, trapped in the tunnels of the prison and feasting on those I had once called friends.

But even as I felt myself dragged off to the infirmary I swore that it wasn't over.

Just don't forget your name, Monty had told me. I wouldn't.

I died in that room.

I would be reborn as something else, something terrible.

But I was Alex Sawyer.

And I would have my revenge.

THE IV

Welcome back, old friend.

I thought I heard the tunnel walls laughing as I was carried through them – deep chuckles that could have been distant earthquakes. Somewhere inside I knew it must have been the echo of the blacksuits, but the injuries in my mind were just as bad as the ones on my skin and reality was a distant memory. I was living inside a nightmare now, a place where Furnace was a creature that howled with delight as we were pulled back into its belly, dragged to the infirmary.

Every atom of my being was in agony. God knows how badly I'd been burned when I'd hit the incinerator flames. I would have opened my eyes to see if I'd been barbecued, but they wouldn't obey. I would have lifted a hand to check that I still had my eyes, but I couldn't find the strength. I would have screamed, but there was barely enough air in my smoke-ravaged lungs to breathe.

So instead I tried to shut down my brain. Tried to forget that I'd ever been alive. Tried to flood my body with absence – a black tide that would douse the pain in my flesh. Maybe if I could do that then death would sneak in, snatch me up right from under their noses. It worked for the fraction of a second until I heard the voice.

'Oh no you don't, Alex,' the warden hissed, snapping me back into my body. 'Death can't have what belongs to me.' The whisper grew louder, accompanied by wicked shrieks I knew all too well. 'Get those wheezers to work. We haven't got long. And find me an IV, *now*!'

I was lowered onto something which should have been soft but which felt like acid against my burned skin. I tried once more to leave my head. Maybe if I could just escape my skull for an instant then death would take me, carry me up through the rock towards that sliver of daylight I had glimpsed only minutes ago.

Then I felt the needle in my arm, and something cold rushed into my veins. I knew exactly what it was, I'd seen it before on Gary, on Donovan – a drip full of evil, not quite black, not quite silver, with specks of starlight floating in its dark weight. It was the warden's poison, the stuff that turned you into a monster.

I tried to fight it, to buck my body until the needle came out, but the pain was too great and I could feel the leather straps holding me tight against the infirmary bed. The panic grew like a living thing in my chest and I made one last mental effort to escape, to leave my flesh behind and vanish like smoke. But the liquid nightmare flowed into me like molten lead, filling my veins and arteries and weighing me down. And it's impossible to escape anything when the chains are inside you.

It was only a matter of seconds before it reached my brain. To my surprise it numbed the agony. I felt the same way I had years ago – a lifetime ago – when I'd broken my wrist and the doctors had given me morphine. It was like I was no longer connected to anything physical, like my mind was free.

I should have known better than to hope. For a blissful instant I felt nothing, then the floodgates opened and something far worse than physical pain burst into my head.

This time I managed to scream.

It was as if the warden had ridden into my mind on the wave of poison, because I could swear his voice came from inside my skull.

It's over, he said, the sound of him causing rotten images to sprout from the shadows in my head. I saw something that looked like flyblown meat, something else that could have been a dead dog, there for only a second before evaporating. The warden continued: *Everything you ever were, everything you are now, and everything you ever wanted to be, it's over.*

I wanted to argue, wanted to open my mouth and tell him he was wrong, but his words were like maggots burrowing into the flesh of my brain. They gorged and grew fat on his dry laughter, revealing visions so horrific that I couldn't bear to make sense of them.

There is nothing to be gained in fighting. What flows inside you now is far more powerful than that fallacy you call a soul. Let it take you, for without it you are nothing.

'I am something . . . I am Alex . . .' I tried to say, but even inside my own head his voice was stronger than mine.

You are nothing, you can be nothing. Surrender yourself and be done. You were never Alex Sawyer, because Alex Sawyer never existed.

'You're wrong. I'm . . .' I began, but my words were so weak I could barely hear them. He cut me off with another laugh, and this time when he spoke his voice was like fingers sliding into my brain.

Alex Sawyer never existed. You are one of us.

The fingers flexed, as if they were pulling something out of me, and with nothing more than a whimper I fell into the gaping emptiness that had once been my soul.

I was standing in a muddy trench, and for a moment I thought I was free. Then I glanced up at the sky and saw an endless void of darkness and knew that I was dreaming.

To my left and right were slick earth walls the colour of blood, sheer and too high to climb. Not that I'd have wanted to – beyond I could make out dull explosions which shook the air and caused a fine rain of soil. I was about to take my eyes from the sides of the trench when I noticed a vague shape in the mud. I couldn't quite make out what it was until two slits appeared and a pair of eyes stared back at me.

By the time a mouth had opened up beneath those eyes and unleashed a groan of desperation I was already running. The ground gripped my feet the way it always did in dreams, slowing my escape. And when I looked down it was hands I saw pushing from the mud – cracked and broken fingers snatching at my legs. I kicked out at them, trying not to lose my balance, trying not to fall.

But there were simply too many, dozens of hands and faces emerging from the soil like the living dead. I felt the world spin, saw the ground rush up to meet me. There was no impact. Before I could land the trench seemed to freeze – all except for a puddle of filth right beneath my face. The muddy water bulged up, then slowly parted to reveal a face beneath, caked in dirt but still familiar.

'What do you want?' I asked it, although my voice made no sound.

The mouth opened and moved as though it was speaking, but again I could hear nothing.

'Who are you?' I asked wordlessly, studying the eyes, the nose, trying to remember where I'd seen the face before. It didn't stop talking, but there may as well have been a sheet of soundproof glass between us. I focused on its lips, caked in mud but visible.

Don't . . . I made out, reading the way they moved.

forget . . . It could have been any of a million words but somehow I knew. Just like I knew what was coming next.

your name, the figure mimed. I opened my mouth to

reply, but before I could do so the face morphed into an expression of pure terror, its eyes like diamonds set into the wet earth. It was only then that I recognised myself in the mud, the face a mirror image of my own. It – *I* – tried to say something else but my mirror face was sucked back into the ground, mud filling its mouth and nose, flowing over its still-open eyes until nothing remained.

'Wait!' I yelled. 'Wait!'

Then the rest of the trench once again found life, zombie hands grabbing my legs and clothes and head and pulling me down into the grave. My heart lurched, the sensation of being buried alive too terrifying for my sleeping mind. The trench exploded into dust, darkness flooding in like water and propelling me back to the surface. I rose from the dream like a drowning man, gasping for air and clutching at the night.

It didn't take long for me to remember that the real world was even more horrific than my nightmare.

But far worse was the fact that, for several seconds after waking, I couldn't remember who I was.

UNDER THE KNIFE

Even though I was still blind I knew the warden was watching me. I squirmed, like an ant trying to escape a lit match, but the bed held me tight in its leather grip and his only reaction was another hateful laugh.

'Did you dream?' he asked, his voice at once distant and whispered in my ear. Part of me was glad that I couldn't see. It meant I didn't have to look at his eyes – or the place where his eyes should have been if anybody had been able to meet them. 'Everybody dreams the first few times.'

I opened my mouth, hoping that some words would tumble out, but it was so dry that my defiance lodged in my throat.

'Dreams of dark places,' the warden went on. I could hear the tap of his shoes as he moved around my bed, right to left. Behind that was another sound, a heart monitor matching my own weak pulse beep for beat. I remembered the machines I'd seen by the beds in the infirmary, knew that's where I was now, just another test subject for Furnace's bad science. The thought should have terrified me, but the poison in my veins imprisoned my emotions the same way the straps gripped my body.

Again I tried to speak, spitting out a dry husk of a word that even I couldn't have interpreted. But the warden seemed to know exactly what I meant.

'Zee? Yes, he is here. And that freak who let you out of your cage. But they, like you, are about to pass from this fitful existence into something far more meaningful. Tell me.' The bed creaked as the warden sat on the edge of the mattress. 'Tell me what you saw when you slept.'

Already the dream had drained from my mind, leaving nothing but a residue that sat in my gut like a cannonball. I remembered a trench, bodies buried in the mud, and my own twisted reflection sucked down into the grave. I kept my mouth shut, not wanting to give the warden the satisfaction of an answer, but again he seemed to scoop the thoughts right out of my head.

'The trench,' he whispered, the glee in his voice like rancid honey. 'The fallen army. Fascinating. But then I was expecting no less from you.' The bed shifted, the rustle of the warden's suit as he once again continued pacing. 'That's twice now you almost escaped. Once, that was impressive.' For the first time since I'd been caught I heard an edge of anger in the warden's voice and I pushed myself back into the bed to escape it. But I could sense his face right above mine, his foul breath on my skin. 'Twice? That was just rude.'

He spoke again and I struggled for a moment to hear what he was saying until I realised it wasn't directed at me. A wheeze rattled across the room and I felt the panic rise up even through the cloud of poison. The warden spoke a few more whispered words before his voice returned to me.

'Of course it all seems to have worked out. I have you to thank for leading the vermin to us. We managed to cull quite a few of those rat bastards, and others have been rounded up. You'll see them again soon. A few of my men perished, and a few more had to be . . . *put down*. But we can always make more.' He laughed, a childish snigger that made my charred skin crawl. 'Speaking of which, we should get started. The nectar will keep you alive for so long, but only the knife can save you.'

Another wheezed groan cut across the room, followed by one echo, then two. Against the black canvas of my blindness I pictured the creatures staggering towards me, gas masks stitched onto rotting faces, filthy needles strapped to their chests, and scalpels held out to my face. I fought against my restraints until I felt the leather cut my skin, until my muscles cramped, but I was powerless.

'Don't fight it,' the warden said, his voice fading as though he was walking away. 'It is a new birth.'

Then something cold pressed itself against my mouth, gas choked its way down my throat, and once again I tumbled into oblivion.

12

This time there was no trench, just a bare room. Lined up facing one wall, on their knees, were six figures. Each had his hands cuffed behind his back and his forehead pressed against the chipped bricks. I couldn't see their faces but, this being a dream, I knew what they looked like – all boys about my age, their expressions drawn from hunger and stained with tears. They were dressed in dirty cloth overalls that could have been Furnace uniforms except there were only two numbers stencilled on the back of each. The same two numbers: 36. And beneath them, almost unrecognisable against the filth of the fabric, a symbol that sent chills down my spine even in my sleep.

Swastikas. The unmistakable insignia of the Nazis.

'Who are you?' I asked them, but nothing escaped my mouth. I shouted the question once more, then screamed it, but the room's heavy silence remained undisturbed. There was no movement, either, the scene as still as a photograph – until one of the boys started to move. It began as a tremor that made his overalls ripple like water. Then his head started to shake wildly from side to side, his body soon following until he was thrashing wildly against the wall.

Within seconds another of the boys was suffering a similar fit, then a third, until every one of the kids resembled a marionette being jerked by a lunatic puppeteer. Their convulsions became so violent that their hair was torn loose, their skin started to split. Their heads smashed from side to side so quickly that I could no longer make out their faces, each a blur that painted the wall red.

The boy who had first started fitting suddenly stopped, snapping his cuffs as though they were paper. He lurched to his feet and turned, and I saw a face that was right at home here in a nightmare. His skin hung off him in strips, his jaw dislocated and drooping, and his silver eyes blazed into mine with pure, undiluted hatred.

Rats.

The other kids stopped spasming and wrenched their way free from their restraints, leaving bloody handprints on the wall as they stood. I found myself face to face with a line of vermin ready to tear me limb from limb. The fear which made me want to run was also the thing that kept me rooted to the spot, and I could do nothing but watch as they staggered towards me.

Something exploded in my ear, the noise so loud that my heart missed a beat. It came again, the blast of a shot, then again and again as bullets tore through the air and punched into the transformed boys. In a heartbeat the room was full of smoke and the kids were nothing but corpses.

A voice replaced the gunshots, a language I didn't speak but a tone I could easily understand. I felt the sting of the hot gun barrel against my temple and closed my eyes, praying for silence once again so that I wouldn't hear the shot that killed me.

When I woke the sensation of being executed was almost real. The front of my face burned as it had when

I was lying in the incinerator, a pressure in my eyes that felt like something was trying to crawl into my head. My arms were still locked tight, and there was nothing to stop the panic spewing up from my gut – until I realised that instead of darkness I was bathed in a halo of weak light.

I snatched in a long breath, tried to clamp down on the fear. I blinked, hoping that the fuzzy glow before me would focus into something recognisable. It didn't, remaining a featureless cloud of milky grey. I scrunched up my face, feeling something tied tight around my head, and suddenly knew what had happened.

When they took off my bandages I would have eyes of cold silver.

I wanted to cry, but the warden's poison – what had he called it, *nectar*? – still lay heavy across my thoughts and stopped the emotions breaking free. Even so, the image of myself with the eyes of a blacksuit, of a rat, danced against a backdrop of smoke and shadow and it was all I could do not to scream. I'd rather be blind.

It was the first thing they did to you, I knew that much. I thought back to when I'd gone into the infirmary and found Gary lying in a bed the same way I was now, bandages strapped to his face and dark stains spreading out from his eyes. Next they would butcher my body, my face, stuffing me with muscles until I was big enough to fill one of their black suits. And by that time the nectar would have done its job, destroying my brain just as the scalpels had destroyed my body. Making me one of them.

And all I could do was lie here and dream. Nightmares when I slept, nightmares when I woke.

As if trying to distract me from my thoughts a weak groan fluttered up over the beep of my heart monitor, hanging in the air for a second before dying. Someone else repeated it, closer this time, ending in a choked sob. I opened my mouth, flexed my jaw, took as deep a breath as the pain would let me.

'Zee?' I whispered, a word as dry as my throat. I tried again, managed a hiss. 'Zee?'

The only response I got was a wheezer's song, a tuneless squeal like a broken engine. There was a shuffle of boots on stone, the clink of needles as it walked my way. I blinked again, the pain a pressure that threatened to crack my skull. Being here was even worse than being locked in the darkness of the hole. At least I knew I was alone there.

'Zee?' I said, distress giving strength to my cry. 'Simon?'

'Hush.' The reply was so soft that I wondered if I'd imagined it. Only it came again, close enough to be from the next compartment. 'Alex, if that's you you've got to stay quiet. They'll kill you if they hear you talking.'

'Zee?' I asked, quieter this time. The voice was too soft to place it, even with Zee's accent. There was no answer, only the clink of curtain rails as the screen by my bed was pulled aside. I heard the wheezer right above me, that grotesque purr like it was gargling blood. For what seemed like an eternity nothing happened, then I felt a stabbing pain in my arm. Before I could even cry out I felt something rush into my veins like cold smoke, the poison flushing every last thought from my mind.

I called out again, yet this time it was nothing but an echo in my head which pulled me back into the boundless night.

SECOND SIGHT

'Why do you fight it?'

It was words that had pulled me under, now it was words wrenching me back up. Even as I woke from more nightmares – the same visions of boys becoming monsters – I recognised his voice. The way it hung in the air made me realise we weren't in the infirmary any more, that and the absence of any other sound.

'Why do you resist it? What I'm offering you is power, something you've never had before. Open your eyes.'

I realised I was sitting up, my arms and legs still bound. The pain was now a dull throb, the light streaming through my eyelids still a featureless fog. I shook my head, knowing that to obey the warden would only bring more agony.

'Open your eyes,' he repeated, and this time his voice carried the promise of something worse than pain. I swallowed hard, taking down nothing but air, then tried to open my eyes. For a second nothing happened, then with a sickly sound the lids parted. It felt like somebody was holding a welding iron to my retinas and I screwed them shut again.

'It only hurts for a moment,' the warden said, and the compassion in his tone threw me. I opened my eyes a crack, gritting my teeth as the torture became discomfort, then discomfort became nothing more than an itch. Gradually the world swam into focus, and I saw to my surprise that what I thought had been light turned out to be something else entirely.

I was in a room made up of silver lines. It reminded me of one of those pictures you got when you were a kid and you had to scratch off the black layer to reveal the metal underneath. Only this picture was three-dimensional and laid out in intricate detail. I squinted, making out every scratch on the stone walls, every crack in the low ceiling, every mote of dust on the floor. There was too much information to take in and I gagged, although there was nothing in my stomach to come up.

'Take it easy,' the warden said from behind me, his voice still laced with a kindness that I never thought I would hear. 'It's a lot to get used to.'

He placed a gentle hand on my shoulder, then walked round until he entered my field of vision. To my new eyes he resembled an angel, his skin radiating a platinum glow, every stitch of fabric in his suit as large and as clear as the Grand Canyon. Even though I still couldn't look him in the eye I could see what lay there – two portals of cold fire which cast light onto the room and made everything appear to be made from molten lead.

'What's happening?' I asked, wishing I could lift a hand to shield myself from the intensity of his glare.

'I told you,' he said, his words appearing as a light mist which hung in the air before him like breath on a cold morning. 'I'm offering you power. Power you never could have imagined.'

I shook my head, knowing that he was lying, trying to lower my defences.

'There is no trick,' he went on with a laugh. 'Don't you trust your own eyes?'

'They're not mine,' I spat back, screwing them shut.

'Oh, but they are,' he said, and I felt his smooth fingers grab my chin, turning my head to face him. 'It's only natural to fight, but think about what I am offering. Did you ever dream you would be able to see in the dark?'

I snapped my eyes open and this time my quickening pulse had nothing to do with fear. I looked again at the walls and their network of silver veins, saw the pores on the hand that held me.

'Lights,' the warden said, and instantly the room turned inside out – silver becoming substance, shadows blasted away by colour. I felt the world spin but the warden's fingers on my flesh kept me steady. Only when my vision had settled did he let go, pacing back and forth as if deep in thought. I took in my surroundings, a small room with the chair I was sitting in and a screen on the wall in front of me. Everything still seemed to carry far more detail than was possible, as if seen through a magnifying glass.

'This is just the beginning,' the warden continued.

'You'll soon see what true power is. Tell me, is there not a part of you that hates the world for what it has done? That hates being the child who can be pushed around, treated like dirt, who has no control over his life?'

I knew what the warden was doing, knew he was trying to manipulate me, but something in his words struck home with a force I couldn't deny. He was right. The world had forgotten me, locked me up and thrown away the key. I thought about all the times I'd dreamed of being able to fight my way out of Furnace, destroying everything in my path until I broke into the sunlight.

'No,' I said, trying to recover my thoughts. It was the warden who had taken my life, him and his blacksuits. If they hadn't killed Toby and framed me for his murder then I could have taken control, I could have straightened out. 'No, this is your doing. You did this to me.'

The warden stopped pacing and turned to face me once again. In the cold light of the room his gaze was sickening, and even though I closed my eyes and turned away I could feel his thoughts inside my own. He began to tut like a mother scolding her child.

'I know, I know. It is because of me that you are here. But think about what I am offering you. If you surrender to me then nobody *up there*' – he almost spat those two words – 'can ever tell you what to do again. The world is changing, and is it not better to be with those who wield power than those who are subjects to it?'

'I won't let you turn me into one of them,' I shouted back. But again the warden's words burrowed into my heart, made it pound not with terror but with something else. Excitement.

'Everything you have ever wished for, and all we ask is that you forget your old life. Think about it, think long and hard. What are you giving up? A history of weakness, of crime, of being told what to do. Would you really miss it?'

'But, my parents . . .' I tried, causing him to bark with laughter.

'Your parents? The ones who abandoned you when you needed them most, who left you here to rot without even fighting for an appeal against your sentence. They are part of the disease that was your old life. Give it up, give it all up, and embrace something new.'

'It's who I am,' I said. 'I won't let you have it.'

'How can you stop me unless you surrender to me? Without my help you are powerless. There is nothing for you in your past. Forget it, forget who you were, and give yourself to me.'

For a horrible instant I almost succumbed. Something in my blood bubbled up in response to his words. I could see myself as one of them, too strong to be told what to do, too fast to be caught. An unstoppable force that could take revenge on anyone who wronged me.

But it wouldn't be me. *It wouldn't be me.*

I thought about Donovan, who must have been put through this same process. I saw him fighting it again and again until he had no strength left. And I saw what he had become, his soulless grin, his overstuffed body, his dead eyes.

22

'Never!' I screamed, wrenching at the straps which held me to the chair. 'My name is Alex Sawyer. My name is Alex Sawyer. Alex Sawyer, Alex Sawyer, Alex Sawyer.'

And I kept saying it, over and over, even when the warden's fury erupted, even when the wheezer that had been standing silently behind me jabbed another needle in my arm. I kept saying it until the poison once again smothered my voice, and even then it burned through my mind chasing every other thought into the darkness.

'So be it,' said the warden. 'We can do this the hard way. *Pin his eyes, start the reel.*'

I fought the hands that grabbed me, but what could I do? I felt my head clamped to the back of the chair, felt something jab into the flesh around my eyes. And when the screen in front of me came to life in a blur of reds I discovered that I couldn't blink, couldn't turn away.

'Everyone wants power, whether they admit it or not. Let's see how you feel after a day in here.'

Then, with a clatter of bars and the squeal of a door, they were gone, leaving me alone with the worst sights of the world.

It started with animals, somewhere on the open plains of Africa, I guessed. The footage was scarred and faded, as though the reel had been played a million times before, but it couldn't hide the violence displayed on screen. Lions chased springboks, claws through tendons to bring them down then teeth in throats to make sure they couldn't get back up. Packs of wild dogs ganged up on baby wildebeest, charging in with drooling jaws for the kill. Gazelles were slaughtered in high-speed chases by cheetahs, the muzzles of their killers caked in blood.

It could have been something from the Discovery Channel, a highlight reel of nature's most ferocious kills. I almost laughed at how ridiculous it was. Except I could feel something inside me churning at the sights. At first I thought it was pity for the creatures that died. When I watched shows like this as a kid I rooted for the quarry, prayed that it would make it to safety. I used to hate it when the predators won, hated their smug expressions as they feasted on raw flesh. I was always on the side of the chased.

But now, bolted to a chair with the whole world pinning me down, I no longer felt pity for the prey. Every time I saw a wide-eyed antelope tumble into the dirt, the flurry of white and red as the lion literally tore its life away, I grinned with sick satisfaction. My stomach clenched like it used to do when I'd robbed a house. Goosebumps broke out on my skin and I felt my pulse beat a little bit faster. When I saw the light ebb from the eyes of a rabbit, crushed beneath a giant paw, I felt nothing but hatred for the creature's weakness, and nothing but admiration for the beast that had bettered it.

The sensation was so intense that it soon made me forget about the pain in my eyes. For the first few minutes they had burned, but as kill followed kill followed kill the agony seemed to become a part of me, a small sacrifice I had to make to grow into a stronger person – the same way lions and cheetahs and wild dogs had to go through hell and back each day just to survive. I don't know how much time had passed, and how much blood had flowed, before I admitted to myself I wouldn't have looked away even if I'd had the option.

I tried to tell myself that it was the poison in my blood which had altered my thoughts. And there was some truth in that – I could feel the nectar push its way around my body with every beat of my heart, the dark liquid alive inside my veins as though the footage on screen was calling to it.

Deep down, though, I knew why I savoured the slaughter before me with such relish. The warden was right, I was powerless. I was one of the pathetic grazers of the Serengeti, a rabbit or an antelope too cowardly to do anything but run when danger threatened. Every moment of my life I had been tense, ready to bolt – when I was breaking into houses, when I was framed for Toby's murder, when I found myself face to face with the gangs in general population. I was always the prey, never the predator.

And this was never more true than when I was chased by the blacksuits. Fast, powerful and fearless they were the ultimate hunters, the true kings of this under-ground jungle. I could never be anything other than the quarry caught helpless and screaming beneath their shoes.

Unless I became one of them.

I wasn't sure if the voice in my head was mine or the warden's, and the shock of it brought me back. I tried to blink, to twist my head, but the movements only gave the pain a fresh hold on me. Desperate to escape any way I could, I let my vision swim out of focus so that the pictures on screen became blurs. But my new eyes were too efficient to lose sight of the world so easily, and with each sick detail they took in I found myself drawn further into the warden's trap.

It might have been an hour later, maybe two or three, that the reel ended and a new one began. This time there were no animals, only people, but the raw violence was the same. I could do nothing but watch as gangs of police clubbed their victims into the tarmac, as thugs overwhelmed smaller opponents with dull laughter, as endless lines of soldiers marched in perfect time through ruined city streets, their conquered enemies cowering beneath them.

Again and again and again the strong beat down the weak, the powerful overcame the powerless. My horror soon became excitement once more, which then became envy. By the time I blacked out, ushered into restless sleep by the rhythm of steel boots, my envy had become a hunger for power far greater than any found in nature. And the hollow shriek of my own laughter sent chills down my spine as this new nightmare swallowed me.

VOICES

I drifted in and out of consciousness while the endless film played on, unable to tell which of the horrors I'd seen on the screen and which had life only in my dreams. Once, when I woke, I could feel the warden standing beside me. I couldn't turn to look at him, but I could sense the smile on his face as he watched a platoon of black-jacketed soldiers throw an emaciated corpse onto a pile of bodies.

'The world has always worked this way,' he said. 'And it always will. Most people don't get to choose whether they can take the side of the predators or the prey, but you can.' He leant in closer, the stench of his breath the perfect accompaniment to the horror projected before my eyes. 'I know you feel it. It's impossible not to. For far too long now you've been the victim.'

Grainy footage in shades of grey showed a ghostly teenager, not much older than me, escorted in front of a firing squad. Even past the snowstorm of scratches and burns on screen I could see that he was terrified, and there was no hood to hide his screams as the anonymous riflemen raised their weapons and fired.

'I'm offering you the chance to be something so much more,' the warden went on, his dry whisper against my ear. 'You don't have to let them trample all over you any longer. You can be in charge of your own destiny, too powerful to let anyone tell you what to do. Anyone but me, that is.' His words hit home with the same horrible temptation, and by the time I remembered to open my mouth to fight him he was already gone.

Later, maybe much later, I woke to feel the needle slide out of my arm, replaced by a fresh one. I could hear the wheeze of the creature standing beside me, felt its filthy fingertips on my skin, and I cried out for as long as it took the nectar to flood my arteries again. It was as if I'd been injected with pure caffeine and all of a sudden the images on screen became even sharper, the poison like a living creature inside me that thrived on pain and suffering, that wanted to witness through my eyes as much death as possible.

I wasn't sure when I fell asleep again, but the next time I stirred I was shocked to see that the film had finished, replaced by a blurred darkness. At least that's what I thought until the darkness moved and I realised it had been a hand. Before me stood a blacksuit, and in his silver eyes I saw a reflection of my own, echoing each other into infinity. He grinned at me, but it showed none of the malice I was used to. Instead the smile was almost one of pity.

'It's hard to watch at first,' the suit growled, the thunder of his voice echoing round the small room.

He lifted his hand again and bathed my eyes in the lightless warmth of its shadow. 'But it's not for much longer. We all went through this. It made us stronger, more powerful. I'll give your eyes a rest but, when I go, don't fight it.'

I tried to speak but my throat was as dry as sandpaper. I coughed, tried again.

'You were like me once,' I hissed, barely audible over the sound of the footage, the crack of breaking bones. 'A kid. They turned you into a monster.'

'I was never like you,' the blacksuit said. 'None of us were. We were born in Furnace, born from pain into power. And you will be too. Don't fight it.'

And then he too was gone. With no hand to block it, the floodgates opened once again and the mayhem cascaded into my head. I fought it, fought to remember who I was and what had happened to me. But the film on screen was a tide of violence that consumed me, and as I drowned in the endless parade of blood and bruises I realised I could no longer remember what I looked like. All I saw in the charnel house of my mind was a blacksuit I knew was me, kicking and punching my enemies until there was nothing left of them.

And the true horror was that it felt great.

The pattern of violence from the film must have been burned onto my new retinas because, even though I could still see it played out in front of me, I realised I was lying in my bed back in the infirmary. I blinked, the relief blasting through me as I realised I could close my eyes. When I opened them again the illusion was gone, and I found myself staring at the shadowed rock of the ceiling. The only movement was the lights, which swung gently as if buoyed by the gentle sobs that rose up from all around me.

I looked from side to side, wincing as my neck muscles cramped. Gritting my teeth, I eased my head in a gentle circle until the pain had gone. God knows how long I'd been strapped to that chair. It could have been hours, it could have been days, it could have been weeks. In the guts of Furnace, so deep beneath the ground, there was no way of telling how much time had passed. It might as well not have existed at all.

I tried to move my arms, knowing without looking that they were bound to my side by leather straps. I felt the frustration build up inside me and swore under my breath, hating myself for being so useless. When I got out, as soon as the straps were loosened, I'd tear the warden and his blacksuits to pieces.

The thought of it filled me with a kind of euphoria, one so powerful that it made my head spin. Adrenaline surged through me and I felt the poison alongside it, pumped with such force that every single muscle turned to fire. Beneath the thin sheet I could see them knotting, the leather straps creaking as my limbs swelled. It lasted only a couple of seconds before my strength abandoned me, leaving me an empty husk on the bed. But the exhilaration of it left me smiling.

Behind the drum roll of my heart I could hear a

wheezer somewhere in the infirmary, its clumsy steps accompanied by the clinking of glass syringes and the dry hiss of its breath. There was also a noise coming from somewhere to my left, a voice as faint and annoying as a dying fly. I ignored it, diving once again into the maelstrom of my thoughts.

Yes, as soon as I was free I would set about my vengeance. And it wouldn't end with the freaks of Furnace. I'd kill them all, the inmates in gen pop who'd given me a hard time. The police who'd brought me in, accused me of a crime I hadn't committed. A crime I *couldn't* have committed, not back then, anyway. Now I'd have no trouble pulling the trigger if my enemies stood before me. I'd make them wish they'd never picked on me. They'd be screaming by the time I finished with them.

I pictured myself storming into the police station. They'd go for their weapons but they wouldn't be quick enough. I'd have my hands around their throats before they could call for help, and they'd be dead before they hit the floor.

The noise from my left came again, distracting me from my fantasy. I ignored it, wanting to be back inside my head where I was no longer powerless, where I called all the shots. After I finished with the police I'd go after the jury who'd condemned me, and the judge who'd sent me here. Nobody would be safe. And lastly, my parents. They hadn't been there for me when I'd needed them most, when my life was at stake. They hadn't fought for me, they hadn't even believed my innocence. Well, they'd pay just like everyone else.

The voice came again, whispering a word I didn't recognise.

'Quiet,' I said, my own speech little more than a growl. I liked the sound of it. It was no longer the whining mewl I'd known all my life. This was something greater, a voice that could strike terror into people. I uttered it again, a throbbing snarl that sounded like one of the warden's dogs. It ended in a twisted laugh, behind which I could make out the strange word again.

'I said quiet,' I spat, feeling the power in the words even though they were slurred. 'I'll kill you.'

In my head my threats took on their own life and I watched myself tear free of my restraints, march into the next cubicle and stay true to my promise. It was just like in the warden's film, only instead of the thugs and the police and the soldiers I saw myself as the predator, as the victor, and the whole world lying broken at my feet. My excitement rose from my stomach, bringing with it another burst of insane laughter.

But the voice next door wouldn't give up. It repeated the word, then repeated it again, and again, until it was a constant barrage of whispered sound. Unable to return to my imagination I tried to focus on it, tried to make sense of what I was hearing. The word was familiar, but I couldn't think from where. I opened my mouth, tried to wrap my mouth around it.

'Al-ex,' I said, feeling the syllables like lumps of chalk against my tongue. 'A-lex. Alex. Alex.'

Each time I spat out the sound the darkness in my head grew softer. The image of myself as a blacksuit, as a killer, began to break apart. For an instant I saw my parents, cowering on the floor and bleeding from the wounds I had dreamed upon them. Nausea gripped my gut with iron fingers, followed almost instantly by a sense of shame that brought tears to my eyes. I shook my head wildly to clear the last of the waking nightmare, letting my sobs come freely.

'Alex, you've got to keep fighting,' said the voice. I thought I recognised the accent but I couldn't think from where. I pictured a boy, saw us jumping into a river, saw us hugging each other outside the solitary cells, saw us climbing the incinerator chimney together, but the knowledge attached to those memories scattered into pieces like birds taking flight. 'Alex Sawyer, don't forget it. Okay? You can't let them win, just remember Donovan, remember Monty.'

Names that should mean something but didn't. But it wasn't important. I had mine, Alex Sawyer, and so long as I did the warden and his army couldn't reach me.

Not unless I wanted them to.

TRUTH

More darkness, more dreams.

An animal pound, row upon row of cages drenched in shadow. I moved amongst them, peering through the rusted bars to see the creatures inside cowering in the corners, shivering in clouds of their own breath. None of them turned to face me, but there was no mistaking them for the boys they were. Each was dressed in the same cloth uniform as before, marked with a '36' above the twisted cross of the swastika.

A noise rose up from the other side of the room and a metal door swung open. Before I could find a place to hide two men marched in, decked in heavy leather jackets and gas masks and carrying a bundle of rags between them. They looked right at me but there was no trace of emotion in their eyes as they dumped the heavy rags onto a motionless pile on the floor.

The guards strolled along the row of cages, breathing loudly through the contraptions strapped to their faces. As they got nearer I was surprised to see that they were younger than I'd assumed, maybe in their twenties, but there was something in the lines around their foreheads and the dull weight of their eyes that made me think their youth was a lie.

I felt something grab my leg and staggered back, staring into the cage beside me. Bony fingers led to a skeletal arm which in turn was connected by shadow to two white, round eyes. The boy glanced at the guards, who still marched this way, then fixed me in his terrified gaze.

You have to let us out of here, he said. *There isn't much time.*

The kid in the cage sniffed, wiping an emaciated hand under his nose. He leant forward into the light and this time I recognised my own face instantly, the shock of witnessing myself so weak making the bile rise in my throat. I hadn't seen my reflection since I'd arrived in Furnace, but after everything I'd been through here I knew I looked more like this wraith than the healthy kid I remembered staring back at me from the mirror at home.

And I hated myself for it.

I looked at the guards, almost upon us. They walked with strength and with purpose, their eyes fixed in determination. There was no weakness there, only force, and more than anything I wanted to feel it.

Please, Alex, my ghost said. *Don't forget who you are.*

'I'm not Alex,' I replied, and in my dream my voice thundered around the room like a bomb had been detonated. The guards reached the cage and unbolted it, the kid inside scrabbling back against the bars. 'I'm not Alex, he never existed. *You* never existed.'

You do exist! The kid screamed as the men dragged him from the cage, the wiry muscles in his arms powerless to root him in place. *You do, Alex, it's not too late.*

Then he was out, just another bundle of rags held between the two guards as they strode from the room.

I rose from the dream to feel something cool against my eyes, a wet cloth that was pulled away as soon as I jerked into consciousness. My new eyes snapped into focus without hesitation, revealing the warden perched on the side of my bed. He laid the cloth gently across the heart monitor beside him then lifted a glass of water and held it to my lips. I drank greedily, relishing the fluid as it quenched the desert of my mouth.

'Easy now,' he said quietly, pulling the glass away. 'It's been a while since you've ingested anything. The body can't process water for the first few days after the nectar has been introduced. And it can't process food full stop.'

I slurred a few words which turned into growls as they hit the back of my throat. The warden's face peeled open when he heard them, yellow teeth like tombstones behind the cadaverous smile.

'You're making excellent progress,' he said, resting the glass on his knee and looking at me like a teacher might look at his favourite pupil. 'You were dreaming again; tell me what you saw.'

I snatched out at the tornado of thoughts that spiralled around my waking mind, catching hold of a question.

'Why does it matter? They're only dreams.'

The warden laughed, offering me another sip of water which I swallowed too fast. I coughed half of it back up onto his outstretched arm, but instead of reprimanding me he reached around and patted my back until the spasms had subsided.

'I told you to take it easy,' he said. 'Your body is changing, you can't do things the way you used to.'

Somewhere deep inside me the warden's words set off an alarm bell, but the poison in my veins quickly smothered it. He rested the glass on the floor and brushed the liquid from his sleeve, then he returned his attention to me. I could feel his eyes boring into my head the way I always had, but this time instead of the nausea it usually produced the sensation made me feel safe, protected.

'They're not just dreams,' he went on. 'They're something more. Half memories, half nightmares, from a long time ago.'

'Whose memories?' I managed, the warden's words getting caught up in the confusion in my head, their meaning torn apart before I could grasp it.

'People like you,' he explained. 'People who sacrificed a life of weakness to become something much greater. The first of their kind, the creators of us all. You must have already felt their touch, up in the cells. Everybody has bad dreams in Furnace, but sometimes the nectar is so strong it seeps into the very air.'

I remembered the nightmares that had plagued me in general population, images of a prison with glass walls, and my reflection that of a wheezer.

'But they are mere glimpses,' the warden went on.

'Fragments. Only when the nectar is in your blood do you see the whole picture. Tell me what you were dreaming just now. The trench?'

I shook my head, fighting to remember.

'A room,' I whispered. 'Cages, and guards.'

'Interesting,' the warden said, nodding gravely. 'The transformation is occurring more quickly than I thought. Do you remember who was in the cage?'

I thought back, probing the fog that had been the dream. There had been a boy in the cage, skinny to the point of starvation, too weak to stop himself being taken. I couldn't picture his face, only the whites of his eyes.

'A boy,' I said eventually. 'A weak boy. Nobody.'

This time the warden's smile made him look like he'd been sliced open from ear to ear.

'Good,' he hissed. 'Very good. You're ready for the next stage of your treatment.'

He made to get up but I muttered a few more words and he lowered himself back onto the bed. For an instant his face fell and I saw past the façade, saw the monster lurking beneath the leathery skin, but then the black cloud of my mind shifted again and I found myself staring into his smile.

'What?' he asked.

'The nectar,' I said, stumbling over every word. 'What is it?'

'It isn't important what it is,' he replied without hesitation. 'Only what it does. It frees you, frees your primal self. It shows you the truth. I think you're beginning to understand what that truth is. Maybe you always knew.'

I thought about the film, about the never-ending parade of sadism, violence and force, and the nectar inside me seemed to pulse with dark energy. I felt a tight pain in my cheeks and it took me a moment to realise I was grinning.

'Yes, you know,' the warden said, as if sensing my excitement. 'The nectar feeds on those emotions, and in doing so unleashes them. The more you hate the world, the more bitterness you feel at the way life has treated you, the more power the nectar will give you. The weaker you were, the stronger you will become.' He stood, walking to the curtain that sealed off my cubicle from the rest of the infirmary. 'Don't question it, just accept it. The nectar will show you what really lies at your core.'

He had almost gone by the time I put together my next question.

'But who are you?' I said to his back. He paused, then turned to face me, the white curtain a shroud around him. For an instant I met his eyes, raw pits that seemed to have no end and which radiated power.

'Who am I?' he repeated, chewing on the question. 'I am the man who made you. I am your father.'

Then the white fabric flapped and he was gone, leaving me alone with my smile.

FLESH

They came for me while I was sleeping.

I opened my eyes to see the illuminated ceiling flow past above me like a river of molten rock, the gurney rattling against the stone floor. There was a flap of plastic as I was wheeled through the slats that marked the exit from the infirmary, towards the operating theatres, the rooms where the wheezers worked their sick magic. I felt no fear, even though I knew where I was going.

And why.

I heard the staccato song of an electronic lock, followed by the hiss of the door sliding open. A chorus of wheezes fluttered from the room ahead as the surgeons inside greeted my arrival. I didn't have to look up to picture their faces, the rusted gas masks sewn into their decaying flesh, the gleam in those black, piggy eyes. I felt my skin crawl at the thought of them, but I ignored the sensation. After all, it wouldn't be my skin for much longer. I'd soon be a new man, far stronger, iron muscles wrapped in a jacket of steel.

My head lolled to one side as the blacksuits hoisted me onto the operating table and I saw the warden stride into the room. He beamed at me – an expression I was getting used to – and walked over.

'Good, good,' he muttered. 'No fights, no protests. You know this is the right thing.'

He glanced up and I followed his line of sight to see three wheezers preparing equipment, the light reflected from the scalpels and bone saws dancing across the red walls. The tools all looked familiar, but I couldn't think from where. For a fleeting moment I saw myself climbing, hammers and pins in the rock, but the image couldn't anchor itself and soon fell away.

'Run a test,' the warden said to one of the wheezers. 'Then start on his legs.'

He looked at me once more and smiled, but the way his mouth twisted upwards made me think of hunger rather than affection. Then the view was blocked by a blacksuit, the hulking figure strapping my torso to the table and fixing my head into a brace. The guard checked over his shoulder, and from the click of shoes I knew he was watching the warden leave. He looked back at the last buckle, giving it a tug to make sure it was secure, then bent down and put his mouth to my ear.

'I'm not going to lie to you,' he said, his voice a sonic pulse that echoed around my brain. 'The procedure hurts like hell. You'll feel like your body is being pulled apart piece by piece, then sewn together again with hot needles. I guess that's not too far from the truth. But stick in there, ride out the pain. Because when you're done you'll be one of us.'

Something swelled in my chest, a feeling I hadn't experienced for a long time. I don't know if there was a name for it, but I knew what it meant. *I belonged.* The blacksuit patted me gently on the shoulder, then cast a suspicious look at the wheezers as they moved in.

'Ride it out,' he said without looking back, then walked out of the door. I turned to watch the surgeons approach, a wall of filthy leather and ancient syringes. One slid a needle into my arm and the welcome numbness of the nectar swept through me. The other two lifted glinting weapons in their tattered gloves, the pitch of their wheezes even higher than usual. But I wasn't scared. I welcomed them. Because they were here to give me what I wanted.

Very soon now I'd join the ranks of the powerful, the blacksuits.

My brothers.

He hadn't been lying: it did hurt like hell.

I must have blacked out with the first incision, the sensation like somebody holding a blowtorch to my skin. But even under a shield of sleep I could feel them working on me, as though the nectar wanted me to sense the pain in my muscles, in my bones, to feel the transformation taking place.

The agony filled my head with images that must have been memories, but which I couldn't place. I pictured a boy being beaten to a pulp in an old gymnasium, other kids with skulls on their bandanas letting loose with kicks and punches. I saw the same boy caught in the jaws of a foaming river, only luck keeping him from being torn to pieces on the knuckled walls. I saw him falling into the flames of an incinerator, pulled from the fire before it could take hold.

And that same boy – whose face I knew so well yet at the same time didn't – followed me into my dreams, where he pleaded with me to remember who I was. But even as the guards carried him off into the black recesses of my nightmare the kid couldn't tell me what my name was.

He too had forgotten it.

The pain was so intense that it consumed every other emotion. Except for the anger. I lay on the table, alone in the small room, while the fury inside me grew. It was as if the searing heat in my legs was a fire, one that literally made my blood boil.

I didn't know what fuelled the hatred inside me. It wasn't directed at the wheezers, or the warden. Certainly not the blacksuits. It was everything else. All the pathetic people of the world who led their lives as meekly and quietly as possible, who had no idea of the forces at work beneath their feet. All those who relied on others to fight for them, who didn't have the strength to survive by themselves. The thought of them, the idea that I used to *be* one of them, made me sick with revulsion.

I shifted my body as best I could beneath the leather straps, the movement causing a fresh explosion of pain in my legs. I couldn't lift my head high enough to see what the surgeons had done to them but I knew anyway. They would resemble immense slabs of muscle, barely contained by the skin stitched around them. As soon as they healed I'd be able to outrun anyone, catch any prey. And I would show no mercy to those who could not defend themselves.

I wanted to see past the anger, to remember how I'd got here. Surely I hadn't always been like this, so full of rage. But there was nothing in my head other than Furnace. I must have been born here, in this place. Yes, this was my home, and the warden my father.

And yet still something tugged at the back of my mind, a nagging thought that came and went too fast to make any sense of, like a bluebottle smashing its haphazard path from window to window. There was something else, something I had forgotten, something important.

How important could it be? I had the nectar swimming in my veins, giving me strength I never knew I could possess. And I would soon have the body to match my mind, one that would never know what it was to be weak.

Again the thought fluttered and I saw the boy from my dreams, his whine like the furious beat of the bluebottle's wings. I pictured myself reaching into my head and snatching the image, crushing it beneath my heel until nothing remained but a gritty smear. There was no other world, only this one, only *my* one. And here I would be king.

I laughed, but the sounds were pistol shots fired out from the anger in my gut. I squirmed against my restraints, desperate to be free so that I could unleash the fury I felt on the first thing I saw. Opening my mouth, I shouted for the wheezers to finish what they had started, but all that came out was the deep, throbbing growl of an injured lion. It didn't matter. I had no use for words, only violence. What good was speech when you were getting pounded by broken knuckles? What use was language when you faced the monsters of the world?

I growled again, this time using every last drop of air in my lungs. It rose in pitch like a jet engine, so loud that I heard the scalpels on the tray beside me tremble against one another. It felt good, and I unleashed another, a devil's roar which blasted from the room and chased its own echoes down the corridor. I opened my mouth for a third but my lungs were starved of air and all I could produce was a weak groan and a string of spit which trickled from my mouth.

'It feels good, doesn't it?' said a voice from the door. The warden was standing there, half in and half out of the room. He wore that same empty smile, like the painted face of a Punch doll, but I could sense the pride emanating from him. I still had no words, but he didn't wait for a reply. 'To feel the power growing from your pain, to feel your body become something nature never could have made.'

He ducked out of the door and I heard him bark an order. By the time he looked back at me I could make out the slap of booted feet on rock behind him.

'I can sense that hunger for strength in you, more than most. I can *smell* it. The world will pay for what it has done to you. Together we will make it suffer.'

He must have noticed the gleam in my eye as my imagination gave life to his thoughts. The warden nodded at me, then stood to one side as a pair of blacksuits marched in, one wheeling a gurney. They gently unfastened the buckles that held me, lifting my body onto the wheeled stretcher. As they did so I caught a glimpse of my legs, like two tree trunks wrapped in crimson gauze. The pain still radiated from them but I relished it because it meant they were a part of me.

'They've done a good job,' the warden went on, gently smoothing down the bandages. 'These will heal up in no time.'

My arms, I tried to say, coughing up another snarl.

'Patience,' the warden said, obviously delighted. 'The rest will come in time. Too much, too soon, and you won't be able to cope. Your body is young enough to handle the nectar, the surgery. But your genes are only so flexible. And you don't want to find out what happens when they're pushed to the point of meltdown.'

The blacksuits began to wheel me out of the room, and as I passed the warden he rested a cool, dry palm on my forehead.

'Rest, and dream of darkness,' he said. 'It won't be long.'

He lifted his hand but I could still feel the cold

weight of his fingers as I was pushed out of the door and down the corridor.

I heard the infirmary long before we reached it. Something was screaming inside, not in pain but in anger. The sound was loud enough to make my ears ring as the suits pushed my gurney through the plastic slats.

I tilted my head to get a better look, saw the curtains of one of the cubicles billow as vague shapes wrestled inside. There was another scream, then the dull thump of a fist on flesh.

'Number 195 again,' growled one of the blacksuits by my side, running over to the cubicle and disappearing inside. The other guard wheeled me across the stone floor, muttering something under his breath. It was as he was preparing to lift me from the gurney that all hell broke loose.

Another scream blasted from behind the curtain, this one followed by a blacksuit crashing back through it. He tripped over his feet and spun through the air, a delicate double helix of dark blood spiralling from his nose. He hit the floor hard, racked with spasms that made him resemble an overturned beetle fighting to right itself.

Swearing, my blacksuit porter dropped me back onto the gurney and raced across the room so fast that he was just a charcoal smudge against the row of white curtains. But he didn't even have a chance to enter the cubicle before an arm of solid muscle punched its way out, catching him on the jaw and snapping his head round with a crack that could have been the earth splitting. He dropped like a sack of bricks, the light fading fast from his silver eyes.

I sat up, the anger in my blood extinguished by fear. From behind the curtain came another scream, but this time its pitch was lower. I heard something tear, like a wing being pulled from a cooked chicken, and a splash of red bloomed on the white material.

Behind the trails of colour that dripped slowly towards the floor I could see the silhouette of a hulking shape stagger forward. It reached out and pulled the curtain to one side, revealing something surely too large, too misshapen to be a face. Eyes like polished coins blinked into focus, dropping to the blacksuits on the floor then slowly grinding up to look at me.

And with that look something came flooding back. I knew it, recognised the cold, soulless touch of that gaze. In my head I saw a boy who had once terrified me far more than any wheezer, a kid who had taken lives with the casual ease of a wrestler snapping matchsticks.

Gary Owens.

There were shouts from outside the infirmary, the thunder of boots on stone. But I couldn't take my eyes off the creature in front of me. It pushed its way through the curtain and I saw a body of knotted flesh, muscles sprouting from muscles like a gnarled oak tree, all barely held together by a coat of stitched skin. Even as I watched, something seemed to swell beneath its flesh, its arms bulging outwards as though they were being pressure fed with water.

A cavern of darkness opened up in the centre of its face, freeing another hellish scream. Even as it ended, the creature was bounding towards me, the very rock shaking with the sheer strength of it.

Panic took over, propelling me from the gurney before I could even think about what I was doing. I hit the ground prepared to run, but as soon as I landed the pain clawed up my new legs and into my spine. I sprawled across the cold stone, barely even finding the strength to look over my shoulder, to face my death.

The creature swiped out at the gurney with a giant hand, sending it flying across the room. Then it was on me, fingers like hot iron around my chest. It picked me up as though I weighed nothing, drawing me close to the pit of its mouth.

It was as if the fear purged the nectar from my blood, pure adrenaline stripping the poison from my arteries. As I hung from the creature's fists the heavy curtain across my mind was pulled back and I remembered who I was, and where I had come from. And with that knowledge came language.

'Gary,' I wheezed, the word nothing but breath. I sucked in more air, tried again. 'Gary, remember your name.'

The creature paused, its platinum eyes swimming in and out of focus like a blind man learning to see. Its breath came in short, ragged bursts, each one carrying the stench of decay from inside it.

'Gary,' I repeated. 'Gary Owens. It's your name.'

The hammered footsteps reached a crescendo as the

blacksuits poured into the room. The creature looked up and screamed again, blasting me with so much rancid breath that I gagged. I felt its fingers tighten, felt my ribs bend under the pressure. Black spots began to appear in the corners of my vision, as in a photograph held over a match.

The first shot caused the creature to spin back. Its arm jerked and I found myself airborne, crashing down onto my shoulder before rolling into a curtain. I looked up, trying to make sense of the cartwheeling room, saw the creature take another shotgun round to its chest. The flesh erupted, but it might as well have been stung by a bee, and with a roar of defiance it charged towards the guards.

This time they were prepared. The nearest suit fired his weapon again, taking out the creature's legs. Another two ran forward with a pole topped with a hoop that danced and sparked with electricity. Before the freak that had once been Gary could get back up the wire was looped around its neck, its skin rippling as the charge pulsed into its body. After a couple of attempts to rise, the creature let itself drop limply to the floor, its arms twitching uselessly in a pool of its own blood.

Two of the blacksuits ran to check on their fallen comrades, the shaking of heads as they pressed fingers to necks making it obvious that they wouldn't ever be getting up. It was only then that they seemed to notice me, the nearest of the guards striding over.

'Leave him.' The words came from the far side of the room, spat out like wormwood. I looked round to see the warden approach, all trace of a smile now scrubbed from his leather face. He loomed over me, and I could feel his eyes bathing me like an icy shower. I cowered before him, shrinking as far into myself as I could while the gooseflesh erupted on my skin.

'What a disappointment,' he grunted before turning his attention to Gary. Or the thing that had once been Gary. 'Patch up Number 195. Take him to general population tonight, let him sate his bloodlust on his old cellmate. And when he comes back down, make sure he's secure.'

He crouched, and grabbed my chin with smooth fingers.

'I thought you'd left your old life behind,' he hissed, his eyes black holes that led into the abyss of his soul. 'If you remember his name then I take it you remember yours. Well, I guess we'll have to try a little harder to destroy that pathetic mind of yours.' He used his other hand to ram his finger repeatedly against my temple before dropping me to the floor and standing. 'Take this maggot back to the screening room. Lock him in there for two days and double his feed.'

The warden stormed from the room, looking back only once as he reached the main door of the infirmary, screaming at the blacksuits. 'And get this mess cleaned up!'

ARMS

My head was a war zone, memories of an old life that I had almost forgotten battling with the fantasies of power that had threatened to consume me. I fought to make sense of things but the confusion was too great, a seething mass of images and thoughts that threatened to drive me insane.

'My name is Alex,' I told myself as one blacksuit retrieved my gurney and another lifted me onto it. Even as the words spewed from my lips they made no sense, sounding to my ears like a foreign language, but I knew that I had to keep saying them. 'My name is Alex. My name is Alex. My name is —'

A gloved hand clamped down on my mouth, so hard that I struggled to breathe. I flailed against it as the guards wheeled me back across the infirmary, but the grip was too powerful.

'One more word from you and we'll be seeing just how long you last against a shotgun,' said one of the suits, ducking beneath the plastic strips that led out towards surgery. 'You've got some nasty little memories that just won't go away. Well, they'd better do soon or you'll end up in there.'

He gestured towards a steel door at the end of the corridor and I remembered a room full of bodies, and a raging fire. I ignored his warning, tried to speak, but he pressed his hand down until I felt my teeth cut through the back of my lips.

'That's what happens to the ones who can't forget,' the blacksuit continued through his shark's grin. 'We burn them along with the other trash.'

I could still feel the sting of flames on my flesh, the memory of pain enough to make me keep my mouth shut. We swung right at the junction, rattling along the uneven floor until we reached another door. It opened into the same room I'd been locked in before, the one with the screen, and although I panicked at the thought of having my eyes pinned open again I was powerless to stop the suits as they strapped me into the chair.

'If you have to keep one thing in that head of yours then let it be this,' growled the giant man as he lifted my eyelid. 'You're either one of us, or one of *them*. And believe me, you don't want to make the wrong decision.'

He stood to one side to let a wheezer in, and I felt the sting of the needle once again. This time the nectar poured into me like I was hollow, filling me from toe to forehead with its cloying darkness. My mouth drooped open, a weak cry like that of a dying bird the only protest I could make as the freaks left the room.

Before I arrived in Furnace, I never would have imagined that there could be so much horror in the world. But here it was, carried from celluloid to screen by flickering light, seemingly every act of senseless violence ever to have been committed. It was a different film from the last: no animals this time, just humans. But the things they did to one another were crimes that not even the lowest beast would inflict upon its enemies.

Again I tried to close my eyes, to look away, to think about something other than the nightmare unfolding in front of me. But I couldn't shut my burning eyelids, I couldn't move my head, and when your worst fears are paraded endlessly before you, how can you force your mind away?

I don't know how long I was in there before the images started to seep from the screen, suspended in the air as though I was wearing 3D glasses. It was like the madness of what I was seeing was too much to be contained; it overflowed its origins and polluted everything around it. I knew I was hallucinating, that the nectar was making me see things that weren't there, but as the punches flew, the guns fired and the bodies fell all around me it was as if I was standing in a hurricane of bloodshed and cruelty, one that battered and blasted against my mind.

And it wasn't long before my mental defences were stripped away completely. One by one the clips of film tore through the air and into my head, pushing out all other thoughts. I fought to hold on to my name, to the memories that had returned when I'd seen Gary, and what he'd become. But the nectar was a black tar pasted over my old life, onto which the images on screen stuck like feathers. No scrap of memory was spared. Everywhere I looked I saw only aggression, only anger, only death.

And if there is nothing left of you but darkness, how can you not become a monster?

When you're seeing things that aren't there, there is no line between being awake and being asleep. I looked down, saw that the leather straps were now loose, and knew I must be dreaming. My suspicions were confirmed when I stumbled to the door and opened it up onto hell.

At first I thought I was outside, but before the elation could rise higher than my stomach I knew it was an illusion. Ahead of me, stretching to a horizon lost in darkness, was a muddy field. Above it, where the sky should have been, roiled a ceiling of smoke the colour of dried blood, and so thick it could have been made of rock.

The wet earth was littered with forms that might once have been human, like a graveyard where the dead have floated to the surface. Scattered at uneven intervals were huge craters, some half filled with water like stagnant ponds. Even as I watched, something fell from the heaving sky, exploding into a ball of burning colour as it struck the earth. Dark water fell, carrying with it a heavy hail of rock and bone.

By the time the light from the fireball had sputtered out I saw the shapes in the mud start to move. They were crawling forward in slow motion, and past the filth that covered them head to toe I made out uniforms of worn cloth, round metal helmets and belts laden with equipment. Each of the writhing forms gripped a rifle in one bony hand, holding it up towards the distant horizon, towards a hidden enemy.

Another explosion rocked the earth a stone's throw away, pumping more smoke into the glowering sky. Silhouetted against the flames were three figures who marched across the mud without missing a single step. Each was dressed in a leather trench coat, a gas mask strapped to his face. Two held a stretcher between them, the third scanned the ground with beady eyes, like a vulture looking for flesh.

They stopped by a shape in the dirt, close enough for me to see a boy there. His uniform was in tatters, mud disguising the wounds that had been opened up beneath. He looked up at the stretcher and I thought he would be relieved to see it, happy at the thought of leaving this carnage.

But when he saw the men who carried it, their wheezes audible even over the distant sound of gunfire and the patter of falling shrapnel, he began to scream.

I'm not injured, I can fight! came his voice, and even though I didn't understand his language I knew what he said. The men didn't reply, simply laid the stretcher on the ground and started to peel the boy from his casket of wet earth. He fought, yet despite his claims he was too weak to stop them. Seconds later he was strapped in place and the men in gas masks were carrying him into the darkness. I watched them go, saw the red bands strapped to their arms, the swastikas blazoned there.

And then they were gone, the boy's shrieks the last thing to fade as he was carried off – taken to somewhere far worse than this landscape of madness and mud.

I don't remember leaving the screening room, although I must have done because the next time I woke I could feel the same pain in my arms as I had done in my legs. I looked past my shoulders to see two slabs of meat, so immense that the bloody bandages wrapped around them were threatening to split.

I flexed my new muscles, enjoying the strength I could feel there behind the pain. These weren't the sort of limbs used to cover your face as you curled into a ball, bleating, they were the limbs of someone who struck fear into his enemies, the arms of a survivor, a killer.

Blinking out the haze of sleep, I swung my head round to see that I was back in my cubicle in the infirmary. Instead of a bed, however, I was lying almost upright inside a metal coffin tipped back against the wall. Welded into the dark steel were thick chains which secured my arms, legs and chest. I knew without even trying that I wouldn't stand a chance of breaking out of them, despite my new strength.

Something about the sarcophagus rang a distant bell

in my memory, but the poison – still dripping into my veins from the IV bags beside me – was plastered over every thought and the nagging doubt soon popped like a bubble in tar. I tried thinking back to my dream, back to anything that had happened before I woke, but the same impenetrable darkness covered it all.

'It isn't taking . . .' The voice was faint but close, maybe from the next compartment over. I let my head swing to the side, tried to make out the whispered words. 'Double his feed, and if nothing happens, send him to the incinerator. I'm not willing to waste any more nectar on a lost cause.'

There was a muffled response, but even if I had been able to make out a word it was masked by a wheeze. I heard a curtain open and close, followed by footsteps. Then the white wall in front of me peeled apart to reveal the warden's face. For a second I caught his eye and suddenly I was back in the screening room, a sick procession of morbid images splashing across my retinas. I looked away and the world reasserted itself.

'You're awake,' he said, pushing into the compartment. I didn't look up to see if he was smiling or not and he made no effort to approach. 'For a while there I wasn't sure you'd make it. They filled you with more nectar than I thought was possible. I wonder . . . do you know who you are?'

I pushed into the shadows of my mind looking for a response, but the truth was the warden's question didn't make any sense. I was me, and I was being made better, and that's all there ever had been. I shook my head, each movement slow and exaggerated.

'What about a name?' the warden asked. 'Do you have one?'

Again I fought the confusion, trying to understand what he might mean. I knew what a name was, of course, but as for mine . . . Surely I had never needed one, because I had just been born. And in this world, where force was everything, what good was a name? Why did you need a word to identify you when you could define yourself with strength? I shook my head again.

'Good, good,' the warden said. 'You got there in the end. It's a positive sign. The ones who fight the most take more work, but when you fall you fall hard. How are your arms?'

They hurt, I wanted to say, although my mouth refused to shape the words and instead they spilled out as one long, low groan.

'They look strong,' the warden went on. 'They're healing already. You know, an operation like that would kill the healthiest adult, even if he were an athlete, or a soldier. Even if he had been pumped full of nectar. Human genetics truly is a miracle. If you could only see what you were becoming.'

I *knew* what I was becoming. Stronger, faster, better. I didn't need to see it when I could feel it in every fibre, in every burning nerve.

'One more procedure,' came the voice, all smoke and steel. 'The most difficult but the most rewarding.

One more operation and the transformation will be complete. Then we'll give you a little test to see how far you've come.'

I watched his legs turn and move towards the curtain, but he paused before leaving.

'And to make sure there's no going back.'

INTRUDERS

I waited for that final procedure with murder on my mind.

Strapped upright in my metal coffin, the screams and wheezes of the infirmary around me, all I could think about was breaking free of my chains and unleashing my new-found strength. Nobody would be safe because I was the predator and they were my prey. Blood would spill, and it would not be mine.

Whenever I had the energy I would test my muscles, feeling the power that lay in the swollen flesh. I didn't know what they had done to me – whether it was my own body which had grown, sprouting coiled tendons of steel under the skin, or whether somebody else's tissue had been grafted to mine. It didn't matter. All I knew was that I now possessed a raw might that could tear the world to pieces if it wanted.

A picture floated into my head of a boy – the same boy I sometimes saw in my dreams. He was pale, his arms and legs like twigs, his ribs showing even through his prison overalls. A distant part of me, buried deep beneath a lake of poison, knew that somehow I had once been this boy. But the only emotion this knowledge produced was nausea.

How could I have ever let myself be so weak? So pathetic? The scrawny ghost that pleaded silently in my head was not fit for life. He did not deserve it. That's why he had died, so that I could be born. The child was gone, his name was gone. All that existed was me, the beast that had grown from his corpse.

I let the growled laughter come, hearing the deep pulses reverberate from the stone like thunder. Nobody would ever disrespect me again. Nobody would ever bully me, or lift a finger against me.

Distant words distracted me from my fantasies and I let my heavy head swing round. Sobs and choked cries were heard frequently in the infirmary, but words were rare. Especially hissed, urgent commands like these. I listened out for the clack of the warden's shoes, the breath of a wheezer, but other than the wavelike symphony of whispers rising and falling there was nothing.

'. . . hurry . . .' I made out, the sound of metal scraping against metal. 'Come on . . . Cut the other one.'

There was a scuffling sound, the slap of leather on stone, then the patter of footsteps. I felt my heartbeat quicken, the nectar coming to life in my veins. I gripped the chains that held me, tried to force them from their steel casings. I didn't know what was going on out there, all I knew was that I wanted to be part of it. The metal squealed in protest but held tight.

'Where are the others?' one of the voices said.

'There's no time!'

'Just find them . . .'

More footsteps over panicked breaths, then the sound of curtains being pulled back. The noises grew closer until it seemed as though they were right next door.

'You okay? Quick, cut the straps.'

A slurred response, followed by the grating of a serrated blade through leather. I heard more words that I couldn't make out, then something pale and wraith-like pushed its way past the screen to the side of me. I snapped my head round and opened my mouth, letting loose a guttural growl that sent the face skittering back into the next compartment.

Seconds later it returned, and there were two more with it. I knew them, although at the same time they were complete strangers. The first was half boy and half beast, one arm grotesquely muscled the same way mine were. His silver eyes were wide in disbelief and he shook his head as though I was a nightmare that had visited him in the flesh. The two kids standing next to him were tiny by comparison, and they looked unmarked.

'Jesus,' said one, smoothing a hand through his hair. He had turned three shades paler in the time he'd been standing there.

'We've got to go,' said the smallest kid. 'Wheezers'll be back any minute.'

'Is that him?' said the freak with the giant arm. The other kid walked forward and I wrenched at my chains again, growling at him. He had no right to look at me the way he was doing now, as if I deserved pity. He was the weak one, they all were. Weak and incomplete. If I could escape I'd show them what strength was. I'd show them power.

All three seemed to recoil at the sound of my growl, but they didn't leave.

'Simon, what do we do?' said the youngest. 'Can we get him out?'

'No,' answered the bigger kid. 'He's too far gone. Look at him, for Christ's sake. I've never seen that much nectar hooked into the vein.'

'We can't leave him,' said the third boy. I studied his face and was surprised to see that every trace of weakness had gone. His expression was set in stone, a look of fierce determination, and it sent chills down my spine. I knew that look. I knew it because I had worn it once. A memory swam through the nectar like a whale trying to breach the surface of a frozen sea. I couldn't grasp it, but I knew that I'd been in this situation before. Only . . . Only it had been different.

The kid vanished into the next cubicle and returned a second later with something in his hands. I couldn't quite twist my head round far enough to see what it was, but somehow I knew.

It was a pillow.

'What are you doing?' said the small kid. 'You're not going to . . .'

'Ozzie, shut up,' snapped the one they called Simon. 'It's the only thing we can do. He's gone.'

The boy with the pillow took a step forward and I felt the terror wash through me. I thrashed against my chains but they were solid steel fingers that held me tight. Opening my mouth, I screamed at him, the sound like the roar of a jet engine. But he didn't stop, didn't take his eyes from mine.

'Alex, are you in there?' he asked. 'Because if you are then you have to let me know, right now.'

I growled again, throwing my entire body at him in the hope that my bonds would snap. There was nothing called Alex here, there was just me, and I was going to kill the child in front of me. I was going to kill them all. I was the powerful one, the predator. They were nothing but loose skin on bone, not even worthy of being prey. I felt my face split open at the thought, my grin like the sneer of a lion that knows it is about to feast.

'Jesus, Zee, hurry up. I can hear them coming.'

Zee. I knew the word, the name, although I couldn't think from where. It floated before me like silk in water, surrounded by thoughts and images I could make no sense of. I had almost grasped one – the kid called Zee in a lift, alongside me and two others, being carried down into the guts of the earth – but by the time it had taken shape I felt the pillow on my face.

I almost laughed at the thought that I could be killed by such a pathetic weapon. Then I tried to draw breath and my lungs stayed empty. I bucked, snapping my head back and forth, but the kid must have had all his weight on my face because the pillow didn't shift.

'I'm sorry,' I heard him say. 'Forgive me, Alex.'

I struggled to draw breath, feeling the panic radiate from my starved lungs. All the pillow gave me was dust and the stench of sickness. If I could just get an arm free then I'd stand a chance, I could kill him before he killed me.

'Oh God, they're here,' said one of the others, his words accompanied by a familiar wheeze which swept in from the back of the infirmary. I tried to scream again, to draw the gas mask's attention, but with nothing behind it my cry was silent. I felt the pillow press with greater insistency, heard the boys argue amongst themselves as the dry wheezes grew closer. Even with the cloth against my face I could feel the edges of my vision growing darker, the sounds fading like I had cotton wool in my ears.

'It's too late.' The voice pushed through the numbness in my brain, and all of a sudden the darkness was ripped away. I found myself staring into the twisted face of a wheezer. It had one gnarled hand wrapped around Simon's throat and the other held the scruff of Zee's neck. The smallest kid was curled up in a ball on the floor screaming the same three words over and over. 'It's too late. It's too late. It's too late.'

And it was. Even as the boys fought to free themselves the blacksuits ran into the infirmary, fierce silver eyes aiming down their shotgun barrels. They flew into the cubicle like a dark tornado, the butts of their guns causing the boys to fall like pins. It was over before I could draw in my first stuttered breath.

'Get them back to their beds,' a blacksuit said, wiping

the blood from his gun before using it to point to Simon and Zee.

Before anyone could move, the sound of the warden's shoes drifted up from the back of the room. The black-suits straightened, their faces steeled against the storm that was coming.

'What now?' came his voice. He appeared at the open curtains of my cubicle and I turned away before I could meet his eye. 'Is a little order around here too much to ask for? Go on, get them back before the feed is damaged too much. And that kid, find out how he got in, and if there are any more of them out there. When I asked for the perimeter to be secured I meant just that.'

I felt his glare scuttling up from Ozzie to me like a spider.

'What about Number 208?' he asked, his voice directed at me.

'I think they were trying to kill him,' replied one of the blacksuits. 'Same way they killed Number 191.'

'Any damage?' This time it was a wheezer that responded, although there were no words in its gargled purr. The warden stepped forward. 'Find out if there's brain damage. I don't know how long he went without oxygen. He looks weaker than he did.'

My fury had lifted my head before I even knew what I was doing. *Weaker?* Even the warden had no right to call me that. I met his eyes, felt the world peeling away like wallpaper, felt the cold touch of death in the swollen pits of his pupils. But I didn't look away. I held his gaze until it felt as though my soul had been pulled out of me, and the devil's breath had taken its place. Only then, when every last drop of strength had been drained, did I let my head drop.

'Well, I take it back,' he said. 'Not weaker at all, just angrier. Good, good. You'll soon have a chance to get even.'

I heard him stand to one side while the blacksuits hauled their catch from the floor. Even though I didn't have the energy to move I caught a glimpse of the kid called Ozzie as he was dragged away. His eyes were distant and unfocused, his mouth silently shaping those same three words. Then a giant hand engulfed his head and he was lifted out of my line of sight.

'Once you've done interrogating the intruder, take him to the chamber.' The warden's voice grew fainter as he walked away, but I could still make out what he was saying. 'As soon as Number 208 has had his final procedure we can try him out on the child, see just how powerful that anger makes him.'

There was more, but it came from too far away. It didn't matter. I understood what the warden had said. One more procedure and I'd be let loose, I'd be free. And neither hell nor high water would stop me tearing the life from those who had tried to kill me.

208

In my dream I lay next to the same kid who had haunted my sleep since the nectar had entered my veins. His bony body was strapped to an operating table, a splinter of shadow compared with my own muscled form as I lay beside him. I thought at first that the room we were in was empty, but then the darkness started to move and I realised there were wheezers all around us, their twitching limbs like insects running up and down the dark walls.

'It's time,' said the kid, the one I knew had once been me. His face was calm, but beneath his tattered overalls I could see his ribs jutting up like rock through snow, rising and falling too fast. He was scared, and even in the fog of sleep it angered me.

'Time for what?' I asked, my growl so deep it made the table beneath me tremble.

'Time to let go of me forever,' the kid answered, and I could see that he was trying to hold back the tears. 'If that's what you want.'

Before I could answer the wheezers were approaching,

their staggered movements making them look like puppets. Several grabbed hold of the kid's arms and legs, but none tried to twist his gaze away from mine.

'I don't want to be you any more,' I answered as another wheezer lifted a scalpel from the tray beside the table. 'You're weak. You're pathetic.'

'You're wrong,' the boy answered, and at last the fear broke through his paralysis and he started to struggle. The rest of his words came in short, sharp bursts as he fought the arms that held him. 'It's an illusion. I wasn't strong, but at least I could think for myself. You're the weak one, you're letting them win. You can still stop them.'

I looked at his limbs, nothing more than matchsticks, the whites of his eyes so bright they seemed to light up the entire room. The thought that he was still in my head somewhere, still alive after everything they had done to me, made my stomach churn. He had no right to be there. I was done with him.

'Please, Alex,' he pleaded. 'I don't want to die.'

The wheezer lowered its scalpel towards the boy's chest and held it above his heart. Then it raised its piggy eyes to me and I nodded.

'You died a long time ago,' I said, watching as the scalpel blade vanished into the boy's skin, a geyser of blood reaching skyward like one last bid for freedom. The kid screamed, and as much as I wanted to see him die I couldn't bring myself to watch. I turned away, losing myself in the artificial night of the ceiling until the last wet breath had faded.

There was a shuffle of feet as the wheezers approached me, and I offered no resistance when the butcher pressed his dripping scalpel against my chest. There was pain, but pain was nothing new to me and I didn't so much as flinch as the blade cut through my skin. Because it was a dream there were no bones beneath, just a hole stuffed with straw and twigs – almost like a bird's nest. The wheezer laid the boy's heart down in its new home, the organ still pumping despite the fact it wasn't connected to anything.

'Am I done?' I asked, watching another wheezer thread some surgical wire through a hooked needle and start to sew me back up. They didn't respond in words, but I could see from their gleaming obsidian eyes that their work was finished. The last stitch was knotted and they stepped back.

I looked round at the kid, sprawled on the table, dead eyes seeming to stare at the world a mile or so above him. It looked as though something had exploded from his chest, and blood pattered like rain onto the floor around the table. There was no room in this world for a boy like him – like the one I had once been. There was only space for the creature that had been born from him.

I lifted an arm and felt the tight zigzag of stitches that marked my chest. The kid had been killed so that I could live. His heart was now mine. I was finally complete, finally whole.

But even in my dream I couldn't shake the feeling that, despite the immense layers of muscle that bound me and the stolen heart that ground against my sternum, I was now empty inside.

There was a moment when the world of my dream and that of real life seemed to overlap. I felt myself stirring, saw the wheezers peel away as I bubbled to the surface of sleep. I looked back at the body of the kid one last time, but after a single blink the murdered boy had become a stone wall and the last trace of nightmare drained from my head.

I tried to move but it felt as though I had been stabbed in the chest. Looking down, I saw that the truth wasn't far off – my entire torso had swollen to twice its normal size, a network of scars and stitches decorating the bruised skin. My face, too, radiated pain, and all I could do was open my mouth and utter a scream, a pathetic croak that barely made it out of my mouth before tumbling unheard to the floor.

Panic gripped me, doubling the agony in my chest and stomach. I had never felt this weak, not ever. Even if I wasn't held down by leather straps I doubted whether I could have climbed off the operating table. I was as helpless as a newborn baby, ready to be picked off by the first enemy that walked in through the door.

What if something had gone wrong? What if the wheezers had somehow injured my spine as I lay sleeping? What would happen to me now? Bait for the rats, or maybe just incinerated along with the rest of the failures.

Something moved behind me, the flap of a coat and the tail end of a dry wheeze. Oh Jesus, they were coming already. *Wait*, I tried to say, but this time my words were so timid even I didn't hear them. The noise grew louder, then I felt the sting of a needle as it slid into my arm. Almost instantly the pain began to fade, the strength returning to my new body as the nectar filled me. The relief was so great I swore I could hear thunder in my head, loud enough to drown out the warden until he was standing right next to me.

'The pain is what kills most people,' he said, perching on the edge of the steel table. 'Or what drives them insane. Take the rats. They couldn't handle the pain so they lost their minds, became animals. The nectar, and the operations, they can have that effect.'

He noticed a trickle of blood that was slowly winding its way towards him. Pushing himself up, he paced around the room as he continued.

'I was worried about your mind. You see, if you try and resist too much it's like using a stick to barricade a door. It will only last so long before it snaps into splinters.' He walked over, pressed a hand on my forehead. The touch released a fresh wave of pain that scoured its way down my face and torso. 'But you seem to have survived with all your mental faculties intact. Well, the ones we wanted to keep anyway. You dreamed again while they operated on you, right?'

I was in too much pain to nod but the warden didn't seem to be expecting an answer.

'It will be the last one. It always is. From now on

there will be no more pain, no more nightmares. Only power. It hasn't been an easy journey, I know that. But it will be a rewarding one.'

He walked round behind my head and I felt the topmost strap loosen. He appeared on my other side and unfastened the buckle that held my arm. Slowly and methodically he released the bonds that held me, then offered me his hand. I couldn't look him in the eye to see what his motives were, but I knew he meant me no harm. Grimacing against the ache in my chest, I took his hand and let him pull me into a sitting position.

'I'm proud of you,' he said, resting both palms on my head the way a priest might do. 'You have embraced a new life, our life.'

I felt my chest swell, not with pain this time but with pride. The warden took a step back, checking the sac of nectar which hung from a stand beside the table. When he spoke again the warmth was gone from his voice, taking me by surprise.

'But we are not ready to accept you, not quite yet.' I opened my mouth to protest but he stole the words with a single glance. 'Simply staying alive this long isn't a guarantee that you are ready. Some of those who make it through the procedure are still weak at their core, they do not have what it takes to join my family.'

He nodded at the door and a wheezer entered the operating room. I watched the creature as it staggered to a tray beside the table and picked up a long syringe. This one was full of clear liquid.

'Some lack the physical strength to make it as one of my soldiers,' the warden went on as the wheezer tapped the tube and squirted some of the liquid into the air. 'Others cannot handle the . . . responsibilities that their new life entails.'

The wheezer shrieked, and before I could object it jabbed the needle into a vein in my forearm. There was none of the cold rush of nectar, just a pleasant buzz that permeated my entire body. When the warden's voice came again it was muffled, as if heard through gauze.

'This is a mild anaesthetic, nothing to be worried about. When you next wake we'll find out how far you've come, and how strong you really are.'

His voice continued to fade as I plunged deeper into the silence of my mind.

'Get the chamber ready, divert the river, and prepare the rats. Let the test begin.'

THE TEST

Something was dripping on my face and it was driving me insane.

I snapped open my eyes, saw that the world was made of silver. I was confused for only a moment before I remembered my new eyes, the night vision letting me know I was in a small room made of rock. At first I thought I was back in the hole, in solitary confinement, until I looked to the side and saw a narrow passage leading off into shadows.

Another trickle of water brushed down my cheek and made my whole face itch. Looking up, I saw a hatch embedded in the rock maybe ten metres above my head. Even as I watched, two more globules peeled their way loose from the metal and fell, every detail perfectly sharp as they danced then merged with one another – platinum teardrops against the dark stone. I went to move out of their way but a cold grip on my wrists stopped me. Manacles, bolted into the wall.

What the hell was going on?

I thought back. Remembered the warden's last words. *Let the test begin.* What kind of test was this?

Tugging on my chains did nothing but almost deafen me in the small space. I waited for the echoes to die out before searching the floor for a key. The cracks in the rock were laid out like a spider web of light, and there was nothing there but my own bare feet. I noticed the scars on my skin and remembered the surgery, the way my torso had looked the last time I'd seen it. I don't know how long had passed since the wheezer had sent me to sleep, but it must have been a while because the pain had vanished completely.

And the warden was right. There had been no more nightmares.

Something groaned above me, so loud that I felt my heart stutter through a couple of beats before finding its rhythm again. I clambered to my feet as the trickle of droplets became a steady flow, as if somebody had turned on a tap on the other side of the hatch. The groan came again and this time I knew what it was. I felt my blood run cold, and it had nothing to do with the freezing downpour that was already starting to form puddles in the rock.

It was the sound that metal makes when it is under a huge amount of stress. The kind of stress that might come from an immense weight of water.

Before the third groan died out I had wrapped the chains around my hands and was pulling on them with all my might. There was now a veritable waterfall slui-cing down the narrow shaft, making the floor slippery and preventing me from getting a grip on the metal. Although the passageway next to me meant that the water wasn't getting any deeper, I knew it was only a matter of time before the hatch gave out under pressure and I was crushed beneath a fist of white foam.

Swearing at the top of my voice, I braced my leg on the rock and leant back, tensing my arms and shoulders until I thought the muscles would burst through my skin. I could feel the strength inside me, feel every fibre of my being put to work. It was power I had never dreamed of possessing, but it wasn't enough.

The hatch groaned again, then one corner popped loose from its casing. I looked up in time to see a jet of water cut down the cell, slapping me hard enough to make me lose my footing. I scrabbled up, screaming in rage as another hinge snapped above me and the jet became a blade.

This time I wrapped the chains around my chest and turned away from the wall, pulling on them like I was hauling a cart. The adrenaline pulsed through my veins like acid, and I could feel the nectar in there too, giving me strength, urging me on.

I wasn't going to die like this. Not now that I finally had power at my fingertips. *I wasn't going to die.*

I gritted my teeth so hard I thought they might snap, pushing my foot back into the join between floor and wall and putting every muscle to work. There was another groan, and I almost dropped earthwards, thinking it was the hatch finally giving way. But then I felt the chains stretch and knew that this time they had made the sound.

I stopped for a second to recover my breath, then threw myself forward again. The chains cut into my wrists, into my chest, but the pain was good, spurring me on. With the squeal of metal on rock one of the bolts in the wall flew loose. Facing my strength alone, the other bolt didn't stand a chance, ripping out a head-sized chunk of stone as it surrendered.

Momentum caused me to fly into the passageway, which probably saved my life. Above me the world seemed to collapse in on itself, a sound like the sky falling. The floor trembled as the water struck it, but by that time I was running along the passageway at full pelt, my chains dragging behind me.

My legs were like jackhammers, the silver cracks in the walls and floor flashing by like catseyes on a midnight motorway. I could feel the wind on my face, the sheer exhilaration of being able to run this fast making me grin despite the fact that death was right behind me. I risked a look over my shoulder, the unleashed river like a swirling torrent of mercury, gaining quickly. Too quickly.

I forced myself to run faster. There was nothing but rock ahead, no sign of a door or a junction or anything that might let me escape. I was stronger and faster than I had ever been, but my lungs were burning, my heart was threatening to burst its stitches, and I knew I couldn't go on like this forever.

I felt the first cold tendrils of water on the back of my neck, the roar like some vast creature that saw its prey was trapped. I knew why it sounded so triumphant. It had held me in its teeth before, this river, an age ago.

I had escaped, and now it wanted to finish the job.

And it would. Up ahead the passageway was sealed, a dead end of solid rock. I was strong, but there was no way I could pummel my way through it. Not before the seething mass of water ground me to a pulp against the stone. This wasn't a test, it was an execution.

I thought of the warden, his cold laughter as I died, and the anger clawed its way up from my stomach. Uttering an animal cry of pure rage, I charged at the wall, my fists raised. The water was almost upon me, its cold fingers the touch of death. So this is how it would end. Crushed between the unstoppable force of the river and the immovable weight of the rock.

I had almost smashed into the end of the passageway when I noticed the tunnel angling upwards. I reacted instantly, propelling myself off the ground and bracing myself in the narrow chute. The water flooded the space I'd occupied only moments ago with a sound like an atomic bomb being detonated, flecks of foam resembling pale talons reaching up for me. The river wasted no time in continuing the chase, bubbling up against the rock with frightening speed.

Snatching in a lungful of air, I began to climb, my silver eyes picking out cracks and crevices in the rock and my massive arms pulling me up with ease. The heaving breath of the river made the stone slick and slippery, but every time I thought I'd lost my grip I rammed my legs against the sides of the vertical tunnel, locking myself in place. The water was fast, but I was faster. I was going to outclimb it.

And then the top of the shaft came into sight, sealed tight by a hatch.

I vaulted up the last few metres with a grace that surprised me, leaping from side to side like an ape. Wedging my feet in opposite corners, and hooking one hand into a crack in the ceiling, I reached up and felt the ring of metal. A single touch told me the hatch was solid steel, at least as big and as heavy as the one that had kept me in solitary. The water was still rising, maybe five metres between its icy depths and me. I had only one chance.

Furious, I bunched up my fist and threw it at the hatch. I don't know what I'd been expecting, but the sound it made when it connected almost made me lose my footing. The crack of bone on steel, and my cry of pain, were twin echoes that dropped down the shaft until they were swallowed by the roar of the river.

It felt like my hand had been put down a garbage disposal, the pain unbelievable, even when compared with everything else I'd been through. But when I looked at the hatch I was amazed to see a dent in the metal, as though it had been struck by a sledgehammer.

Grunting, I smashed my other fist against the hatch, this time causing the edge to buckle. Blood dripped from my knuckles, turning the white foam red inches beneath my feet. This time I wrapped the heavy chains once around each hand and lashed out again, and again, left and right, the steel barricade bending out of shape with each strike.

The water reached my ankles, its touch seeming to drain all warmth from me. I gripped the ceiling harder, tensed my legs and my back to give my arm more leverage as it blasted upwards again. The hatch bent even further outwards, but still it didn't break. Past its warped edge I could see the flickering light of torches, and more than anything I wanted to be out there. I didn't want to die like this, swallowed whole by a beast of ice.

But the river was up to my waist in seconds, so cold it made me feel as though all the bones had been filleted from my body. By the time it had reached my chest, my muscles had no strength left in them. I tried to take in one last breath but the water was too eager, filling the top of the shaft in a heartbeat and sliding its cold fingers down my throat.

I choked, spasms ripping through my body as it fought for air. But there was none to be had. No air, no warmth, no strength. All I had left was my anger. It seethed and coiled inside me like a living thing, telling me to bunch up my fist again, ordering me to lash out one last time.

The punch was slowed by the water, but not by much. It tore towards the hatch, impacting with enough strength to send a shock wave pulsing down the river. I felt something snap – a pistol shot, deafening in the maelstrom – and thought it was my bones breaking.

Then the hatch swung open and I was pushed through it by the very force that had sought to drown me. I landed hard, slapping my still-bunched fists against the rock as I fought for breath. The water continued to pump through the hatch, but I was lying in a huge chamber full of rocks and the tide pooled harmlessly on the uneven floor.

It couldn't touch me here. I was safe. I'd passed the warden's pathetic test with colours flying, if a little ragged. I started to laugh, hacking coughs that were more liquid than air, and so loud that I didn't hear them approaching until too late.

And it was only when a dozen needled teeth sunk into my flesh that I realised the test wasn't over yet.

It had only just begun.

SELF-DEFENCE

I kicked out, connecting with something soft and sending it reeling back. The needles slid from my flesh but I
barely felt them, my survival instinct forcing me to my
feet in time to see a constellation of silver lights turning
towards me.

Rats. The chamber was full of them.

The one I had kicked shook itself like a dog, its long
forelegs flapping limply from side to side. It wasn't
particularly big – smaller than me – but its bulging jaw
was packed full of teeth which glinted in the torchlight.
It opened its maw and let loose a chilling scream that
echoed round the large room. Then it charged, pounding across the wet rock and throwing itself at me.

I threw up my arms to protect my face as the creature
slammed into me like a freight train, locking its jaws
around my wrist. We tumbled back, rolling into a pillar
of rock which jutted out from the floor. Luckily the rat
took the brunt of the impact, the shock loosening its
teeth from my flesh long enough for me to wrap a hand
around its throat.

It snarled, its entire body bucking against my grip, but I held on as tightly as I could. My knuckles were already starting to swell, the bones grinding against each other inside my torn skin, but I had no other weapons. Pulling back my chainmail fist like a spring, I unleashed another punch, this one catching the rat on the jaw. It sounded like a gun had been fired inside its throat, its head snapping round at an impossible angle and the convulsions becoming weak death throes.

There was no time to gloat. I spun round at the sound of claws on stone, saw a second rat hurtling my way. This one was so disfigured I couldn't tell what it had once been, its skinny legs and body that of a dog but its face too flat to be canine. Its hairless form glistened in the soft light, every strand of muscle flexing then contracting as it bounded this way.

It was on me in seconds, straightening up from four legs to two and slashing at my chest with razor-sharp claws. I leapt out of its reach, preparing to turn and run, but before I could I heard a growl behind me.

Something slammed into my back, pushing me into the path of the rat. This time its claws raked my stomach, pulling loose stitches. I yelled out as the pain flared, but the sound was cut off by a filthy paw inside my mouth. It ripped at my jaw, jagged claws against my tongue as it pulled me to the floor. Then they were both on me, their hands like some monstrous machine tearing chunks of flesh from my torso.

A long time ago, in another life, I would have laid

down and died. But not now. I was the predator, not the prey. I was the hunter, not the meat.

I bit down on the thing inside my mouth, feeling hot blood gush into my throat. I spat it out, heaving in a breath before letting my rage explode from me as a guttural roar. It was a howl of pure animal fury, the cry of a killer, and the rats knew it.

The first leapt off my chest, backing away with a feeble whimper. The other wasn't so lucky. Before the ghost of my battle cry had faded from the walls I had my hands around its head. The first time I smashed it against the rock it let out a squeal of pain. The second time it was silent. By the fifth time there was nothing left in my fingers but mush.

I got to my feet, the nectar pumping me full of strength, full of anger. Arching my back, I let out another cry, this one tearing around the chamber like a demon. I had never felt so alive, so powerful. This was my domain now, my territory.

The second rat bolted, its razor-clawed feet skidding as it swung round the rocky pillar and vanished. I cracked my swollen knuckles, tightened the chains around them, then charged after it. Anything that tried to mess with me now would pay the price.

I rounded the pillar to see the floor moving. There must have been a whole nest of rats in here, almost a dozen of them squirming across the rock. Most were clustered in one corner and I soon saw why.

Tied to a wooden post like some sacrificial offering was a figure far smaller than any of the rats, a boy whose face was covered in blood but still familiar. I thought he was dead, but as the creatures turned to face me the kid raised his head and opened his mouth. Even from across the other side of the chamber I could understand what he said.

'Help me.'

I charged, too fast for the rat in front of me. Snatching it up in my giant hands I hurled it across the room, its squeal dying out as it slammed into the main pack. It was like watching skittles fly, the creatures lurching to either side as they saw their brother dashed to pieces on the rock. I didn't give them a chance to get angry, throwing myself into their midst with my arms flailing.

I caught one with a blow to the temple, hard enough to crack its skull. The second had its teeth in my shoulder before I could stop it, but pain was a distant memory and I used my other hand to pull it loose, barely noticing that it took a strip of skin with it. I threw the creature at the wall, not needing to look to see whether it would get up again.

The rats were starting to panic, crashing into each other as they scrabbled out of my way. I caught one by its hind legs, swung it round like a club and took down two more before launching it into the air. Before they could get to their feet I had a knee on each of their backs, wrenching their heads up until their spines snapped.

'Jesus, Alex – is that you?' said the kid tied to the pole. I looked up from my killing ground, fixed him a glare that made him shrink back against his chains. 'It's

Ozzie. Simon's friend. Remember? Help me, get me out of here.'

I heard the patter of feet behind me. The last three rats had closed ranks, charging forward as one. The two on the outside were savage but small, running upright. One must have had surgery on its arm, the overstuffed limb hanging uselessly from a narrow shoulder. The other had a monster's legs attached to its skinny torso.

But the one in the middle was big and mean, every limb except its left leg stuffed with muscle and its torso so huge it looked like it had been chiselled from rock. The creature limped, but that didn't stop it covering ground like a bear. None of them took their eyes from me and I recognised the expression in their twisted faces. They were angry, they were furious. And it gave them strength.

I ducked my head and charged, knowing that to show any sign of weakness would mean death. One of the smaller rats skidded to a halt, shaking its head and whimpering, but I didn't care. I kept the big one in my sights, never breaking eye contact with its silver gaze. Travelling this fast, the distance between us shrank away in a split second, and we collided with a thump of flesh on flesh.

The impact ripped the breath from my lungs, giving the rat the advantage. It grabbed my face in one giant paw, slamming it down against the rock, then rammed its knees into my chest. Stars exploded in my vision, fading into blackness. I felt the other one grab my arm, its jaws snapping like a bear trap on my flesh, but with the huge creature pinning me down I couldn't get leverage to shake it off.

Snarling like a rabid dog, the huge rat lunged towards my throat, its teeth glinting like broken glass. I barely got my other arm up in time, wedging the chains into the corner of its maw and pushing it away with what little strength I had left. The rat lost its balance, toppling from my chest. I saw my chance, swinging my leg round and ramming my knee into its head.

I didn't wait to see what damage I had done before wrenching my arm free and backing off. Blood was pouring from me with the same force that water had been leaking from the hatch back in the tunnel, and I was starting to feel light-headed. I knew I couldn't last much longer. I had to finish this.

With another cry of rage I threw myself back into the melee. Using my left hand this time, I smacked the smaller rat square on the nose, sending it sprawling back onto the rock. Before it had landed I lifted my right arm in an uppercut, catching its bigger friend in the stomach. It was like punching a wall, the muscles like paving slabs, but it was obviously winded as it staggered away from me, growling weakly.

I took my eyes from it for a second, scoured the floor for something I could use as a weapon. It didn't take long. The chamber was littered with scraps of broken rock, and I hefted one the size of a watermelon. Both rats turned to run, but I was on them in a single leap, molten fury turning my vision white and making my body act as though it had a mind of its own.

The first went down with a sickening whack, somersaulting twice before coming to a rest. The bigger rat almost outran me, but there was nowhere for it to go in the chamber. It didn't have time to turn and face me before I crushed its head between the wall and my rock.

Turning, I spotted the last rat bolting to the corner where the kid had been tied. I don't know what it was doing, but there was no escape from the anger that drove me. Three huge strides and I was across the chamber, a scream of defiance bubbling from my bloody throat as I brought the rock down onto its skull. It sagged, its death instantaneous.

'Thank you –'

Still drunk on adrenaline, I had turned and lashed out before I even knew what I was doing. Somewhere in my head I knew the rats were all dead, knew there was nothing left to kill. But my mind was so exhausted, so filled with fury, that I couldn't stop myself.

The kid, Ozzie, looked at me in disbelief. His mouth dropped, and from it ran a single thread of dark blood. It trickled down his chin, arcing under his throat and merging with the crimson tide which flowed from the wound in his temple.

'Alex,' he said, and although his lips continued to move there was no breath for them to make words with.

I dropped the rock, staggered back, unable to take my eyes from his, even when the light had left them, turning their sky blue to pale grey. He slumped, held up by the wooden post as though his body was refusing to acknowledge its own death.

What had I done? Even though the nectar still seared my mind with darkness, my heart pumping with my victory against the rats, I knew I had committed a terrible crime. The kid had been helpless. He wasn't a rat, he was a person. And I had killed him.

'No,' I growled, fighting against the burning wave of emotion that rose from my stomach. 'You deserved to die. You deserved to die.'

He *did*. He had been pathetic, too weak to even free himself. He had been nothing but prey for the rats, nothing but prey for *me*. I pictured his face, doe-eyed as the vermin closed in on him, too scared even to scream. This was how all the weak of the world would meet their end, devoured by predators like me. Ozzie had been nothing, a nobody, and he had deserved to die.

And I kept telling myself that, even as I stood in the middle of the chamber, racked by tremors that caused my teeth to chatter and sent blood showering from my wounds. I kept telling myself that because it was the only way to survive the guilt. It was the only way to survive the knowledge of what I had just done without taking the rock and stoving in my own brain. It was the only way to survive the test.

Because the warden was right. I was a monster now. And there was no going back.

BELONGING

I wasn't aware of the blacksuits entering the room until the electrified wire had been looped around my neck. The charge wasn't strong, like the tickle of a million insects scuttling down my spine, burrowing into my muscles, but I was on the floor before I even knew I was falling.

I couldn't have fought back even if my life had been at stake. I just lay there, silent but for the hoarse whispers that rattled in my throat, watching the warden's feet splash across the bloody rock and stop in front of me. He squatted, ducking his head down until it came into my line of sight.

'Now that was impressive,' he said, and I couldn't see his grin so much as feel it. He gently pulled the dripping chains from my knuckles, unlocking the manacles and throwing them across the room. 'Very impressive. Such bloodlust, such ferocity.' He stood, and for a second I caught a glimpse of myself in the polished black leather of his shoe – my face too big, like a Halloween pumpkin carved with stitches, my eyes twin candles whose silver light looked on the verge of sputtering out. Then the warden walked off and it was gone. 'Get him up,' he shouted over his shoulder. 'Get him to his bed. He's earned it.'

The loop of wire around my neck disappeared, strong hands beneath my armpits guiding me back to my feet. I barely remembered how to put one leg in front of the other, but the blacksuits weren't going to let me fall.

'That was good work,' said the one to my left, his bass tones echoing round the chamber. 'When we saw the water bubbling up from the hatch we didn't think you were going to make it. That's where most of them fail.'

'But you punched through it like it was paper,' said another. 'And those rats never stood a chance.'

They chuckled, their laughter so deep I could feel it tremble across my skin like another electric charge. One kicked the limp corpse of a rat out of his way and I watched it slide through a pool of its own blood before folding itself around a rock. Bodies lay everywhere, their silver eyes now the colour of lead, claws and teeth still bared as though they hadn't quite noticed they were dead. Wet stains bloomed across the walls and the floor like some strange subterranean fungus, looking almost black against the dark rock. The smell of decay already hung in the air, the metallic tang of blood mixed with the dying breaths of the rats, trapped forever in this tomb.

I couldn't believe I was responsible for such carnage. It had started as self-defence, yes, but surely even the rats hadn't deserved to be culled so brutally.

We reached a metal door almost completely concealed by a pillar of stone, the warden leading the way through it into a bright corridor beyond. I took one last look into the chamber, saw Ozzie still propped up on his stake, watching over his legions of twitching bodies like he was lord of the damned. Then the scene was lost behind the heavy door, my thoughts drowned out by the thunder of boots.

It was only then that the pain started to seep in. Inside the chamber the adrenaline and the nectar had kept me going, but now that the fight for my life was over my body seemed to just give up. It started as a cramp inside of me, as though every muscle was protesting about what I had put it through. In places that deep, burning agony became something sharper, and in my delirious state I pictured the wounds on my shoulder, in my back and across my stomach and chest hanging open like mouths, screaming.

I glanced down, watching a red rain fall from me as I was dragged along the corridor, the blood steaming as it hit the rock. I tried to draw attention to it, but the warden didn't seem concerned.

'You won't die,' he said, looking back at me without breaking his stride. 'You can thank the nectar for that. Your body is, for want of a better word, superhuman. It would take something far more serious to terminate you now. Your wounds will heal in a couple of days, maybe even a few hours. And it will always be that way, just so long as you keep taking the nectar.'

He reached a junction, guarded by a blacksuit. The

giant grinned at me as he wrenched open a metal door and ushered us through.

'Glad you made it,' the guard said.

His words sparked the tiniest of memories, the ghost of something in my former life. I couldn't quite picture it, but I knew it had something to do with playing a game, feeling like I was part of a team. I did my best to return his smile, and although my bruised face prevented my lips from parting I could feel the gleam in my eyes.

Thanks, I tried to say, but only blood escaped my open lips.

The room ahead was darker than the corridor we'd just left, the substantial shadows sweeping from corner to corner as though trying to hide what lay ahead. But nothing could be concealed from my new eyes, and as they focused I made out a long, narrow dormitory lined with what must have been fifty or sixty beds. It could have been the infirmary except for the absence of screens around each patient. That and the fact that the hulking giants in these beds weren't strapped down.

'These are your quarters from now on,' said the warden, his soft voice matching the quiet darkness of the room. 'You will operate in shifts, but we'll worry about that tomorrow. For now, you just need to rest up and let those wounds close.'

He nodded at the blacksuits who held me, and they eased me gently across the room before laying me down on an empty bed. I winced as the change of position caused the pain to flare up again, feeling the immaculate sheets turn warm and wet. Then somebody slid an IV into my arm and the dusk of the room began to seep through my pores, collecting in my mind.

'Sleep,' said the warden, his voice the sound of a razor on a whetstone. 'When you wake you'll feel better than you ever have before.' He turned and marched from the room, the blacksuits a dark cloud in his wake, but he stopped before reaching the door. 'Because then you'll truly be one of us.'

I don't know how long I slept for. Devoid of dreams and nightmares the featureless abyss of time could have been crossed in one night or a hundred years. Even when the darkness parted and I found myself staring at the ceiling I wasn't sure I had actually woken. My body felt completely numb, the absence of pain surely too miraculous to be real.

I lifted a hand, surprised to discover that I hadn't been strapped down, pressing my swollen fingers against my chest, then my face. I could feel the touch, but that was all. There was no scream of ravaged flesh, no sting of stripped skin, no burning of strained muscles. It was as if my battle with the rats had never taken place.

Maybe it hadn't. Even now the memory seemed vague and distant, like something I had watched in a film or dreamed many years ago. It didn't seem possible that I had escaped a tunnel of ice-cold water by pounding my way through a metal hatch. It didn't seem possible that I had taken on an entire nest of deformed, rabid creatures and won.

And surely it wasn't possible that I had ... had killed an innocent kid.

I clamped down on the thought before it could unfold, refusing to let the image of Ozzie's face enter my head. I had done what I'd needed to do to survive, that's all. Ozzie hadn't been one of us, he'd been one of *them*, one of the weak. He had died so that the killer in me could live, so that I could be whole.

All blacksuits had to go through the same thing, I knew that now. I remembered Monty, way back in another life, when I was a different person. He'd been taken, his body ripped apart and put back together the same way mine had been. And he'd been brought back to the cells in general population, let loose on his cellmate Kevin. I'd never been able to figure out why, but it made sense now.

Because once you'd killed in cold blood there was no going back. It changed something inside you. It turned you from one of them into one of us, a blacksuit. That was the true test, I realised. Not the water, not the rats, but the taking of an innocent life.

It was an accident, a part of me argued. But had it been? I'd known the rats were all dead. I'd known there was nothing more to fear. Something else had made me lash out – anger, yes, and hatred of what I had once been, what Ozzie still was. Somewhere in the darkest part of me I'd known exactly what I was doing.

I felt a sudden pang of guilt. Not over the death of Ozzie, but of Monty. He had shed his weaknesses and become a blacksuit, and I had killed him. If only I'd known then what I knew now, known the truth about the warden and his prison, known what it could offer me, I never would have tried to escape.

I heard something stirring and looked across the room to see ten or so blacksuits rising from their beds. They moved as one, pulling back the sheets and getting to their feet, stretching their knotted muscles before donning suits and boots. In less than a minute they were dressed and filing from the room. One caught my eye as he passed and flashed me a silver wink.

'You're awake. Good,' he said without stopping. 'I'll inform the warden.'

They vanished through the door, before returning seconds later. At least I thought that's what had happened until I studied the men walking into the room and realised these blacksuits were a different bunch. Their suits were creased, their faces drawn, their hands dirty. None of them looked my way as they slouched to a set of beds further down the ward, pulled off their suits, collapsed onto the mattresses and hooked IV needles into their arms. With a shudder of exhaustion they all seemed to drift into sleep together.

I sat up and swung my legs over the side of the bed. There were bandages across the areas where the worst injuries had been inflicted, but although each showed a halo of dried blood there was no other indication that I had been so much as scratched. Even the surgery wounds had lost their stitches, now nothing but faded scars beneath fresh skin.

The warden was right. I was superhuman. And it felt great.

My grin must have been visible from the far end of the room, because it's the first thing the warden seemed to notice when he entered.

'I told you you'd feel better after a good sleep,' he said. I looked up, saw that he was carrying something over his shoulder.

'How long was I out?' I asked, my voice like treacle. I was relieved to find that I could form words again.

'Only a night,' he replied, 'though it probably feels like a lifetime.'

I nodded as he reached the bed, careful not to look him in the eye. I had changed, become far stronger than I had ever been, but the warden was still the warden, and his eyes spoke of truths that I never wanted to discover. He stood before me, using his free hand to pull my eyelid back, studying something beneath.

'You've recovered fully,' he said. 'No pain, no aches, am I right?'

I nodded again.

'Then you're ready for this. Stand up.'

I did as I was told, pushing myself off the bed. For an instant I thought the warden had shrunk, until I realised it was me who had grown taller – by at least half a metre. I had obviously been too exhausted to notice the previous night. The warden looked me up and down, then lifted the object from his shoulder and held it out like a gift.

My heart seemed to explode with joy, causing my

muscles to lock and my throat to tighten. I couldn't believe what I was seeing, what the warden was offering me.

'This is yours,' he said. 'Wear it with pride, and know you were one of the first. Because when the world turns and the strong have their way, then you will be amongst us. Here, try it on. It will fit.'

And I knew it would. Because surely nothing in the world could fit me more perfectly than the white shirt and black suit draped across the warden's arms. I choked on my thank you, but neither of us seemed to notice as I reached out and slotted an arm into my new uniform. The linen shirt was cool and soft, a new outer skin against my new inner one, and in my excitement I fumbled with the buttons. The warden cuffed my hands aside, straightening the jacket over my shoulders then doing up the shirt like a father dressing his child.

Seconds later I stood before him fully dressed while he knotted the tie around my neck. He patted it down against my shirt and took a step back, and I swear I could see my glowing pride reflected in his face as he looked me up and down once again.

'Perfect,' he said eventually. 'Welcome home, Soldier of Furnace.'

THE TOUR

I followed the warden with my head held high, enjoying the sound of my new boots as they beat out a rhythm on the stone, and the crisp coolness of the suit that clung to my muscles like silk. Every time we passed a guard in the corridor he would nod at me, and I returned the gesture, knowing at long last what it meant to belong, to be a Soldier of Furnace.

'You have seen most of the prison, from one side of the bars or the other.' The warden spoke over his shoulder as he walked, with only a trace of annoyance in his words. 'But we shall forgive your past trespasses. Only now will you understand the truth of what takes place here, of what we have created.'

He reached the end of the passageway and turned left, stopping at another guarded door. The blacksuit released a huge lock, then pulled the gate open, slamming it as soon as we had passed. I recognised the corridor we were in by the junction up ahead – the right passage ending in the incinerator, the left heading up past the surgery rooms into the infirmary. But the warden led us straight ahead.

I'd been up this way before. The ghost of a memory haunted my thoughts, showing me a corridor leading off to the right, and dozens of crooked creatures in filthy jackets and gas masks staggering down it.

'Wheezers,' I said, fear slowing me down. The warden looked over his shoulder and spat out a dry laugh.

'So you have been down here,' he said. 'Did you get as far as their cells?'

'No,' I replied, picking up speed again and joining the warden. 'No, there were too many of them.'

'You had just killed one of their brothers. They don't take too kindly to that. They won't recognise you now, though.'

The corridor ahead was deserted, with no sign of the creatures who had infested it before. It ended in another door, this one unmanned. The warden gripped the handle and twisted, opening it with a squeal that sounded almost human. As soon as that had faded I could make out music beyond, the sound chillingly unfamiliar after so long in Furnace. I moved towards it but he held out a hand to stop me.

'As I said, the wheezers won't remember that you're the one responsible for the death of their brother. But that doesn't mean it isn't dangerous. Stay in the middle of the room, don't approach any of the cells, and don't look them in the eye.'

It might have been my imagination, but I thought I could sense the slightest trace of anxiety in the warden's voice. However, without another word he turned and walked through the door, his broad steps if anything more confident than before.

Beyond was another room the same size as the infirmary. The music came from an old-fashioned gramophone perched in the middle of the rock floor, a record spinning unevenly on the turntable and the sound spiralling out from its large horn. A woman sang in a strange language, the same one as from my dreams, her voice scratchy and faint but beautiful all the same. I felt something inside me melt at the sweetness of her song, the melody like a knife that cut through the fog and let distant memories bob to the surface of my mind. It lasted only a second as I let my eyes take in the rest of the room.

There were no beds this time, but the ward was far from empty. Even with my new body and the strength it contained I felt my step faltering. It wasn't quite fear, more a faint echo of it, but it still made my legs weak.

Lining both sides were open metal cages, almost like cattle stalls, bolted into the wall. And inside almost every one stood a wheezer. They all seemed to be convulsing, their bodies juddering and spasming, moving too fast for any human. As soon as they saw us, their piggy eyes narrowed and they let loose a collective wheeze, a chorus of hoarse screams that made me want to run from the room, black suit or no black suit.

The warden must have sensed my hesitation, ushering me on with an urgent wave of his hand.

'Don't stop,' he hissed over the music. 'Don't attract their attention.'

Even as he spoke, one of the wheezers staggered forward from its cell, moving like somebody who had just been stabbed. It lurched across the stone floor towards us, using one unsteady hand to pull its jacket aside, revealing the needles strung up beneath. The warden seemed to shrink away for an instant before collecting himself.

'Back!' he barked, moving towards the wheezer with frightening speed. 'Get back to your cell, now!'

The wheezer ground to a halt, watching the warden through the lifeless lumps of coal that served as its eyes. It twitched a couple of times, its head snapping back and a sickening gargle rattling out from behind the gas mask stitched into its skin. Then it slowly turned, traipsing like some zombie back to its cell.

'Come,' the warden said, his voice much quieter but carrying the same authority. 'Before they all start to take an interest.'

I followed him down the length of the room, barely able to take my eyes off the legions of convulsing wheezers. There must have been fifty in here, at least, all identical with their pale, wrinkled skin and their filthy jackets. Luckily none seemed remotely concerned as we opened a door embedded in the far wall, and the only thing that chased us out was another symphony of wheezed screams that concealed the end of the song.

'The north wing is theirs,' the warden said once the door had been sealed. We were in another corridor, this one lined with several openings that resembled the storerooms on the other side of the prison's underbelly.

He marched down the passageway, casting his words over his shoulder. 'It isn't wise to come here alone, only if they call on you.'

'But what are they?' I asked, my heart still running up and down my ribcage. I thought back to my dreams, visions of young men in trench coats and gas masks, and found myself answering my own question. 'They're the same as the men in my nightmares, aren't they? They used to be soldiers.'

The warden peered back at me and I caught his eye. In the space of a single heartbeat, time seemed to unravel, the world disintegrating into a mosaic of brutal images – bombs exploding in mud, dead bodies in trenches, and the same wheezing figures stalking the shadows. Then I blinked and reality reasserted itself with such force that I felt my head spin.

'Soldiers?' the warden asked, stopping beside yet another door. He made no move to open it, staring at the worn metal as if lost in thought. 'We all used to be soldiers.'

'But where? When?'

'A long, long time ago,' he replied, his face suddenly as old as his voice. He was still for a moment more, obviously dwelling on some distant memory, then he seemed to remember I was there. 'Come, let me show you something. It might help explain.'

He turned the lock, pulled open the door, and led me right through the gates of hell.

My first thought was that the room ahead was some kind of grotesque zoo. The air was filled with screams, roars and strangled growls, the sound seeming to battle for supremacy with the stench of waste and decay that clawed its way into my nose, making me want to puke. I reeled back, but the warden stopped me with a scowl.

'There is no escaping it,' he said, gesturing forward with a leather glove. 'This is your destiny now, your home.'

My hand dropped but I kept my back pressed firmly against the cool metal. It was the only thing stopping me from sinking to the floor. I let my gaze wander, but I didn't truly see anything. It was as if my eyes were too scared to settle on the horrors that lay before me in case they were dragged into the madness.

The room was the same as the other wards, red stone walls stretching into shadows above my head, lights hanging down from the ceiling and painting every sick detail in their crimson glow. But while the infirmary and the blacksuit ward were ordered and still – and while even the wheezers had largely remained in their stalls – this place was bedlam.

To the right of the room were a dozen or more cages, like the ones I'd seen in my dream. Glowing silver eyes peered at me from the darkness that swelled at the back of each iron box, and when the figures inside moved I saw that they were dogs. Some were covered in fur and cowering against the bars, others were twice as large, their skin peeled away to reveal the muscles beneath. These monstrosities threw themselves at us, causing the cages to bend outwards, their teeth serrated knives already stained with blood.

Directly opposite them lay a canvas screen, much larger than the ones in the infirmary. Behind it I could glimpse more cages, although the pale forms that lay lifeless in these had none of the characteristics of dogs. I turned away before I could make sense of what I was seeing, the horror boiling up inside my throat.

The warden paced slowly forward, his hands clasped behind his back. I wasn't sure what to do so I trotted after him, eyes on the floor to avoid the sights that surrounded me.

'Don't hide from it,' the warden's voice curled up from the cacophony, a bell-clear whisper in my ear. 'You are part of this place now, just as it is part of you. And it *is* part of you. It flows in your veins, an infinity of power brought about by an eternity of suffering. Because all progress must come from pain. Look.'

I reluctantly obeyed, raising my head to see another cage on the same side of the room as the dogs. This one was much larger, at least three metres high and half as wide. And the creature inside almost filled it completely, its misshapen head ducked low to avoid touching the top, and its immense frame so grotesquely muscled that it bulged through the bars. There were four IV stands positioned around the cage, each with two bags of nectar connected to needles in the creature's arms.

It howled, rattling its cell so hard I was convinced the metal wouldn't hold, but then stopped when it saw us, cocking its head. I looked at its face, at the dripping, drooping maw, at the sunken eyes like silver pennies pressed into a ball of pink dough. And although there was no way I could have known who this creature was, somehow I did.

Gary, I thought, and almost spoke the word aloud before remembering what had happened last time. I couldn't quite recall why I wasn't supposed to know its name, the knowledge like an itch inside my skull. The warden stopped and I could feel his gaze on my skin, scouring me for any sign of emotion.

'Do you know who this is?' he asked.

'No,' I lied. The warden studied me for a moment longer before nodding.

'Another subject,' he explained. 'Although this one has had an unusual reaction to the nectar. The procedure has wiped all trace of humanity from it, all its powers of rational thought and cognitive reasoning. It has become a creature of pure destructive power.'

'A rat,' I said. Again the warden nodded. Another memory flashed across the darkness of my mind: a boy called Gary, devoid of emotion, willing to kill for nothing more than a thrill. The nectar hadn't turned him into a monster. How could it? He had already been one. Again the itch seemed to burrow into the bone of my skull, a tide of memories wanting to be released, and I spoke just to chase it away. 'If he's a rat, then why hasn't he been incinerated?'

'Look at him,' was the warden's reply. 'Physically he is far superior to the other specimens who have undertaken the procedure. The nectar has made his body grow at almost twice the normal rate. And it doesn't seem to be stopping.'

The warden approached the cage and held out a hand. The creature took the bait, lashing through the bars with hooked fingers. The warden was too fast, ducking out of range with a humourless snigger.

'I want to know why, and so do the wheezers. We've had a number of specimens react this way, but we don't yet understand it. If we can find out what it was about his body that reacted so effectively with the nectar, then we can change the formula, we can ensure that all our new *recruits*' – he said the last word with the same chilling laugh – 'match his size and strength. Besides, specimens like this are of extreme interest to Alfred Furnace himself. They are his personal project, the berserkers. He takes very special care of them.'

'Here?' I asked. The presence of Gary alone was enough to strike terror into me, but the idea that there might be more like him, more killing machines of mutated muscle and uncontrollable fury, was enough to make me want to leap right out of my new suit and cower in the corner. The warden sensed my discomfort and flashed me another crooked smile.

'No, even this place cannot hold the berserkers. They exist in a far more secure compound. Dr Furnace's domain. A place you may one day see, if you are lucky.'

I stared at one of the IV bags, saw the darkness inside, and beyond that the golden dust that sparkled like distant galaxies. Even as I watched I felt the nectar in my own blood respond to the sight, fuelling my heart as it beat a little faster, sharpening my senses so that the smells and sights and sounds of the room became almost unbearable. I wrenched my eyes away, focusing on the floor once again until the sense of vertigo had passed.

'But what is the nectar?' I asked, if only to hear my own voice. 'Where does it come from?'

'It comes from the very worst places of the world,' the warden said, walking as he talked. 'And the very best. I couldn't tell you exactly what it is. Neither could the wheezers, even if they spoke. Only Dr Furnace knows, because he was the one who discovered it.'

'Discovered it?' I started. We passed another screen and he pointed inside. I followed his finger, seeing an operating table beyond. On it, unconscious and twitching in its sleep, was a dog. Half its body had been blown up like rotten fruit, the veins in its skin pumping black as the nectar pulsed through them.

'Alfred Furnace was there at the beginning.' The warden laughed that sick laugh again. 'Well, we all were, but he was the mind who engineered the nectar, who created the first of us. He was the one who discovered that war does not just have to create horrors, but wonders too.'

'I don't understand,' I said. 'You're saying that Furnace created the nectar during a war?'

'During *the* war,' the warden replied.

I shook my head, seeing more images from my dreams: the boys with swastikas on their prison uniforms, the soldiers with the same emblem emblazoned across their jackets. I knew what period in history those sights belonged to, but it was too long ago.

'That's impossible,' I said. The warden's face split open into a smile that seemed too wide, too gleeful, like a child remembering a seaside holiday.

'With the nectar, nothing is impossible,' he replied. 'It makes the human body a machine of infinite possibilities. Even age has no hold on us with the power of Furnace in our veins.'

I studied the warden's skin, like old leather, my new eyes letting me see every tiny crack and wrinkle in his face. He seemed ancient, older than time.

'But,' I tried again. 'You can't have been alive . . .'

'I was,' he said, once again letting his eyes crawl over my face. 'The nectar was created during the Second World War, and I was there to witness its birth.'

TRUTH

'I don't believe you,' I said when I remembered how to speak. 'It can't be.'

'But it is,' the warden replied without missing a beat. 'There is no need for lies and exaggeration when the nectar is involved.'

He began to walk again and my silent bubble of shock burst, letting the chaos of the room back in. I drew back as the creature that had once been Gary stretched out a hand towards me, trying to hear past its nightmare screams to keep hold of my scattered thoughts. The warden looked old, yes, but not old enough to have fought in the Second World War. It would have meant he'd been alive for a century.

'You more than most should know what it is like to have the nectar inside you,' the warden went on. 'Know how it changes you, how it improves you. How does it feel, knowing you will live far longer now than you ever could have dreamed?'

I tried to get my head round the thought but it was impossible. He was right, I had all the evidence I needed to believe him. The nectar had completely changed my body, after all; it had let me shrug off wounds that would have killed a normal person. And it had obviously kept the warden and the wheezers alive for far longer than they had any right to be. Maybe it would make me immortal as well as invulnerable. I smiled at the thought, my shark's grin imitated by the warden.

And yet the itch still ground itself against the back of my head, the thought that something here wasn't right.

'Alfred Furnace discovered a way to harness the nightmares of war, the anger and hatred of the soldiers,' the warden continued as he strolled further into the madhouse. 'He was experimenting on troops, ones who had been injured, and those driven insane. You saw this in your dreams too, did you not?'

I remembered the vision of the battlefield, the young soldier lying on the edge of death in the mud, scream-ing as the men in trench coats and gas masks carried him away. The warden knew my answer without look-ing at me.

'He found something in the weakest men, in those who feared death the most. He found something *inside* them.'

'The nectar,' I said. I didn't understand anything that the warden was saying, but the truth of it sat in my gut, swam in my veins.

'It was the essence of the nectar,' the warden corrected. 'The darkness that lies at the heart of it. Dr Furnace realised he could take that darkness and replicate it artificially. And that's what led to the nectar.'

The further we walked into the room, and the deeper the warden progressed into his story, the greater the horrors around me became. It was as if his words were so terrible that they morphed the world around us, turning it into a hideous parody of itself.

Past the operating table, half hidden by a blood-stained screen, was another huge cage, this one occupied by two rats who tore at what might once have been a limb – just a few scraps of flesh on dirty bone. Beside this, propped up next to each other like dominoes, were several stiff, pale corpses which didn't resemble anything human, yet unmistakably still were. Beyond them, on the other side of the room, a wheezer sat on a wooden chair picking the filth from its gloves. It didn't seem to notice us as we passed, but the figure still made me so nervous that it took a moment for me to realise that the warden was talking.

'His moment of triumph came when he discovered what happened to the human body when the artificial nectar was introduced. It stripped away all of the weaknesses that plagued the mind. It transformed his subjects into killers, true soldiers, without fear and without remorse; without any emotions, save those from which the nectar was derived – anger, cruelty, and hatred.'

The warden's speech was growing louder and faster with every word, as though he could barely contain his excitement.

'And with the weaknesses of the mind now under control, the body could become what it was truly meant to be, could grow to the size and strength that nature intended it. With a little help from the knife, of course. Thanks to Alfred Furnace, mere mortals – those pathetic souls known as men – could become gods.'

He aimed the last word at another cluster of cages piled high against the wall to my right. These all stood empty apart from one, where yet another body pleaded back at me with dead eyes – one silver and the other brown.

'Not that there weren't sacrifices to be made,' the warden said, once again coming to a halt. He locked eyes with the corpse. 'Dr Furnace soon realised that the adult body couldn't cope with the nectar, or the surgery. The cells only lasted so long before they literally disintegrated. Only a young body, one that hadn't fully matured, had the strength to recover. And even then there were those whose bodies rejected the nectar, who died on the operating table.'

'Or who became rats,' I added.

'That's right. Because there is a fine line between erasing a person's mental weaknesses, their emotions, and wiping out every last trace of humanity. Too little nectar and they die from the surgery. Too much and they become monsters. Dr Furnace thought he could find the right balance in time to win the war, but by the time he had perfected the nectar the Allies had taken Berlin and he was forced to flee.'

'Flee?' I said, suddenly realising what the warden was saying. 'Because he was a war criminal, a Nazi war criminal, right?'

I could sense the anger charging up inside the warden,

his entire body seeming to swell. But he took a deep breath and the tension dissipated.

'Dr Furnace was a genius. He managed to do what nature could not. He created a race of beings far superior to humankind. Soldiers who could fight without fear, without pain, without pity.'

'But –'

'But nothing,' the warden spat back. 'Do you know what it's like to throw yourself into battle knowing that you are going to die? To see your friends fall by your feet, their heads split wide open, or blown to mist by a mortar shell? Do you?'

He swung round, grabbing my face in his hand before I could turn away. In his eyes I saw his words take life, becoming visions of pain and fear and violence that poured into my head. I fought him but his grip was too strong, and I was forced to relive his horror as he spoke.

'I do. I was there, in the mud and the excrement and the blood, with a gun that wouldn't fire because my hands were too cramped to pull the trigger, with a uniform too tight to let me run, with bullets screaming towards me from friend and foe because nobody could see what they were supposed to be shooting at, with the skies opening and bombs falling from it like God crushing insects, with darkness all around us, so deep, so endless that we might as well have been blind, or dead. And the pain when you're hit, when you feel that sliver of red-hot metal puncture your guts and set fire to your insides, knowing you can't go on and you can't go back because your own men will cut your throat for cowardice, knowing that you're going to die with your face trampled into the dirt so far from home, so far from everything you know.'

He let go of my chin and I snapped my head away, reeling as the last of the images bled from my mind.

'I was your age when I was forced into war,' he went on, his tone softer. 'And I would have died was it not for Dr Furnace. He showed me what it was like to feel no fear, to be a creature of pure power, of unlimited strength. If he'd been allowed to carry on his work then terror would have become a thing of the past. War too, for that matter. Because when the strong inevitably overcame the weak, and the powerless were scrubbed from the face of the earth, then who would be left to fight?'

He set off, entering the final third of the room, and I followed – part of me terrified of hearing the rest of his story, part of me desperate to know what happened next.

'After the war Dr Furnace came to this country. We all did. And we found a way to carry on his work, continue our research into the nectar.'

'Why here?' I asked, somehow managing to find the words. 'Why a prison?'

'Why do you think? Where better to replicate the panic, the hatred, the anger of a battlefield than a place like this? A place with no mercy, no sanctuary, where violence lies around every corner, where the powerless are persecuted by the powerful, and where your enemies will kill you simply for the joy of watching you die. Although for many years we tried to accomplish our goals by various means, there was no way of accessing the numbers we needed, and the ages that were so vital. But eventually, when your government finally saw that liberalism was no way to run a country and Furnace Penitentiary opened its doors, we had an unlimited number of subjects to work on, with absolute immunity.'

I felt the room start to spin again, and closed my eyes for a moment to recover my balance. I couldn't believe what I was hearing, yet what else could explain everything that I'd seen here, and everything that had been done to me?

'And we are close, so close, to what we want to achieve,' the warden said, steering me to the left to avoid a puddle of blood that rippled out from behind a screen. I couldn't see past this one, but the gargled cries and dry wheezes beyond let me know what was happening there. 'There will be another war, a great war, and the world will at last fall to its natural leaders, its supreme race. Survival of the strongest, and a total annihilation of the weak. And you, my friend, you will have the honour of being on the winning side. You will have a place in the new fatherland.'

The warden spoke the last sentence with a pride that seemed to explode from his every pore, and it was impossible not be roused by it. I felt the nectar in my blood burn through my heart, and my mind, carrying with it a hunger for power. I could be one of the chosen few, part of a new race that would scour humanity of everything that stopped it reaching its full potential. With the nectar in our blood, nothing could stand in our way.

And yet as soon as that rush of euphoria passed it left a stain behind it, like the slime trail that follows a slug. It was almost as if there was something wrong with what the warden was saying. But how could there be? What could be wrong with a world in which weakness did not exist? Still the feeling persisted, a familiar churning in my gut that I couldn't quite place.

As the warden led the way towards a door at the far end of the room I saw a fleeting image of the boy I used to be robbing a house. With it came the rush of easy money followed by the guilt of what I had done – the latter quickly buried out of sight. I didn't know why, but I was feeling the same thing now, a sickening combination of sweet and sour.

The warden had to flick a chunk of something red and wet from the door handle before wrenching open the huge iron portal.

'But for every soldier like you, every child of Furnace, who has a place in the new world,' he went on, walking into another tunnel carved into the rock, 'there must necessarily be those left behind. The nectar does not work on everybody. It seems that some genetic codes are resistant to the darkness inside it, no matter how much you give them. These unfortunate souls can play no part in the war that will follow.'

I wondered why he was telling me this, but then I

heard shouts from up ahead, an accent I recognised, and suddenly it became clear. The itch in my skull became a stabbing pain and I faltered, bracing a hand on the wall. The warden heard my ragged breathing and stopped, his smile sliding from his face for an instant before he remembered to pull it back.

'Is something wrong?' he asked, and I knew from his tone that there was only one answer I could safely give.

'No, I'm fine,' I said. 'It's just a lot to take in.'

'Indeed it is, indeed it is,' the warden replied, chewing on the words as though deciding whether to believe them. 'It will be easier when this is over. Come, follow me.' He talked as he walked. 'As I was saying, there are those who can never know the power of Alfred Furnace's creation. The only purpose they serve is to make us stronger.'

He reached a door, but this one was already open. Inside I could make out the thump of fist on flesh, and I was unsure whether the squirming in my gut came from fear or excitement. There was another shout, followed by booming laughter, and the warden took that as his cue. He grasped my arm and pulled me through.

'The only purpose they serve is to make us into killers, to help us embrace our destiny.'

The room ahead was small, the rock splashed a deeper shade of red than the corridor we'd just left. Two blacksuits stood in the centre of it, their clenched, swollen fists the same colour as the walls. They were still laughing as the warden continued speaking.

'The only purpose they serve is to die.'

The blacksuits stood to one side to reveal a boy strapped to a chair. His head drooped against his chest, blood still dripping from his nose, but when he heard us enter he looked up and fixed us with a fierce, defiant stare. I knew him. He was the kid who had tried to kill me, tried to smother me with a pillow. What had his friends called him? Zee? But there was something more, something about him that I couldn't quite remember. I fought to access the memory, groaning as the agony in my skull grew worse.

The warden held out his hand towards the boy like he was giving me a present.

'He's all yours,' he said, his teeth glinting in the harsh light. 'Now kill him.'

RAGE

I didn't move. I couldn't. The pain in my head was growing. My memories were a dark tide, my mind a floodgate about to buckle under the pressure.

'Did you hear me?' the warden said, his voice as sharp and cold as a knife edge. 'Kill him.'

All eyes in the room were on me – two sets of silver pennies from the blacksuits, which somehow weren't anywhere near as intense as those that belonged to the kid. He stared up at me from his chair, never blinking, even though tears of blood snaked their way down his cheeks.

But it was the warden's gaze which filled me with terror. I couldn't bring myself to look at him, knowing that his expression would be one of disdain. I'd seen it before, the times I had failed him during my procedure, and I couldn't bear to witness his disappointment in me again.

I steeled myself, blacking out my mind and focusing on the job ahead. What was so difficult about this? I had killed before, after all. I had slaughtered the rats, and murdered Ozzie. I was a killer, a soldier. Taking a life meant nothing to me any more.

More pain in my head, like I was trying to put my mind into a gear it simply wouldn't engage. I screwed my eyes shut, taking a deep breath and hoping that when I opened them again the kid would be gone. Or at least be looking the other way. But when the room swam into focus he was still staring at me, his expression of defiance carved in stone.

'Go on,' the boy spat. 'What are you waiting for? Get it over with, Alex.'

I felt my heart lurch, that last word so close and yet so distant. Before I could grasp why, one of the black-suits lashed out and caught the kid with a savage blow to the temple. His head snapped back, and for a moment I thought the guard had done my job for me, then the kid's eyes opened once again, his gaze swinging blindly around the room before finding me.

'Are you disobeying me?' the warden growled, his rancid breath on my face. 'Did you not hear what I ordered you to do? Kill him, *now.*'

Even before his last word was spoken I felt something slap me across the cheek. Stars exploded in my vision and I staggered back across the room. The blow hadn't been hard so much as shocking, and I could feel the anger clawing up from my stomach. My pulse accelerated, the room growing darker as the nectar laced every vein and artery.

I swung round to the warden, my teeth clenched as tightly as my fists. He slapped me again, his hand moving so fast I didn't even see it, and this time the anger flared like a fireball inside my head.

'That's better,' the warden said. 'Feel that power, that anger. You are a Soldier of Furnace, and I your commandant. You will do as I say.'

The nectar began to flood my mind, erasing everything but the hatred, the rage. I looked down at the kid, so small and weak. He was just like Ozzie, cowering for his life – a life that belonged to me, that was mine to spare or take as I wished.

Only he wasn't cowering. He wasn't weak. He was still glaring up at me, his eyes so bright that it was I who broke contact with them. I glanced at the blacksuits, their smiles wavering along with my will. They could finish off this kid with a single blow, and so could I. What the hell was wrong with me?

I turned to the warden for support. I could feel the panic surging through the anger, swimming up my throat like bile. His hand flashed, a solid punch that rocked me back. He followed it with two more slaps, one across each cheek. I roared in pain, a sound that seemed to come from every fibre in my body, and held up my fists to defend myself.

'This is pathetic,' the warden was screaming, specks of phlegm exploding from the corners of his mouth. 'Are you so stupid that you don't remember him trying to kill you, pushing a pillow over your face? The nectar has rejected him, it does not work on him. He can never be one of us. *He must die!*'

The warden slapped me again, and again, a flurry of

strikes that made my blood boil. Then he took my arm and swung me round, pushing me towards the kid.

'Now do it, or I swear I'll kill you both myself and throw your corpses into the incinerator.'

I lifted my hand, feeling my muscles swell against my suit with such force that I thought I heard the fabric tear. The nectar thrashed inside me, desperate for blood, for vengeance, and before I knew what I was doing I had grabbed the tattered overalls around the boy's chest. His body was brittle against my skin, nothing but parchment and dust. How could he die when he wasn't properly alive?

I let one hand snake up to his throat, my huge, scarred fingers engulfing the twig of bone that served as his neck. One squeeze, one snap, is all it would take.

'That's it,' came the warden's voice from behind me. 'Do it.'

'You'll feel better when it's over,' added one of the blacksuits. 'Don't think about it, just one hard twist and you're done.'

I tightened my grip, the sting of the warden's slaps like a branding iron on my face, fuelling the anger that stewed within. And still the kid didn't look away, his eyes so fierce that they seemed to burn right through me.

'You may as well just kill me,' the boy said. The boy called Zee. 'Because if you don't then they will. And I'd rather it was you, Alex, even though you're not you any more. After everything we've been through, I'd rather you killed me than them bastards.'

'Shut up,' I growled, feeling the pain like a blade across the surface of my brain. It opened up a hole in the darkness, letting out a memory that was so bright, so vibrant, that it took my breath away – me and Zee sitting on a bunk packed with gas-filled rubber gloves, laughing. It was there for an instant and then it vanished, plunging me back into the night.

'Do it now,' said the warden, his impatience like a fuse burning down to its last millimetre, ready to blow.

'Yeah, just do it,' Zee said. 'I don't want to be here any more. There is no way out except this way. You did it for Donovan, now do it for me, Alex. Do it for me. Let me go home.'

He thrust his head forward, pressing his throat against my hand, his eyes never leaving mine. I could feel his pulse against my palm, soft and fast like a bird's.

'Let me go home.'

Home. I didn't even know what the word meant, but again the knife drew across my mind, freeing the memories imprisoned within. I saw the pair of us jumping into a river, saw us climbing a chimney, saw the glint of sunlight above us. And suddenly there were words in my head, words that I knew had nothing to do with the warden.

'All for one,' I spoke them aloud, my voice little more than a whisper. Something in Zee's face seemed to change, his eyes widening.

'And let's get the hell out of here, Alex,' he mouthed, so quietly that even I couldn't hear him. But I knew what he meant. I remembered us saying it before. Gradually the nectar was ebbing away, sluiced from my mind to reveal the memories beneath. Donovan, Monty, my mum and dad and . . .

'My name,' I said, loosening the grip around Zee's throat. 'I remember my name.'

'You have no name,' the warden shrieked, his voice deafening in the small room. He spun me round and this time it was his hand around my throat, his grip like a vice. 'You never had one. You didn't exist until I made you. You belong to me!'

He raised his other hand as if to slap me, but before he could I snapped up my arm and caught his wrist. I looked him in the eye, and this time all I saw were two watery pupils which blinked at me in shock.

'My name is Alex Sawyer,' I hissed.

The warden opened his mouth but before anything could come out of it my fist connected with his nose. I let go of him and he staggered back, blood the colour of tar spraying from between the fingers he held up to his face. I followed with an uppercut to his stomach, sending him crashing down onto the stone.

The blacksuits were on me before I could turn round, a giant hand on the back of my head slamming me into the wall. I felt something inside my face crack but I'd been in this situation before and I knew how to handle the pain. The nectar pumped back into my heart, into my head, only this time it was on my side, the anger giving me strength.

Bracing my hands against the stone I pushed back as hard as I could. The guards were caught off balance, stumbling across the room. I turned in time to see Zee stick out a foot, sending one of the suits somersaulting into the far corner.

The other swung his head round to see what had happened, and when he looked back at me all he saw was my elbow. It caught him in the throat with a blow so solid I could feel the tremors travel through my spine, but it worked. He dropped to his knees, gasping for breaths that wouldn't come.

I leapt across the room in a single stride, landing on the other suit's chest as he tried to get up. His silver eyes became as wide as goblets, unable to believe what they were seeing, then they faded to a dull grey as I snapped his head round.

'You were right,' I said, getting to my feet. 'One hard twist.'

'Oh Jesus, oh Jesus, oh Jesus,' I heard Zee's chant and remembered that he was there, running to his chair and unfastening the straps that held him. He staggered to his feet, never taking his eyes off me. 'Oh Jesus, Alex. What have they done to you?'

I looked at the dead blacksuit in the corner, then at the dying one by my feet, and finally at the warden who was leaving a trail of dark blood behind him as he crawled towards the open door. Then I looked at my hands, stained red.

'They've given me what I need,' I said, grinning. 'They've given us what *we* need to get out of here.'

Even past the bruises and the blood I could see Zee's smile blossom. He ran forward and wrapped his arms around me, his head now only reaching my chest. Then he sprung back, shaking his hands like they'd been stung.

'Man, you're burning up,' he said.

'Yeah,' I replied. I was about to add more when I saw the warden pull something from his jacket. Too late I noticed the square box he was holding with a panic button at its centre. He turned and glared up at me, his face curling into a sneer. Then he pressed down with his thumb and a siren blasted into the room.

'Lockdown!' said Zee, the deafening klaxon turning his shout to a whisper. 'What do we do?'

I looked once again at the carnage inside the room, then grabbed Zee's arm and dragged him towards the door.

'We run.'

A DISTRACTION

We flew from the room, Zee kicking out at the warden's head as we passed like he was taking a penalty. There was a jarring crack and the warden's body flailed into the wall, more of that thick, black blood spurting from his lips.

'Don't you dare get up,' Zee screamed, his face twisted into an expression of pure hatred. We didn't hang around long enough to see if the warden would take our advice, swinging left into the corridor beyond and bolting towards the door.

'Where are we going?' Zee yelled over the siren. I stopped at the end of the passageway, twisting the handle and opening the door a fraction. My mind was a mess, my thoughts smashing against each other like boats in a hurricane, the nectar a storm cloud that threatened to plunge everything into darkness.

'I have no idea,' I said. 'But we have to get out of here.'

And we did. Because when reinforcements arrived there would be no more tests, no more questions, no more torture. The warden would have us killed on the spot.

The room ahead was just as it had been when I'd walked through it minutes ago, the only sign of life the monsters in cages. The wheezer that had been cleaning its gloves was now standing, its black eyes watching us suspiciously through the crack in the door. I took a deep, ragged breath and straightened myself out, grabbing Zee roughly by the collar and dragging him into the ward.

'What are you doing?' he said, his tiny hands prising at my fingers and the whites of his eyes showing. He looked afraid and I didn't blame him. He'd just seen me kill two blacksuits with my bare hands and he had no idea what I was capable of. Right then neither did I; the nectar was causing too much confusion.

'Just trust me,' I growled, the words more a vibration than a sound. I marched forward with as much confidence as I could muster, heading right for the wheezer. It cocked its head, its bubbling breath audible even over the alarm, but all it saw was a prisoner being escorted by a blacksuit and it quickly lost interest.

As soon as its head was turned I let go of Zee and charged. The chair it had been sitting on was in between me and it and I picked it up as I ran, swinging it like a baseball bat. It stuck the wheezer in its back, sinking into the porridge of flesh beneath the coat with a sound like feet being pulled from mud. The creature tumbled across the room, crashing into a cage and lying still.

'Good shot,' said Zee, but I could barely hear him because the noise in the room erupted. The creatures in the cages were screaming and barking and growling like it was feeding time, the sound of screeching metal letting me know that some of the bars weren't going to hold.

'Come on,' I said, sprinting down the ward towards the far door. If we could just get out of here then we might be able to hide somewhere until the coast was clear.

But before we had made it halfway the door swung open to reveal six hulking shapes packed into the corridor. A dozen blazing silver eyes swung round the room before focusing on me. Maybe if I'd kept my cool, if I'd acted like one of them, they might have run right past me. But something in my hunched, defensive stance gave me away.

'Get him,' one of the blacksuits bellowed, raising his shotgun and letting off a round before he had even entered the room. I heard the pellets tear through the air, ricocheting off the stone, and dived for cover behind a cage. Zee threw himself to the ground next to me as the space we were standing in was torn to shreds by shotgun fire.

What now? I screamed at myself. I could feel the anger swelling up inside me again, feel the nectar urging me to fight. I'd beaten two blacksuits, but six or more, armed with guns? It wasn't going to happen.

Something to my side bellowed, the roar dwarfing even the siren. I ducked instinctively, peering through my raised hands to see that we were right next to Gary's cage. Even in the time since I'd last seen him he had grown bigger, and when he rammed his deformed fists against the barred door I saw one of the hinges fly clean off. He lashed out again, leaving knuckle-shaped indents in the metal. I could hear the thump of the blacksuits' shoes, approaching cautiously, the pump of their guns.

Talk about being stuck between a rock and a hard place.

Zee's fingers dug into my arm and I turned to see him watching with open-mouthed astonishment.

'That's . . . oh Jesus, Alex, that's Gary,' he said. I nodded, risking a peek round the side of the cage to see that the first wave of guards had been joined by several more. I barely got my head back in time before the air exploded into smoke and sparks.

'We're screwed,' I said, blinking the fire from my eyes. 'So screwed.'

Gary was winning his battle with the cage, using his trunk-like legs to pound one of the bolts from its casing. The door rattled alarmingly, his face behind the bars a mask of absolute rage. I saw the nectar still pumping into him from the IV bags, knew that the only thing going through his head was murder. If he got loose then he'd kill all of us, Zee and me and the blacksuits, without breaking a sweat.

Suddenly I knew what to do.

'Get ready to run,' I said to Zee. 'Head round to the far side of the room, behind those cages. Get to the door.'

'What are you going to do?' he asked, shaking his head as if he already knew.

'Something really, really stupid,' I replied. 'Now go!'

He didn't hesitate, staying low as he ran close to the walls, keeping the cages between him and the guards for cover. I went to move and found that I couldn't, fear rooting me to the spot. Then, with a choked cry of defiance, I threw myself towards Gary's cage.

The creature inside reacted like lightning, angling its gnarled hand down and raking razored claws across my chest. I ignored the pain, reaching out and grabbing hold of the last bolt that secured his cage. I barely had time to slide it open and push myself away before Gary punched the door, snapping the remaining hinge and sending it spinning across the room.

The blacksuits were already firing at me, buckshot like a branding iron as it burned through my flesh. One blast struck me in the leg and I collapsed. It probably saved my life.

Gary burst from his cell like a rhino, unleashing another roar that shook the very stone on which I lay. One vast foot smashed down inches from my head, but before he could start on me I heard the blacksuits firing their weapons, felt the patter of hot blood on my skin as the beast above me was hit. And then he was gone, powering across the room towards his attackers.

'Alex!' Zee's urgent cry forced me up, the agony of my shredded leg already fading as the nectar did its job. I ran directly across the room towards him, looking briefly to my side as I did.

It was a massacre. The creature that had once been Gary was tearing into the blacksuits like a kid playing

134

with dolls. They didn't stand a chance, their weapons skidding across the floor, their punches useless against Gary's raw fury. In the space of a second or two the scene was masked by smoke and a mist of blood.

'Are you crazy?' demanded Zee. 'The old Gary was bad enough, but –'

He didn't get a chance to finish. Something flew over our heads, a black–clad lump that rained blood. I grabbed Zee's arm again and ran, ducking round the back of the cages. Every now and again there would be a flash of red through the bars as Gary continued his work, but I focused on the path ahead, looping round the side of the room towards the far wall.

We didn't stop when we saw the door, hurtling through it without looking back. There was another terrifying scream, but whether it was directed at us or at one of the suits we didn't know and it was soon lost as we slammed the door shut behind us. I grabbed the lock and twisted it, using all my strength to bend the metal round. It would take some effort to open it from the other side but I was pretty sure Gary wouldn't have any trouble.

The corridor was so quiet after the hell we'd just been through that I thought I'd gone deaf. Then the siren broke through the frantic pumping of blood in my ears and I remembered we were a long way from safety. Staggering from the door I set off down the passageway, Zee by my side. We passed one of the storerooms and he pointed inside.

'What about in there?' he asked.

I peered in through the door, my eyes dissecting the darkness to reveal a grainy black and white room that was empty, and far too small to conceal ourselves in.

'It's not big enough,' I said. 'They'll find us in seconds. Come on.'

I set off again before Zee could ask the question I saw in his expression.

'I can see in the dark,' I explained. 'All the blacksuits can. It's why our eyes are silver.'

'You're not a blacksuit,' Zee said over the alarm. I felt his hands on my sleeve, pulling me to a halt, and turned to face him. 'You're not a blacksuit,' he went on. 'You said *our eyes*. But you're not one of them, Alex, you're one of us.'

I nodded, smiling. But I don't know whether I believed him. I mean I looked like a blacksuit, I had the nectar in me. How long would it let me remember my old life before the darkness started to creep back in?

The sound of cages crashing to the floor behind us broke through the moment, spurring us on. Only one of the storerooms along the corridor was big enough to hide in, but even that wouldn't conceal us for long. There was only one thing for it: we had to go through the infirmary, then out into the network of caves that circled the prison. Surely we could find a safe place there.

We reached the end of the passageway and Zee started to open the door. I heard the music first, a different song but the same haunting tone scratched out from the gramophone. As soon as the door was open, though, the woman's voice was drowned out by the bone-dry squeals of the wheezers. I looked inside to see that most were still in their stalls, although some lurched across the middle of the ward as if trying to find the source of the siren.

'Keep running and don't stop,' I said, throwing myself forward. I ran wildly round one wheezer, twisting my body out of the way as it raised a gloved hand towards me. I barrelled into another, sending it sprawling to the floor. The wheezed screams of its brothers grew more urgent as they staggered from their cells, but they were too slow to stop us.

I'll give you something to cry about, I thought, kicking out at the gramophone as I passed it. The woman's voice vanished in a scratch, the record smashing as it struck the stone. The wail of distress that rose up in surround sound from all around me shredded my nerves, but before it could reach a crescendo we had swung open the door and skidded into the corridor beyond.

I pulled the door shut, bending the metal lock round the same way I had before, and was about to head off when I heard Zee's breathless retching. He was puking in the corner of the corridor, nothing but a thin trail that looked like gruel dangling from his trembling lips. He gagged once more, then looked up at me through watery eyes.

'Sorry,' he said. 'I would have waited for a better time but, you know . . . Once it's on the way up there ain't no stopping it.'

I put a hand under his armpit and eased him gently up. The siren was even louder out here, and I could hear

137

the stamp of booted feet on stone. But this time I knew what to do. So did Zee.

'You thinking what I'm thinking?' he asked.

'What's that?'

'The Wookiee gambit,' he answered with a smile. I didn't have a clue what he was talking about, but somewhere in my head a distant memory was forming. He raised an eyebrow. 'Christ, Alex, what have they done to your brain? You don't remember *Star Wars*?'

I shook my head, but even as I was doing so more memories bubbled up to the surface, cut off as the thunder of footsteps grew louder. Zee laced his hands behind his back as though he was wearing handcuffs, bowing his head and shuffling forward. I knew what he was getting at, keeping my hand firmly on his shoulder and straightening my back. We marched round the corner, then took the first right that led up to the infirmary.

A group of blacksuits nearly hit us as they charged out from the plastic curtain. One stopped and lifted his gun, and it was all I could do not to throw myself to the floor as I stared into the bottomless barrel. But I steeled myself, glaring at him as fiercely as I could, and he quickly lowered it.

'Where's the warden?' he boomed over the siren, glancing at the bloodstains on my shirt where Gary had slashed me, then at Zee. 'And why is he here?'

'Number . . .' I thought back to one of the conversations I'd heard when I was in the infirmary, the number they'd given to Gary. '195 is loose. They're trying to contain him. I was told to bring this one back to his bed.' I shook Zee roughly by the collar, hard enough to rattle his teeth, and he glared at me. 'You'd better go help, it's a mess in there.'

Several pairs of suspicious silver eyes looked me up and down.

'I said go!' I growled, as deeply as I could. The suit in front charged off without another word, the guards like a dark shadow sweeping after him. I didn't wait to see what they'd make of the bent lock on the door, letting go of Zee and pushing through the curtain of plastic slats.

'Piece of cake,' he said.

'Piece of cake,' I repeated. And it was a good thing that the infirmary was empty of blacksuits and wheezers because we were giggling with relief as we set off across it.

A RESCUE MISSION

It was Zee who remembered Simon.

I stopped running when I realised I couldn't hear his footsteps any more, spinning round to see him peering through the curtains that hid each bed.

'Come on,' I hissed, expecting the blacksuits to burst into the infirmary at any moment, the warden at their head and ordering our immediate execution. 'We've got to find somewhere to hide.'

'Not without Simon and Ozzie,' Zee replied, ducking behind another screen. 'Check the other side.'

I couldn't move. My mind filled with visions of Ozzie's face as he pleaded for my help, his limp body after I'd snatched the life from him. Zee emerged again, his face falling when he saw my expression.

'What?' he asked. 'You know where they are?'

Yeah, I knew. Ozzie would be in a pile of corpses ready to go into the incinerator, his eyes staring blindly at the ceiling. Either that or he was already ashes lining the chimney that led to the surface. Maybe some of those charred specks would make it all the way to the top. Maybe that way he'd be free.

Or maybe I was just telling myself that so I'd feel less guilty about killing him.

'Alex, if you know where they are then you've got to tell me. They both risked their lives getting us out, we can't leave them here.'

I shook myself free from the paralysis that gripped me, running to the other side of the room and looking behind a curtain. The bed was empty, the ancient bloodstains on the mattress like the shadow of its previous occupant.

'I don't know where Simon is,' I replied. 'But Ozzie is . . . I think he might be dead.'

I looked back across the infirmary to gauge Zee's reaction, and the moment our eyes met it was clear that he knew what I was saying. He froze, his mouth dropping open, but he managed to stop himself asking the question I was dreading.

'Then we have to find Simon and get the hell out of here,' he said eventually, pushing his head past another set of curtains then wrenching it out a split second later. I did the same, seeing a boy with a bandaged face in one cubicle and a couple more empty beds after that. It was as I was peeling back the next that I heard Simon's voice. It was faint over the relentless siren, but unmistakably his.

Zee had obviously heard it too and we set off down the infirmary together, listening for his call in the quiet valleys where the alarm faded into itself. After a couple of failed attempts we ripped open a set of curtains to see him strapped to a bed, his silver eyes as wide as the grin that welcomed us.

'Y'know, you two really don't get the meaning of subtle, do you?' he said, almost laughing. 'I could hear you yabbering away as soon as you entered the infirmary.'

We laughed quietly, Zee popping his head back out to act as lookout while I unfastened Simon's buckles. Although there was an IV drip by his bed, he didn't look like he'd been through any more surgery – his disfigured body and single, enormous arm the same as they had been the last time I'd seen him. He struggled to sit up, a worrying series of clicks emanating from his muscles as he stretched.

'I thought the warden had already given up on you,' I said, remembering Simon's stories of being dumped.

'Guess he figured I deserved a second chance,' he replied with a shrug. 'What about Ozzie? You found him yet?'

I let my eyes drop to the floor, my confession ready on my lips.

'He didn't make it,' Zee said before I could speak. 'Suits got him. I'm sorry, Simon.'

Despite the siren, silence seemed to hang heavy in the room. Simon thumped the bed and I heard the grief choked in his throat. It was almost too much, Ozzie's face once again swimming before mine, his eyes glaring at me. Then I felt Zee's hand on my arm and the illusion vanished.

'He wouldn't want us to mourn him,' Zee said. 'He'd want us to get out of here. Right?'

'Right,' replied Simon, getting unsteadily to his feet. He rested his large arm on my shoulder and we staggered forward like two oversized kids in a three-legged race. Zee checked once again to make sure the coast was clear, then vanished in a flash of white.

We pounded after him, heading for the plastic curtain at the far end of the room. I could hear more shouts beyond, and the barking of dogs, but they seemed distant. We had time.

'Left or right? Which way?' said Simon as we pushed through the cold plastic. Both Simon and Zee turned to look at me, as if by being a blacksuit I knew a secret way out. I hated to disappoint them.

'I don't know,' I shrugged, my pulse quickening as I heard the growl of the dogs drawing closer. 'I don't know. I say we find somewhere to lie low until we can figure out a plan. The caves? The steeple?'

'Okay,' Zee and Simon said in unison. 'Right it is.'

Zee took the lead, swinging out of the door. With every step I thought we'd smack right into a platoon of guards and their dogs but fortunately the sounds seemed to be coming from behind us, back towards the solitary cells. The doors of the storerooms were a blur as we hurtled past them, reaching the T-junction that split off towards the caves.

I expected the vault door to still be off its hinges, the way the rats had left it the last time they'd broken through, but the closer we got to the end of the passageway the clearer it became that the way out had been resealed. There wasn't even a door now, just a slab of solid concrete that didn't budge by so much as a millimetre as we thumped into it.

'No way,' Simon groaned, throwing a pathetic punch at the grey wall. 'They can't do this!'

But they had. The warden had obviously grown so sick of the rats breaking into the compound that he'd sealed off the exit to the caverns beyond. We were well and truly at a dead end. Simon threw another punch, but this time he left his knuckles resting against the concrete.

'Pete's through there,' he mumbled, his entire body shaking. He looked up at me like I might have an answer to his unspoken question, but I just lowered my gaze. If Pete was still alive behind there, which was doubtful given the state of his broken body, then there was nothing we could do for him. Simon left his hand on the wall for a moment longer, his lips mouthing some silent goodbye, then his expression hardened.

'There's another way out, right?' Zee was saying, his words broken into pieces by heaving breaths. 'In the north wing. I remember hearing you talking about it.'

'It's probably been sealed off as well,' Simon said, sucking the blood from his knuckles.

'And even if it hasn't, I'm not going back that way,' I argued. 'That's where the warden is, and Gary.'

Simon looked at me, obviously confused, but there was no time to explain. Instead we paced back and forth along the corridor, listening to the sounds of the guards and the dogs growing louder then receding as they turned into the infirmary. It wouldn't be long, though. As soon as the suits managed to rouse the warden he'd tell them exactly what had happened, then they'd be back here with murder on their minds.

'Okay, let's think,' I said, smashing a palm against my head. 'We need to find a map or something, a security room. Somewhere we can plan an escape.'

Simon and Zee stared back at me, their shoulders hunched and their eyebrows raised as if I'd just said the stupidest thing they'd ever heard.

'Yeah, sure,' snapped Zee. 'Let's find the magic room filled with maps and weapons and escape plans. Maybe a teleporter. Good thinking, Alex.'

I scowled at him, realising he was right. But then I looked over his shoulder, another memory floating to the surface: the warden being escorted down this very tunnel, taken into a room down the corridor. With it came more distant thoughts: a telephone ringing from the same room, a voice on the other end that struck fear into me, even though I couldn't possibly have heard it.

'The warden's quarters,' I said.

'What?' asked Zee. 'Are you crazy?'

'No, they're right there,' I pointed down the passage-way to a door visible in the wall. 'Think about it, he must have plans of the prison, stuff like that. Maybe we can find a way out.'

'Right,' said Simon, turning to look at the door. 'He might have weapons too, keys maybe. But . . .'

Simon didn't have to add anything. I knew exactly what was worrying him. More memories blossomed in my head like dark flowers, the feeling I'd got the first time I'd walked down this corridor, that I was being watched by something bad, something evil. Even now the thought of it chilled me to the bone.

'But nothing,' I managed eventually. 'What choice do we have? Hide in a storeroom until the dogs sniff us out? It's our best bet. It's our *only* bet.'

As if they were twisted mirror images of each other, Simon and Zee's expressions relaxed then tightened again.

'Alex,' said Zee, a tremor belying the calmness of his tone. 'That's the first place the warden's gonna go when he gets back here. I really don't want to get caught in there.'

I smiled at him as best I could. Then I ran towards the door, towards the warden's quarters, yelling over my shoulder:

'Then we'd better be quick.'

LAIR

The door was closed, which was no surprise. But when Zee cautiously turned the handle there was no resistance, the thick barrier of metal swinging inwards without so much as a creak. We looked at each other, not believing our luck.

'I wasn't expecting it to be that easy,' said Zee, pushing the door all the way open. Beyond was a short corridor, like an entrance hall, at the end of which we could make out a dimly lit room.

'Maybe the warden doesn't think anyone is stupid enough to trespass into his quarters,' I said, ready to take a step forward.

'Or maybe it's booby-trapped,' added Simon.

I froze, my leg hovering over the stone floor beyond. I didn't honestly think there were traps there ready to snare us if we set foot in the warden's lair, but there was something stopping me moving forward. I couldn't say exactly what, just a feeling that this wasn't right, that we should turn and run. Suddenly it didn't matter that the blacksuits were after us, or the dogs. The only thing that was important was getting away from this room.

I looked at Zee, the sickly colour of his skin revealing his own fear.

'You first,' he said.

'Papers scissors stone?' I risked, but both boys shook their heads. I tried to swallow, my throat too dry. 'Fine, you chickens, I'll go.'

I finally let my foot drop, the echo surely too loud as it bounced back and forth along the short corridor. There was enough light ahead to make out a large room, drenched in shadow, and although there was no sign of life I couldn't shake the feeling that something inside was watching me.

Come on, I screamed, giving myself a mental kick up the ass. I lifted my other leg and passed through the door, the sensation like stepping into a hot shower. I thought for a moment the siren had stopped, then realised that I could still hear it, only as though from far away. I turned to make sure that Simon and Zee were following and my heart almost missed a beat. They too seemed to be distant, just specks at the end of a vast, black tunnel, their voices nothing more than the susurration of bird wings.

Then I blinked and they were right next to me again, the siren pounding at my ears and the passageway just a passageway.

'You okay?' Zee asked. 'You looked like you'd seen a ghost.'

I didn't reply, just wiped the cold sweat from my brow and led the way down the corridor. Simon closed the door gently behind us, and after just a few paces we found ourselves in another world.

'Christ alive,' muttered Zee. 'This dude is messed up.'

'Like we didn't already know that,' Simon replied, his voice faint, as if the room had snatched his breath away.

Dominating the chamber was a flag. It hung from the ceiling to our left, covering one entire wall. It showed a blood-red background, on which sat a white circle. The bold, black insignia inside could easily have been something else, but instead it showed the Furnace logo, the three circles arranged in a triangle, each with a dot in its centre connected by straight lines.

Beneath the flag was a desk, bigger than a snooker table and made from a wood so dark it looked burnt. Carved into it were figures, and we had to take a few steps towards it to work out what they were. We soon wished we hadn't.

Each carving showed a kid, no older than us, being executed. On one leg was the twisted, emaciated corpse of somebody hanging from the gallows, his face stretched into an expression of pure terror. Above him, decorating the panel between the leg and the top of the desk, was what looked like somebody on the rack, their body already broken beyond repair but the pain detailed in their eyes that of somebody fighting tooth and nail for life. Next to that was a teenage boy facing a firing squad, his face masked by a hood. Everywhere my eyes fell lay another nightmare, the work so detailed I could feel the bile rise in my throat.

And running along the edge of the desk, carved in letters the size of my hand, were four words:

THEY ARE ALL GUILTY.

The desk brought back more memories that I thought had been lost forever – me on a bus with Zee and some other kids, seeing the looming body of Furnace's surface building, the Black Fort, growing larger and larger until it blocked out the view from every window. There had been figures carved onto the stone there, too, the same scenes of torture and death, and that word – *GUILTY* – emblazoned above the door, the last glimpse of the outside world I thought I'd ever have. If any desk belonged in Furnace it was this monstrosity.

But even the desk itself didn't fill me with as much fear as what lay on it. The huge expanse of polished wood was bare but for one thing.

A telephone.

It resembled something from decades ago, something my gran might have had, solid black with a dial in the centre and a small receiver mounted on brass prongs. Just looking at it made me feel like the life was ebbing from me, leaking from my pores, evaporating into the cloying heat of the room. I pictured my soul being ripped from my body, becoming part of the desk in front of me – my screaming face carved into the wood for all eternity.

'Anyone want to make a call?' asked Zee, his voice making me jump. I snatched my gaze away from the phone, scanning the rest of the room. It was empty apart from a leather couch that sat opposite the desk, its surface so clean and crisp that it might never have been used.

'I don't want to go anywhere near that thing,' I heard Simon answer. 'And who would we ring anyway? The police?'

'Maybe there's some papers in the desk,' I suggested. 'Plans of the prison.'

Zee and Simon both nodded, but neither of them took a step forward. For a second we all stood staring at the cruel carvings, lost in our own macabre thoughts. I was the one who broke the collective paralysis again.

'This is ridiculous,' I said, storming forward. 'It's just a desk.'

My confidence stalled when I reached the other side of the vast table. There were carvings here too, but they didn't show executions. I caught a glimpse of a battle-field, the detail surely too realistic for an engraving, a boy being carried away by men wearing gas masks. Below that, adorning one of the thick legs, was another kid on an operating table, screaming as his skin was peeled away by a wheezer. If the carvings on the front of the desk were bad then these were plain terrifying, all the more so now that I knew the scenes they depicted were real. The writing on this side was the same, all except for the last word:

THEY ARE ALL SAVED.

I ran my fingers along the letters, the wood hot and smooth like living skin. There were no drawers in the desk that I could see, no shelves full of plans, no hooks with keys. There was nothing. I was about to report this to Zee and Simon when my finger slid under the bottom of the desktop and made contact with something cold and round. I ducked down, peering into the shadows beneath to see what it was. A button.

I could only think of two functions it might have. The first was to sound an alarm, the same as the warden's portable panic button. If that was the case then it didn't really matter if I activated it – after all, the siren was already blasting through the prison. The other possibility was . . .

I pressed it, standing up in time to see a hidden door opening in one of the walls, the sound of rock grating on rock deafening. Simon and Zee heard it too, screaming in unison as they spun round to defend themselves. All that emerged was a fierce white light which turned them into ghosts of themselves.

'Christ, a little warning would be nice,' said Zee, one hand to his heart. 'I almost cacked myself.'

I laughed, walking round the desk to investigate. For a few seconds I couldn't see anything in the glare; it was like looking into the sun. Then I realised that something in the room beyond was moving, specks of white against the glow that could have been birds swooping and circling. My heart leapt as memories from the outside world hit me, visions of beaches and sunlight and sea breezes. Then my eyes got used to the light and the room swam into focus.

'Jackpot,' said Zee, pushing past me. 'Holy crap, we've hit the mother lode.'

Simon and I followed him inside. He was right. The

secret room was the same size as the one we'd just left, but there the similarity ended. The movement I had made out came from the television monitors that took up almost an entire wall, each displaying a scene from somewhere inside the prison. We stepped closer, letting our eyes drift over each grainy film.

'That's gen pop,' said Simon, pointing at a screen which showed the canteen. It was empty, the inmates confined to their cells. I could see them on the other monitors, pale faces peering through bars, skinny bodies on bunks, and the feeling of nostalgia that washed over me took me by surprise. I never thought I'd feel homesick for my cell up top.

'How the hell did we get away with blowing our way to the river?' asked Zee. 'There are cameras everywhere.'

'Not in the chipping halls,' I replied, seeing no sign of them on the screens. 'They were hacked out after the prison was opened, remember.' I looked for the kitchen, saw that the angle of the camera was directed towards the doors rather than at the oven, only one corner of which was visible. I pointed it out. 'Bloody hell, that was a stroke of luck.'

'And isn't that the warden?' added Zee. We crowded around another screen to see a group of blacksuits hunched over a motionless shape on the floor. The image was fuzzy but the figure was unmistakable.

'You must have knocked him out cold,' I said, patting Zee gently on the back.

'You did that?' Simon asked. Zee nodded, then looked up at me.

'Well, Alex here did most of it, I just gave him a little extra.' He snorted, the noise not quite a laugh. 'I should have killed the bastard.'

'Yeah,' muttered Simon. 'You shoulda. But at least we know he's still out for the count. Gives us some time.'

The sight of the warden unconscious on the other side of the prison's underbelly did take the knife edge of tension from my back. I let myself breathe, studying the monitors for a clue to our escape, a way out. Then I saw something that almost broke my heart.

'Look,' I said, feeling the gooseflesh erupt on my skin. I lifted a trembling finger to the top right-hand corner of the display, at a sight I never thought I'd see again. 'It's still there.'

'What?' Zee started, but the rest of his question trailed away. For what seemed like forever we gazed at the screen, at a live video feed from a camera that must have been mounted on the side of the Black Fort, staring at the world we thought we'd lost. The picture may have only been small, but that glimpse of moonlight and tarmac looked bigger than a football pitch, an endless expanse of ground without walls, without bars. I felt as though I could travel right up those cables, bursting free at the other end and surging into the night like a free spirit.

'It's raining,' said Simon. And that did it – all three of us broke down. I hoped there was no camera in here because we wouldn't have made a pretty sight, the three of us bunched up against each other bawling like babies. I know it sounds crazy, but none of us ever expected to see the outside world again. We didn't know if it even existed any more. And yet there it was, in glorious black and white, right above our heads. I couldn't have stopped those tears if my life had depended on it.

We emerged from the moment together, coughing with embarrassment and trying not to make eye contact. When we finally managed to look at one another that same unstoppable force which made us cry gave us a fit of the giggles, the laughter bubbling up our throats like geysers. Eventually it passed, leaving us exhausted but exhilarated.

'It's right there, boys,' said Zee as the last echoed laughs faded into the walls. 'We can do this.'

'So let's do it,' I added. 'Let's get the hell out of Dodge.'

A PLAN

When we finally managed to drag our eyes away from the bank of CCTV monitors we realised they were actually the least useful thing in the room.

'Oh man,' said Zee, his hushed tone one of awe. 'Oh man oh man oh man. If the warden was here right now I think I'd kiss him.'

He walked towards the right-hand side of the room where a glass and steel cabinet held a selection of weapons that would have made a terrorist blush. Zee reached in and pulled out a shotgun, his skinny arms obviously struggling with its weight. He held it to his shoulder, swinging it wildly around the room.

'Take it easy, kid,' yelled Simon, ducking down and shielding his face with his mammoth arm. 'I don't want no pepper shot in my ass.'

'It probably isn't even loaded,' Zee replied, resting the barrel of the huge gun over one arm while he prodded the various clips and clasps that ran along its length. Still eyeing him nervously, Simon walked to another cabinet next to the first and I saw him slide something long and metallic into his pocket.

I left him to it, turning my attention to the wall opposite. Set in a recess, framed in glass and wood, was a blueprint of the prison, every corridor and room laid out in a three-dimensional network of fine white lines. Even in miniature the place looked huge, the Black Fort on the surface just a speck when compared with the monstrous leviathan than lurked beneath it. The tip of the nightmare iceberg that was Furnace.

And we were right at the bottom.

'You are here,' I muttered to myself, running my finger down the spider web of lines until I found the room we were in. I had to crouch to see it, the warden's quarters the size of a grain of sweetcorn almost lost in the bulk of what lay overhead. I let my finger trail back upwards, through the endless layers of gen pop, rising to the surface, to freedom.

'Somehow I don't think it's gonna be that easy,' said Simon from behind my shoulder. 'You see any way out on there?'

I returned to my starting point, focusing hard on the blueprint. I knew that the prison's underbelly was a warren of tunnels, wards and storerooms, but I'd had no idea how complex it truly was until now. They spilled out in every direction, seemingly at random, like the roots of a tree. But none of them led anywhere except right back where they started.

'Those two doors were the only way out into the caves,' I said, pointing to the place on the map where the tunnel we'd just been in ended, and another on the north side. Both doors had been scored over with a red X. 'But even if we'd found a way through then we'd have just been stuck out there in the dark. There is no way to the surface from there, remember? The steeple was our best bet, and that failed.'

'So what, then?' asked Zee, who had joined us. I could smell the cordite and grease from the gun he still held, the scent making my stomach churn. 'Ain't there no emergency exit from here?'

'Nothing,' I said, scouring the plans for any sign of a back way out or a secret elevator to the surface. An escape route made sense, if not for a fire then certainly for a riot. I mean, if the inmates took over the asylum then the warden would need somewhere to run.

Only that would never happen, not in Furnace.

No, as far as I could see there was only one way to the surface. I drew my hand up the single white line that ran through the prison from the lowest levels of gen pop towards the Black Fort.

'The elevator?' said Simon. 'Hell no.'

'It's the only way,' I replied. 'You see any other link to the surface? Everywhere's a dead end except that.' I rammed a finger against the glass to emphasise my point. 'The elevator, if we can get to it then it's our way out.'

'But that's in gen pop,' said Zee. 'How are we even supposed to get there?'

'And we know it ain't no ordinary elevator,' added Simon. 'We don't just hop in and press the penthouse button and sit back to enjoy the ride. It probably isn't even operated from the car.'

'One thing at a time,' I said, studying the base of the map to try and find a path to the main section of the prison. If the undersection was like the roots of a tree then gen pop was the canopy. Although both sprawled out in all directions there was only one narrow point where they met. I jabbed my finger again.

'This is where we need to get to. It's back down past the infirmary, you know that junction that splits off to the solitary cells? I think that's it. We take the other branch and it leads to this room. That thing there's another elevator, a smaller one, goes up as far as the base of gen pop. Okay?'

'You say so, boss,' said Simon. 'Let's get kitted up and go.'

I straightened up and pulled the frame from the wall, smashing it on the floor and carefully pulling the blueprint from the pool of broken glass. It was as I was folding it up to slide into my suit that I realised Simon was staring at my chest.

'Something got you pretty good there,' he said. I looked down, ran a hand along the claw marks that Gary had made in my shirt, and in the skin beneath. The pain was almost gone, so much so that I'd completely forgotten about it, and a thick black scab had already formed over the wound. Simon flashed a conspiratorial look at Zee, who was still fiddling with the shotgun, then turned back to me.

'Only reason you're still standing is because of the nectar,' he went on. 'That injury there would have killed you otherwise. How you feeling? A little dizzy? A little weak?'

I shook my head, but now that he'd mentioned it I wasn't feeling as strong as I had before. I blinked and for a second the room seemed to spin, although I was pretty sure I was imagining it. Reaching up, I unknotted my tie, throwing it to the floor and breathing deeply.

'Sooner or later the supply of nectar in your blood is gonna dry up, and that ain't pretty. I've been there.' He waved his mutated arm at me as if I'd forgotten it. 'It's like a drug, this stuff. The more you have, the more you want. And without it your body gets weak. Best-case scenario: you stop being a man of steel and you start being just a boy again. Stronger than you were, yeah, and just as big, but no match for a blacksuit. I was lucky, that's what happened to me.'

'And what's the worst-case scenario?' I asked, flexing the muscles beneath my suit just to reassure myself they were still there.

'There are two,' he replied with a whisper. 'First off, you just die. Body can't handle its new shape without the nectar there to fuel it and just disintegrates.'

'Great,' I said.

'That was the good news. The alternative is your body stays the same but your mind goes. You snap, go schizo with bloodlust. You become something a million times worse than what they made you.'

I didn't reply, trying not to think about what Simon was saying. But how could I not? There was a pretty good chance, then, that even if I did get out I'd end up either dying horribly or becoming some sort of psycho monster rampaging through the streets. Simon must have seen my face drop because he rested his hand on my shoulder, squeezing gently.

'Just giving you a heads up, that's all,' he said. 'I've been there, remember. I know what it's like, and I'm still me – well, sort of. True, you've had a hell of a lot more nectar than I ever got, but there are probably doctors on the surface who can cure you, hospitals and –'

In such a small room the gunshot was deafening. I felt like my eardrums had been blown out, the pain so great that I thought I'd been shot. I dived to the floor, feeling Simon beside me, desperately looking to see where the attack was coming from. But there were no blacksuits, no warden. There was just Zee, holding the smoking shotgun in his hands, his face twisted into a grimace of shock.

'Oops, my bad,' he said. Or at least I think that's what he said; the ringing in my ears was like a church bell. I saw Simon jump up, could read the curses on his lips. I got to my feet and threw in a few choice words of my own. Several of the monitors were now lifeless, dozens of ragged holes in the glass where there had been pictures only moments ago. Tendrils of black smoke curled lazily upwards and pooled in the corners of the ceiling.

'You idiot!' yelled Simon, wiping a hand across the back of his neck and pulling it away to reveal a thin red line across his fingers. 'You shot me!'

'It's just a graze!' replied Zee, laying the shotgun on the floor and holding up his hands. 'I don't know what happened, it just went off.'

'You pulled the trigger, that's what happened,' Simon

muttered. 'Almost blew my goddamned head right off.'

I tried to fight the smile but I couldn't. It sprang up on my face like a jack-in-the-box, and it must have been a good one because pretty soon both Simon and Zee were imitating it.

'Don't see what's so funny,' muttered Simon, trying and failing to look serious as he rubbed the back of his neck. 'Zee, maybe you should leave the gun here. Stand a better chance of getting out if we're still in one piece.'

Zee nodded, kicking the shotgun away like it was a poisonous snake. I stared at it for a second, wondering whether we should take it along. I mean, the blacksuits were armed, and we needed all the firepower we could get. But we really were just as likely to shoot each other as we were a guard, and the thought of the warden's smug expression when he found out we'd done his job for him was too much to bear.

I slotted the map into my jacket and took a quick look at the remaining monitors. There were fewer blacksuits with the warden now, which meant that the rest were probably on their way back here. We had to move. I ran for the door, back into the room with the desk, heading for the corridor beyond.

That's when the phone started to ring.

The blast from the shotgun had been loud, but this was a million times worse. Only it wasn't the same sort of loud. This felt like something was exploding right in the core of my brain, a noise so sharp that I could almost see it – a blinding white light that made me stagger and fall. I clamped my hands to my ears but it didn't help, the shrill ring burrowing into my head like a wasp laying its eggs.

And those eggs hatched into visions that made everything else I'd seen look like something from a kids' book, even the nightmares that sprouted from the warden's eyes, even the dreams I'd had when they were pumping the nectar into me. It was as if the carvings on the desk were coming to life, each scene played out in terrifying detail. I watched each of those poor souls die again and again and again, those few short seconds dragged out into an infinity of pain and suffering.

It was Zee who ended it. Past the churning ocean of blood that sat across my vision I saw him lurch forward, one hand leaving his ear to swipe the telephone from the table. Its flight was arrested by the cord that linked it to the wall, the receiver spinning off and hitting the floor by my head.

The ringing ended, but it was replaced by something even worse – a presence that seemed to engulf my mind in a fist of shadow. I stared into the holes of the earpiece, from which there appeared to emanate something rancid and rotten from the darkest part of the world.

Furnace. Alfred Furnace.

I clawed my way up, half running and half crawling towards the door, feeling invisible fingers in my head, probing my thoughts, leaving filth and decay wherever they went. Only when I'd wrenched it open and fallen into the corridor beyond did the sensation recede, literally purged from me as I unloaded my stomach over the red stone. Zee and Simon fell by my side, retching and crying, wiping the blood from their ears and the puke from their faces.

Together we ran, not caring where we were going or who saw us so long as we got away from that room, from that phone. But we couldn't run fast enough to escape the voice, a soulless whisper that seeped from the receiver and followed us down the corridor, which was both silent and deafening, which held no words but which transmitted images of relentless fury, and which all of us understood.

I am coming for you.

RISING

The further we got from the room, the less terrifying the voice became, although it had carved its message into our heads like a chisel on a gravestone. Our pace slowed, the unnameable dread replaced by a much more realistic fear – of being caught in the corridors by a blacksuit. That first might have scared the life out of me, but the second would mean instant death.

Even in our panic we had managed to take the right path, bolting up the passageway that led towards the solitary cells. I could see the plastic slats of the infirmary up ahead, and we all kept our hushed whispers to ourselves until the curtained door was well behind us.

'That didn't just happen, did it?' asked Zee, his voice little more than a rasping breath. 'I mean, it was a group hallucination or something, right? I saw a programme about it once, people imagining the same stuff and thinking it was real.'

'It was real,' answered Simon, his head constantly swaying back and forth as he checked the path ahead and the corridor behind. 'I've heard that phone go off a few times now, always the same thing, like there's a vice around my mind. Alex felt it too, didn't you?'

'Yeah,' I answered, thinking of the time I'd heard the phone before, the pain in my head unbearable yet my body unable to move away. 'I wasn't standing right next to it then, though.'

The end of the passageway was approaching, the T-junction visible up ahead. We slowed to a crawl, tiptoeing in case there was anything waiting for us. I couldn't hear any voices or growls, though, and when we poked our heads round the corner there was nobody in sight in either direction.

Something was glinting on the floor to my right, and it took me a moment to recognise the hatches of solitary confinement. My throat seemed to swell at the thought of being down there, back before they started carving me up, back before the nectar was pumped into me, back before I knew the truth about Furnace.

Back when Donovan was still alive.

It seemed like months ago – years, even. But how long had it been? Days maybe? Weeks, at most. I had no idea how long I'd been unconscious during the procedure, how much time the warden had stolen from me while he turned me into another of his blacksuit monsters.

'Who was it?' asked Zee, his voice louder now, more urgent. 'Who was on the other end of that phone?'

'Furnace,' Simon and I said, and even though we'd spoken it together the word was barely audible, as if we were worried that by saying his name we'd magic him into existence. Hell, maybe we would. I'd seen weirder things here.

'Furnace? You mean the guy who built this place?' Zee went on. 'But how'd he get in our heads like that? My ears are bleeding, for Christ's sake. Yours too. That isn't right.'

'Yeah, tell me about it,' said Simon, leading the way down the left-hand tunnel. It seemed to stretch into nothing but shadow, even my bionic eyes unable to make out what occupied the darkness. 'There ain't nothing right about that man. You ask me, let's just forget it until we get out of here.'

'But he said he was coming for us –' Zee started, the rest of his protest cut short as Simon grabbed him and pushed him up against the wall.

'I said let's forget it,' he spat. 'We got enough to think about just staying alive in here without his mind games messing us up some more. Okay?'

'Okay! Jesus, chill, man,' said Zee, his voice choked. Simon let him go and carried on walking, Zee's scowl shifting from his back to my face. 'What did I say?'

'Simon's right,' I said. 'It's not worth thinking about. We gotta give everything we have to finding a way out. If Furnace comes then we'll just have to kick his ass the same way we kicked the warden's.'

I thought Zee had answered, then I realised the noise hadn't come from him. There were shouts drifting up the passageway behind us, the familiar thunder of blacksuit boots punctuated by the savage barks of their hideous skinless dogs. They were onto us.

Swearing under my breath I doubled my speed, the ache in my legs now nothing to do with my imagination. I was growing weaker, like a car running out of fuel. I could feel the nectar's power ebbing in my blood.

'You remember which way?' Simon yelled from up ahead. The shadows had parted as though we'd chased them off, revealing another split.

I pictured the blueprint. 'Left,' I shouted back. 'Head left and then you should see the door to the elevator.'

Simon reached the end of the tunnel, vanishing to the left. I was right behind him, running so fast round the corner that it was all I could do to duck in time as a shotgun went off in front of my face.

The lead shot missed me, but the plume of fire that followed it from the barrel scored a direct hit. I spun round and collapsed on my back, momentum causing me to skid across the smooth floor into the legs of the blacksuit. He came down on top of me like a tree, his elbow catching me in the gut and knocking the wind from my lungs. The guard was shouting something but my eardrums had been pummelled again, his voice swallowed up by a dull, continuous chiming.

The gun went off again, but I don't think the suit was aiming at anything. I could see arms around his neck, one small and one massive as Simon fought to get the upper hand. I gasped for some air, then lashed out at the suit's face. I don't know what I was trying to do but something obviously worked as the man slid from my chest and crumpled to the floor. Simon's grip was relentless around the guard's throat until I snatched his hand and pulled it away.

'What are you doing?' he asked. 'Gotta finish him off.'

'He's one of us,' I wheezed, pushing myself up. 'Simon, he's a kid like us. We can't kill them, not if we can help it. Maybe they can be saved.'

The guard groaned and Simon wrapped his giant hand around his throat again.

'You really think that when he comes round he's gonna be on our side, see the error of his ways?' Simon hissed, pressing down with all his strength. I saw the look in his eyes, silver slits screwed shut with hatred, and this time I didn't try to stop him. 'Nah, he's gone. They're all gone. You and me, we were lucky, maybe a couple of others might remember who they were. But I'm not going to send a questionnaire round to find out who while the rest skin me alive. They've all got the warden's poison in them, and they're all killers.'

He spoke some more, mumbles lost beneath grunts, as if by talking he could distract himself from what he was doing. The guard juddered, an engine stalling, then he was still – one last bloody breath bubbling up from his lips. Simon rocked back on his knees, then used the wall to help him up.

'Did he give you a chance to prove yourself before he pulled that trigger?' he asked me, not waiting for a reply before turning and walking away. 'Nothing gonna stand in my way – not now we're so close.'

The voices behind us were getting closer, too, and I

looked back in time to see Zee reel away from the corner, stumble past me and then bolt after Simon.

'They're right there,' he shouted over his shoulder. 'Jesus, Alex, they're right on us.'

I didn't wait to find out if he was exaggerating, almost tripping on the dead guard as I legged it. Simon had already reached the end of the corridor, pushing open a heavy steel door and vanishing into a pool of bright light beyond. Zee was in after him, looking back over my shoulder with about the widest eyes I'd ever seen.

'Run!' he screamed, the word lost behind the crack of a gunshot. I felt the pellets slam into my back; it was like being stung by a hundred bees at once. The impact pushed me forward but I kept my feet, literally throwing myself into the room. I rolled awkwardly, catching a glimpse of the view through the door as Simon slammed it shut – a corridor roiling with dark suits and glistening dogs, their silver eyes like the crest of a tsunami crashing and spitting towards us. Then it vanished behind a plate of steel, Simon bending the lock round to jam it in place.

'Grab that desk!' he yelled, the urgency of his words propelling me to my feet again. I saw a metal desk and a chair, presumably a guard post where the blacksuit had been sitting before he heard us approach. By the time I'd grabbed it the door was being pounded from the outside, bulges appearing in the metal as the suits unleashed their full strength. I remembered how I'd punched my way through the river-tunnel hatch. It wouldn't hold for long.

'There,' Simon directed, helping me upend the heavy table and lay it against the door. It rattled and trembled from the force being directed against it, like a picket fence in the path of a hurricane. We scanned the room looking for anything else we could use as a barricade, but it was empty.

Except for one thing.

'The elevator,' Zee said, pointing at the wire gates that sealed off one wall. Beyond was a platform, much smaller than the main elevator that went to the surface, but easily big enough for the three of us.

We ran to it, the thunder of the guards as they tried to break down the door almost matching the wail of the siren. Simon grabbed one of the gates while I took the handle of the other and together we wrenched them open. By the time we had closed them behind us the door to the tunnel was almost off its hinges, two sets of hooked canine teeth bared through the widening gap.

'Get us out of here!' I yelled, seeing a control panel behind Simon's shoulder. He spun round, slamming a fist against the topmost of two buttons. The elevator started to rise, agonisingly slowly. Through the mesh I saw the outer door finally succumb, crushing the desk under it as the guards poured into the room. For a second the elevator floor was alive with sparks as the suits fired their weapons, then we passed from view and the onslaught stopped.

None of us spoke, waiting for the suits to flick a switch that would bring the elevator down, or to rip out the plug and leave us stranded here, waiting for them to come and get us. But the lift just carried on rising, pulling us up towards the lowest levels of gen pop.

'You okay?' asked Zee. I wondered what he meant, then remembered the wound in my back. It didn't hurt so much as itch like crazy, but the fact there was any feeling there at all meant the nectar was running out. I wondered what would happen when the last of it was used up. Would the wounds I'd sustained be healed by then, or would they end up killing me anyway?

'I'm fine,' I said when I realised Zee was waiting for an answer. 'Just a scratch.'

'Yeah, shotgun blast to the back, just a scratch,' he said, although there was no humour in his voice. 'Want me to take a look?'

I shook my head. Better nobody examined it, then maybe I could pretend it would be okay. I turned to the wire gates, my eyes giving light to the rock that passed us by. It hadn't looked it on the map, but gen pop was obviously pretty far above the prison's underbelly. That distance was good, helped me breathe a little easier. I hadn't seen any other way up, the warden and his suits would have to wait for us to get out before calling the car back down. And if we could somehow lock it in place . . .

I heard the gears struggle as the elevator slowed, the entire cabin shaking in protest. Then a room began to fall into view as we gradually drew level with it. There was a blacksuit sitting in a chair with his back to us, and he obviously hadn't been paying attention to events below. Simon and I pulled open the gates before he could turn, running at him like twin juggernauts.

'This siren is getting on my –' was as far as he got before Simon had rammed the suit's head into the desk he was working at. I threw the unconscious guard to the floor, then hauled him into the elevator.

'Help me with this,' Simon said, pulling the metal table from the wall. Zee and I both grabbed the other end and we slid it towards the lift, leaving it half in and half out of the gates. With any luck, when the elevator went down it wouldn't get far.

Only when it was wedged tight did we let ourselves relax, leaning against each other as we surveyed the new room. Like the warden's quarters, it was full of monitors, rows and rows of them covering one entire wall. Beneath them was a bank of electronic equipment dotted with switches and buttons. I saw a few words stencilled onto the metal – *ARMED RESPONSE* and *CELL RELEASE* – and felt my heart lift.

'You know what this place is, don't you?' I said quietly, my heart thumping in the back of my mouth.

'What?' asked Zee, nervously glancing at the motionless suit behind us.

'It's a control room,' I replied. 'And we, my friends, are finally in control.'

NERVE CENTRE

The first thing I did was pull the blueprint from my pocket, smoothing it across the floor so I could check where we were. The control room lay alone at the top of the lower elevator shaft, linked by a short passage to the main prison. I glanced around, noticing a huge door embedded in one wall, at least seven or eight electrical locks securing it to the rock. If we could get through there, and past the one at the end of the corridor, then we'd be back in gen pop.

Back in our cells, I thought, snorting a humourless laugh. *Back where we started. Great.*

The only other door in the room was marked with a lightning bolt, and from the plan I could see it was just a giant junction box for the prison's electricity supply.

'Man, this is sweet.' Simon was hunched over the control panel beneath the monitors, studying the various buttons and dials. He reached out with his normal-sized hand, flicking a large red switch. At first I thought I'd gone deaf, rubbing a finger in my ear. Then I realised he'd turned off the siren.

'Finally,' said Zee, his voice much louder than it needed to be. He put his hands together as if he was praying. 'Praise the Lord, I can hear again.'

'This computer gives us power over every damned thing,' said Simon through a smile that stretched from ear to ear. 'We totally own this place now.'

The sound of crunching metal made us all jump and we wheeled round to see the elevator start to descend. The table rattled but it didn't move, and when the cabin's ceiling reached floor level it ground to a halt, the gears screaming as they fought to drag it down.

'Reckon it will hold?' I asked, watching as the table started to buckle, the weight of the elevator bending the heavy steel like it was rubber.

'You really want us to answer that?' Zee replied. A crack appeared in the centre of the table where the elevator ceiling met the control-room floor, slowly spreading across the surface with a squeal that could have shattered glass. 'Anyone got any other bright ideas?'

'We should run, get back into gen pop,' suggested Simon. 'If we cut everyone loose from their cells first then the suits'll have more than they can handle.'

It made sense, but if we bolted to the prison now, leaving the path behind us open, then the warden would have no trouble rounding us up. A few hundred rowdy prisoners wasn't enough when the guards they were up against had guns and mutant dogs. No, we had to stop the elevator.

I spotted the lightning bolt on the door beside us and

pulled it open. Inside, stretching from ceiling to floor, were dozens of cables — each thicker than my new arms.

'Ain't no way out through there, Alex,' said Zee.

'Hang on a minute,' I replied, studying the white letters stencilled onto each cable. The sound of grinding metal was getting louder, the table was going to snap clean in half any second now. 'Anyone know anything about electricity?'

Simon and Zee were at my shoulders in seconds, but both were shaking their heads. Zee raised a hand and swung it from left to right, pointing at several of the cables.

'We did something like this back in school,' he said, chewing his lips. 'One of these probably feeds the lift. If we can find the right one ...'

'No kidding, Sherlock,' I said with a little more sarcasm than I intended. 'Any idea which one the right one might be?'

The only answer I got was the crunch of the table as it finally surrendered. The scream of gears became the clattering hum of the elevator descending. The ride up, though it had seemed to take forever, had probably lasted only twenty seconds at most, which meant we had less than a minute before the room was full of blacksuits.

'That one,' said Zee, pointing at a cable marked EV132.2. I looked at him, then at it, then back at him.

'Seriously? How do you know?'

'Duh, it says "EV" on it,' he replied, equally sarcastic. 'D'you think that might mean *Ele-V*ator?'

A distant thump meant the object of our discussion had reached its destination. I could picture them climbing on board now, herding the dogs in before cramming as many suits as possible around them. It didn't matter if Zee was right or not, we had to do something. Taking a deep breath I reached through the door and wrapped my hands around the black plastic cable. Both Zee and Simon took a step back, and even though they were behind me I knew they were shaking their heads again.

'Alex, that isn't the best idea you've had all day,' said Simon. 'That's gotta be thousands of volts.'

'It isn't the volts that kill you,' said Zee. 'It's all about amps. But Simon's right, what the hell are you doing?'

I ignored them, pulling on the wire with everything I had. It was pretty well connected, but I had the devil's strength in me and no cable was going to last long. Out of sight behind the wall something began to come loose, sparks flying from the top of the door. They burned my skin, but I didn't let go. The elevator was on its way back up, and I didn't need a degree in engineering to know that the sound of straining gears meant it was full.

'Here they come,' said Simon. 'Forget it, Alex, let's just go.'

But I kept pulling, even when I felt the vibration of an electric current running down my arms, even when the drizzle of sparks became a monsoon. I pulled until that cable came loose, sliding from the wall and thrashing in my hands like a snake. I could see the copper wires beneath the plastic insulation, spitting at me.

Nothing happened. The elevator continued to rise.

'Come on!' screamed Simon. 'Dump that thing and let's get out of here.'

Dump it. I wrenched the cable further from the wall, ignoring the charge that pulsed down my arms, which made my entire body want to fold in on itself. It wouldn't stretch far but that didn't matter. The elevator shaft was close enough.

I launched the cable towards it, throwing myself back in the same movement. It bucked and lurched as the bare copper made contact with one of the lift gates, then it literally exploded.

The room was plunged into darkness and silence, so deep that I might have been electrocuted. Then I saw the odd spark from the direction of the lift shaft, heard the shouts of distress from beneath us, from the black-suits in the cab, smelled the acrid tang of smoke and, under that, something else which made me want to chuck my guts up again.

'Nice going, Alex,' came Zee's voice, and I wasn't sure if he was being serious or not. 'Now what the hell are we –'

Something rumbled a long way beneath our feet, the steady growl of machinery powering up. The ceiling lights blinked once, twice, then fluttered on like candles, their pale light illuminating the room. Gradually, one by one, the monitors on the wall came back to life, and even in their tiny screens I could see the panic erupting behind the cell doors in gen pop.

'Emergency generator,' said Zee. 'Must be.'

'Doesn't matter,' Simon responded, walking to the elevator shaft and peering down, careful not to touch any of the exposed metal in case there was still a current running through it. 'They aren't going anywhere. Hell, Alex, I think you fried them.'

My stomach churned again as I watched Simon hawk up a spitball and launch it into the shaft. The charge might have given the blacksuits in the elevator some nasty burns, but it probably wouldn't have killed them, would it? And did it matter if it had?

Something black and heavy began to pull itself over my thoughts, a hood that shrouded my vision. I slumped back against the wall, feeling the nectar in my veins pumping through my system and trying to pull me back into the darkness. I groaned, shocked to hear the deep growl that crawled from between my lips. It was the same feeling I'd got when I'd killed Ozzie: the guilt, the horror, turning me into a monster. It's what the nectar wanted, what it *needed*. Because the only way it could control me was if I was one of them, a killer.

I thumped a fist against my head, shaking the fog away. When I opened my eyes again Simon was in front of me.

'Fight it,' he said quietly. 'Take a couple of deep breaths and think about something good, okay? Think about getting out of here. Nectar can't have power over you if you don't let it.'

I listened to him, dreaming about the outside world, about the rain that was falling even now. I imagined it on my skin, running down my face and slaking my thirst. Gradually the impenetrable mist drew back from my mind, leaving me alone with my fantasy. I opened my mouth, let the air flood into my lungs, then pushed myself up from the wall.

'Thanks,' I said. He patted me gently on the shoulder.

'Don't mention it, I've been there, like I said. Gets worse before it gets better.'

A medley of scraping sounds was rising from the elevator shaft, almost masking the symphony of groans beneath, and more to escape the noise than anything else I walked to the control panel.

'That will hold them back for a while,' I said, studying the array of electronic equipment before me. 'But not for long. When they find out what we've done they are going to be pissed. We've got to get out of here now before they think of a way to climb that elevator shaft.'

'I hear that,' said Simon. He had walked to the immense door that led into gen pop and was examining the locks. 'First things first, let's get this open.'

A quick scan of the controls revealed two switches labelled *AIR LOCK*. They could both be set to either 0 or 1, and both were currently pointing at 0. I grabbed one and turned it, and from somewhere close by I heard a single long blast of the siren. The floor trembled, as though a huge door somewhere was opening, but the one in this room stayed tightly shut. I tried the other switch, but it wouldn't turn.

'Look,' said Zee, pointing up at a screen on the wall. We followed his finger to see that the vault door in gen pop had swung open. A blacksuit was walking towards it, the expression of confusion on his face visible even on the tiny monitor. 'Air lock,' he went on. 'It must be like in a submarine, two doors that won't open at the same time.'

'Huh?' grunted Simon.

'For security,' added Zee. 'If the outer door and the inner door open together then prisoners could walk right through. If they open one at a time then anyone who breaches the outer door will get stuck in the middle before the inner door opens. Close that one.'

Zee reached over me and switched the first dial back to 0. There was another blast on the siren and we watched the screen as the door swung shut. The blacksuit walked up to it, and all three of us burst out laughing as he scratched his head, obviously mystified.

When we heard the locks slamming shut on the outer door, Zee turned the other switch to 1. Sure enough, the sound of metal bars sliding back filled the room and the door to our side swung smoothly open.

'You are a genius!' said Simon, grabbing Zee's head and kissing him on the forehead. We walked to the door and saw a wide, short corridor ahead. Mounted on the ceiling, and thankfully facing away from us, was a machine gun. At the end of the tunnel lay the vault door, a mist of dust billowing in front of it from where it had just closed. 'So now we just open the big bastard over there and we're home free?'

We all saw the problem at the same time, but it was Zee who said it aloud.

'We can't open the main door from in there,' he said,

nodding at the corridor. 'It can only be opened from the control panel, right?'

'Right,' Simon and I said together.

'So . . .' Zee said, leaving the statement unfinished. It didn't need to be said.

One of us was going to have to stay here.

PAPER, SCISSORS, STONE

'There must be a way of blocking it, tricking the system, wedging it open, anything!'

Simon spoke as he paced back and forth, rubbing his head so hard I thought his hair was going to fall out. The inner door still stood open, the exit to gen pop so close and yet so far away.

'Blocking it won't work,' Zee explained, his eyes focused on the controls. 'If the computer senses that one door is still open then the other remains locked. Makes perfect sense.'

'I don't care if it makes sense,' Simon screamed, turning on his heels and charging across the room like a battering ram. He raised his hand and for a moment I thought he was going to lash out at Zee, but then he thumped it down on the array of electronic equipment, hard enough to leave a dent.

'That isn't going to get us anywhere,' Zee spat, holding his ground against the bigger kid. 'Gotta use our heads for this, not our fists.'

The next words out of both their mouths were two streams of profanities that echoed off the walls like popcorn in a microwave. I stepped between them, and it took more of my strength than I thought it would to push them apart.

'Zee's right, Simon,' I said. 'There's no use in us all staying here until the blacksuits arrive and kill us. Or until we kill each other. One of us has to stay, operate the doors while the others look for a way out of gen pop.'

I didn't point out the obvious: that by then whoever was left in the control room would be nothing but a stain on the sole of a blacksuit's boot.

'Well I ain't doing it,' Simon said, holding up his hands and backing off towards the door. I could hear the fear in his voice, the terror of a trapped animal. 'I've gone through too much to die in here. We can make it out, I know we can. We're so close. I . . . I have to get out.'

'We draw straws,' I said as firmly as I could, making sure I locked my gaze to Simon's. I was bigger than him now, but he'd been in a lot more fights than I had and I knew he was more than a match for me. 'We draw straws or something. Got to keep this fair.'

Zee started to speak but his soft voice was overpowered by Simon's barked response.

'I told you, I ain't doing it.'

'Paper, scissors, stone, then,' I suggested, ignoring Zee as he attempted to speak again. 'Worked before, when I went out as bait for the rats. You remember that? You were happy to do it then.'

'That was different,' he said, pointing at me with one overstuffed finger. 'Whoever did that had a chance. This is certain death.'

'Guys –' said Zee, but I didn't let him finish.

'It's paper, scissors, stone, Simon,' I said, still not breaking eye contact. 'You don't play then you automatically lose.'

'*Guys –*' Zee repeated with more force.

'Fine,' Simon interrupted. He stared me out for a few more seconds, then put a hand behind his back. 'Me and you. Winner plays Zee. On three. One, two, three.'

I pulled out scissors, but my view of Simon's hand was blocked by Zee.

'Guys,' he whispered, putting his hand on my fingers and pushing them down, 'I'm going to do it.'

'But –' I started to protest. This time it was him cutting me off.

'Do either of you know anything about electronics?' he asked. 'No. Do you know how to bypass a circuit? No. Do you stand any chance whatsoever of being able to trick the system into opening both doors at once?' He laughed weakly. 'There's more hope of the warden coming up here and kissing my ass.'

'But –'

'But nothing, Alex. You gotta trust me, I can do this. It's the only way.'

'Then we'll stay with you until you can break the system,' I said, but he shook his head.

'We don't know how much time we've got. Get out there, stir up the prisoners. Maybe if we can cause a big enough distraction in gen pop then they won't notice us looking for an exit. I'll join you as soon as I can.'

I looked over Zee at Simon, both of us too ashamed to hold eye contact. There we were about to screw each other over to be the first to get out while Zee was volunteering to stay behind. And he was the only one who still looked like himself, the only one who hadn't had the procedure. The only one who had any right to return to the real world.

He was right, though. Neither Simon nor I stood any chance of rerouting the circuits so that both doors would stay open.

'Alright,' I said eventually. 'But you be quick, okay? Is there anything we can use to slow them down?'

Zee's eyes ran across the control panel, then looked at the television monitors.

'I don't need them,' he said. 'And if the suits do break through then it's better if they can't see what's going on. Lob them down there, it might slow them up.'

Simon and I did as we were asked, pulling the bulky screens from the steel brackets that held them to the wall and chucking them down the elevator shaft. There was a good few seconds of silence before we heard each one hit. By the time we were finished Zee had already dismantled the top of the control panel and was examining the wires underneath.

'That can go too,' he said, nodding at the pile of

metal he'd pulled loose. I picked it up, chucking it down into the darkness. The elevator was too far below to make out, and even if I could have seen it I knew it would be buried beneath electrical equipment. It wouldn't stop the suits from finding a way up, but it should keep them back for a little longer.

'I hope you can still let *us* out,' Simon said.

Zee nodded, his breath a long, stuttered sigh that made my heart bleed.

'Find a way to the surface,' he said. 'I'll try and work out the controls for the main elevator too. And I'll be with you before you know it, you'll see.'

'I know,' I replied, although I didn't truly believe it. 'Be quick, though, yeah?'

I stepped forward and wrapped my arms round him, feeling his own on my ribs, too short now to reach my back. I was glad my tears had dried up earlier because it was all I could do not to break down again right now. After everything we'd been through, after everyone I'd already lost, the thought of not seeing Zee again was worse than death.

'We got here together, we'll get out of here together, I promise,' I said, my voice trembling. 'I promise, Zee, I won't leave without you.'

'If you can go, go,' he replied, the words broken up by another sigh. 'You might not get another chance.'

He turned back to the control panel and flicked another switch. I felt rather than heard the sound of thousands of cell doors grinding open.

'That should keep the guards in there busy for a little

while,' he said. 'Now move your backsides before I change my mind.'

'Thanks, Zee,' said Simon, before running into the tunnel. I cast a nervous look at the machine gun over my head as I followed, but Zee shouted after me.

'The armed response has been deactivated,' he said. 'That shouldn't even move.'

I stopped by the main vault door, looking back the way I'd come. I wanted to shout something else to Zee, but the only thing I could think of was 'goodbye', and I couldn't bring myself to say it. Even if I'd wanted to, I doubt I could have forced words up past the lump in my throat. I felt like it was a piece of me I was leaving behind.

But I would see him again, I told myself. I *would*.

The inner door began to swing shut and I automatically started moving towards it, Simon's hand on my arm the only thing that stopped me.

'He'll be okay,' he said. 'He's a hell of a lot smarter than either of us. He'll find a way through.'

Zee suddenly appeared in the closing crack of the door, his skinny hand waving and his pale face doing its best to form a smile. He looked tiny, insubstantial, like he was already dead. A ghost of himself. I pictured the blacksuits flooding in behind him, a dark tide drowning an insect. He wouldn't last five seconds in the face of their wrath.

I shook myself free from Simon's grip and ran towards him again, shouting his name. But the door was too quick, locking his tears behind a metre of solid steel. I felt my ears pop from the change in pressure, the air inside the tunnel suddenly too hot, like we'd stepped into an oven.

'Here we go,' said Simon, and I made my way back to him, doing my best to put Zee from my mind. I pressed my hand against the outer vault door. There was a series of clicks, then with a thunderous groan and a bone-breaking shudder it began to grind open. Behind it I could make out the shouts of a thousand inmates as they escaped from their cells. 'You ready for this?'

'Ready as I'll ever be,' I said, clenching my fists and preparing to run.

The door swung out, revealing the football-pitch-sized yard that made up the base of gen pop. There were already inmates congregating there, and when they saw us staggering out they erupted, shouting and screaming and barging past each other to see what was going on. There were three blacksuits at the front of the crowd, guns cocked, but their attention was taken up by the heated populace.

'Home sweet home,' I said, grinning at Simon. 'It's good to be back.'

Then we put our heads down and charged.

RIOT

I can't imagine what we looked like as we burst from that door, but it must have been a terrifying sight. As soon as they saw us the inmates started to run, darting in all directions as they fought to get out of our way, a shoal of fish parted by sharks.

Their panic provided the distraction we needed. One of the blacksuits fired his shotgun in the air to try to control them and the other two were barking orders at the fleeing kids. They never even knew we were coming.

'Get back in the circle, you freaks,' bellowed one, pointing the barrel of his gun at the huge yellow ring painted on the yard floor. 'Or next time –'

It was as far as he got. I watched Simon thump into him, sending the guard flying. He hit the ground awkwardly, his gun discharging into the crowd. Another of the suits levelled his weapon at Simon but I was on him before he could pull the trigger. I grabbed the barrel with one hand, driving my other fist into his ribs.

The blow was hard, but he didn't seem to feel it. He retaliated like a viper, his forehead connecting with my nose and causing the whole world to explode in white light. I staggered, desperately trying to keep hold of the shotgun as he aimed it at my head. More from luck than skill I kept the barrel vertical, even when he fired it and the cool steel turned red hot.

I blinked away the tears, ignoring the pain in my nose and throwing myself at the suit. This time I aimed a little higher, lashing out at his neck. I could see the confusion in his face, being attacked by one of his brothers.

'You don't have to fight,' I tried to say, but adrenaline tied my words in knots. I don't think he'd have registered them even if they had been spoken. The nectar was in his blood, morphing his face into a twisted mask of rage, turning his eyes to cold fire. It was either him or me. One of us had to die.

One of my punches caught him on the ear and he staggered back, dropping the gun. I didn't relent, my blows like jackhammers. Another shotgun blast ripped through the air and I ducked instinctively, putting all my strength into my brutal attack. The blacksuit tripped on his own feet, tumbling onto the stone.

I was about to finish him off when I saw the other guards bounding across the yard. There were six of them, heading from the direction of the chipping halls, all with guns. Another four were leaping down the steps from the upper levels. Several of them fired together, not seeming to care that there were other blacksuits in the way. They were still too far away for the shots to be deadly, but they wouldn't be for long.

I kicked the blacksuit beneath me hard, then kicked out again to send his gun skittering across the floor. Simon had bested one of the others and was wrestling with the third, his one weak arm giving his opponent the advantage. We were going to lose, be blown to pieces by the suits, unless I thought of something quickly.

I looked around at the inmates, clustered in small groups at the edge of the yard, pressed tightly on the stairs and the landings of the first couple of levels – close enough to get a front-row view of the action but with room to run if they needed to. I scanned the dirty faces and red eyes until I saw what I was looking for, black bandanas painted with crude white motifs.

The Skulls, the worst gang in Furnace, the kids who'd made my life hell back in gen pop. And right now the only thing that stood between me and a lung-ful of lead shot.

I backed off, running towards the side of the yard where they stood. Kevin and Gary were both gone, so I didn't know who was leading them now, but I spotted a tall, skinny kid with a scar running from forehead to chin who I kind of recognised as one of Kevin's lieutenants from back in the day. I aimed my words at him.

'You want out of here?' I asked, my voice tearing across the open yard. Two more shotgun blasts punctuated the end of my question, the blacksuits almost upon us. The Skulls were retreating, all eyes locked on me with a mixture of fear, defiance and confusion. To them I was nothing but a blacksuit, which meant they couldn't trust a word I said.

Another burst of fire crackled behind me, making me jump. I turned to see Simon bolt into the crowd, inmates screaming and throwing themselves out of his way. The suits were right behind him, firing wildly in his direction. They stopped in the middle of the yard, pulling together in a tight circle around their fallen comrades, their weapons never dropping.

'Give him up,' bellowed one, looking at the Skulls but talking about me. 'No need for you to get hurt over this. He isn't worth dying over.'

'And him,' said another of the guards, pointing his weapon at Simon, who was crouched in the doorway of one of the cells. I saw blood dripping from his nose, knew he must be hurt pretty badly. 'Any inmate who helps bring those two in gets extra slop all week.'

A murmur passed through the crowd at the thought of increased rations, and I felt the prisoners close in. If they thought they could get something out of it then they'd turn on us in seconds. And a prison full of angry kids would tear me to pieces a hell of a lot quicker than a few blacksuits. I had to offer them something more. I took a step forward, shouting up to the crowd who watched from all angles.

'I can get you out,' I boomed, my voice bouncing back from the walls with a strength that surprised me. 'I can get you all out of here. Warden's locked below, there won't be reinforcements, won't be dogs. Anyone who wants to escape better start fighting now.'

This time the intake of shocked breath that passed through the crowd was louder, like waves on a stony shore.

'Serious?' said one of the Skulls from behind me. 'You can get us out?'

I didn't know that for sure, but what else could I say?

'I can get you out,' I repeated. 'Everyone. But only if I survive this.'

'You better listen up,' yelled one of the blacksuits, firing his weapon into the air. 'And listen up good. Anyone who even thinks about siding with that traitor will die, right here, right now. Take them down, hand them over, before it's too late.'

But it was already too late. I could feel a tension growing in the prison, like a pressure cooker about to blow, like the electricity in the air before a storm. For the first time since they'd been locked up here the inmates could sense fear in their guards, uncertainty. They knew the tide was turning – there was no siren, no dogs, no reinforcements and, above all, no warden. The prison was theirs.

In that moment all the years of cruelty and brutality that had lain festering in the blood of the prisoners began to bubble over. Every mind was one, a thousand inmates now a machine with a single deadly purpose. That shiver of raw, unstoppable power passed through them like a drug, unleashing a battle cry from behind me. One of the Skulls was howling at the top of his voice, and it spread like wildfire as everybody took up the call, becoming a chant of defiance that could have shaken the prison to its very foundations.

I saw the blacksuits' faces fall, every trace of their usual smug smiles wiped away as the air came alive with the true song of Furnace. Part of me wanted to reach out to them, to try again to remind them that they were once kids like us. It wasn't fair that they had been turned before this moment, that they could never share the freedom that we knew was ours.

But even if I had been able to make myself heard over the banshee wail that rocked the yard it wouldn't have helped. Right then those guards stood for every bad thing that had ever happened to the prisoners around me. Trying to stop what came next would have been like trying to stop the tide coming in.

I don't know who was the first to move but suddenly the prison came alive, the motion of so many people enough to make me dizzy. The suits fired into the crowd but they didn't stand a chance, engulfed from all directions by a foaming wave of white overalls. The movement of arms and legs was like pistons, and although most of those limbs were matchstick skinny there wasn't a creature alive that could have stood up to their combined fury.

I watched for as long as I could, until there was nothing left of the guards but wet, empty suits. Then I turned away, waiting for the bloodlust to subside.

Only it didn't. Something had been caged inside those kids, and now that it was loose there was no stopping it. When they'd finished with the guards they stormed into the cells, their screams enough to split my ears as they ripped toilets from walls and tore their bunks to pieces. If I hadn't known better I'd have said they all had nectar in their veins, their strength surely too savage to be human. Then again, I guess there isn't anything more savage than human anger.

'That was easier than I thought it would be,' said a voice by my side, barely audible over the noise. I turned to see Simon, still wiping the blood from his face and shivering despite the heat.

'You okay?' I asked, seeing his broken nose. He nodded, a smile parting his crimson mask.

'Yeah, no biggie.' We both jumped back as a toilet sailed down from an upper storey, taking a chunk of stone from the yard floor. A cheer rose up from everyone who saw it, which in turn caused a hailstorm of other objects to descend from the shadows. 'What the hell do we do now?'

I didn't have time to answer before I heard a shout from across the yard.

'What about them?'

It was taken up by countless more voices and before I knew what was happening that tide of inmates was flooding right towards me. I felt my blood run cold, tried to back away from the approaching mob. But there was nowhere to go.

'How do we know you ain't with them?' somebody said, the cluster of kids in front of me so thick, and their expressions of rage so similar, that I couldn't tell one from another. They pressed forward, their fists and shoes bloody from what they'd done to the blacksuits. I should have seen this coming. It didn't matter that I had been the one to light the fuse, it didn't matter that I'd promised them freedom. I wasn't one of them, and that meant only one thing.

'He's wearing a suit,' said another.

'Do him!' screamed a Fifty-Niner. 'Do them both!'

They surged across the stone and I closed my eyes, feeling Simon's body against mine. So, after everything we'd been through it was going to end here. At least it would be quick. Nobody, no matter how much nectar was in him, could withstand molten fury like this.

A shotgun went off and instantly the storm of cries and shouts dwindled to a low murmur. I opened my eyes to see a Skull standing between me and the crowd, the smoking weapon held up towards the distant ceiling. It was the one I had earlier identified as their leader.

'This here might be our ticket out,' he said, his voice a lazy drawl that nevertheless carried an icy authority. The inmates glared past him at us, their feet scuffing on the rock like bulls ready to charge. 'I know yous've all got the bloodlust, but anyone lays a finger on him before he shows us the door gonna have me to answer to. Got it?'

A hundred or more heads nodded reluctantly, like a breeze rippling across grass. The Skull kept his eyes on them for a moment longer then swung round to face Simon and me.

'Looks like I got yous two a temporary stay of execution,' he said, bouncing the shotgun barrel up and down in his palm. 'But that only gonna last if what you say is true.'

I knew what was coming, and I knew I didn't have an answer. Not yet.

'How we crack them gates?' the kid asked. 'How we get out of Furnace?'

BATTLE PLANS

We sat at a table in the slop room, every square centimetre of space around us packed tight with inmates.
The Skulls occupied the benches closest to Simon and
me, the kid with the scar – his name was Bodie – resting the shotgun barrel on his legs as he digested what
we'd just told him.

'You're telling me that the blacksuits are . . . *us*?' he
asked eventually.

I nodded, wondering if I was going to have to go
through the whole thing for a third time. I'd already
told them everything about the warden's procedure,
everything about the nectar, and everything about
Furnace's plans to turn us into monsters, blacksuits.
Well, almost everything. I hadn't mentioned the part
about the warden being alive almost a century ago,
about their experiments during the Second World War.
I figured nobody would believe that if they hadn't seen
the evidence with their own silver eyes.

'Every one of them,' I replied. 'Me and Simon
included.'

'Yeah, I know you,' said another of the Skulls. 'You used to bunk with Donovan. You're the one who made it out through the river. You're supposed to be dead.'

I pointed at myself to prove him wrong.

'That's what the warden told you. Didn't want anyone else trying to break out. We made it, most of us anyway. But only as far as solitary. That river didn't lead anywhere but right into the arms of the wheezers. And you can see what happened after that.'

'Yeah, they tried to turn you into one of them,' said a voice from the back of the room. 'But they couldn't.'

'Because you remembered your name?' added Bodie, with more than a trace of disbelief.

'Look, you've seen the evidence, you've seen the blood watch come, the wheezers. Those creatures they bring back, they're us, halfway through the procedure. That's what the nectar does to them.'

'Figured that,' said another Skull. 'Remember what happened to Kevin?'

Bodie chewed on his lip, then nodded. Everyone remembered what had happened to Kevin, slaughtered in his cell by the beast that had been brought up from below, the beast that had once been Monty.

'We don't have much time,' said Simon. 'We can sit here and talk about this all day, but unless we make a move soon the warden's gonna find a way up.'

I thought of Zee, still trapped inside the control room. I hoped he was close to bypassing the doors, and that the blacksuits were still trapped in their hole. The first thing Bodie had done after the crowd had calmed down was station two of his boys on lookout by the vault door, which had swung shut after we'd entered gen pop, and two more by the elevator to prevent any surprises from the surface. Not that I was expecting any.

'And you're sure they won't send the police?' asked Bodie. 'SWAT or the army crawling up in here? I mean, this is a pretty big deal, us taking over the prison. Six o'clock news and all that.'

'They won't,' I said. 'The warden wouldn't dare let anyone else down here, he wouldn't risk them finding out about the experiments, about what they've been doing to us. No, he's screwed himself with his own sick plans. I bet you the world doesn't know anything about this.'

'The world'll find out soon enough when we break outta here,' said Bodie, causing a riotous cheer from the rest of the room. 'Ain't gonna know what hit it.'

'It doesn't mean were safe, though,' I went on. I'd been trying not to think about the phone, about Furnace's message. But it had been engraved on my memory.

I am coming for you.

'My guess,' said Simon, 'is that Furnace will send his own reinforcements, from outside.'

'More blacksuits,' said Bodie. 'Makes sense.'

'But the only way in is using the elevator,' I added, a spark of hope igniting in my head with enough brightness to make me think a crack had opened up in the ceiling. I remembered the blueprint, pulling it out of my pocket and smoothing it down across the table. The gangs leant in to get a better look, some whistling at the sheer size of the prison laid out in blue and white before them. I ran a finger up the long line of the main elevator shaft, the only connection to the outside world.

'So if Furnace wants to get in then he gotta pull the lift up first,' said Bodie. 'And if we already in there when it reaches the top then he's gonna have a nice little surprise when the doors open.'

'True that,' said Simon, imitating Bodie. 'You know if the cabin is up or down?'

'We never know,' said one of the Fifty-Niners. I recognised him from the gym where I'd almost been beaten to a pulp. It felt like decades ago. 'Sometimes goes back up, sometimes stays down. Only way to know for sure is to open it.'

'But those doors are reinforced steel,' added Bodie. 'Ain't no one ever been able to break through them.'

'That's because nobody's had the time to do it before,' I said with a grin. 'You so much as looked at them and the blacksuits would haul your ass off to the hole. But there isn't anyone to tell you what to do now.'

I stood up, causing the Skulls to jump to their feet, fists and guns raised in unison. I held up my hands in surrender, sighing with frustration.

'I might look like one of them,' I said, trying to make eye contact with everyone in the room. 'But I'm not. My name is Alex Sawyer, I'm a prisoner just like you. And if you want me to find a way out of here then you'd better *get those guns out of my face!*'

My calm tone had become a shout by the last seven words, the anger swelling up inside me. I lashed out, smacking the barrel of Bodie's shotgun and sending it spinning to the floor.

'Easy, chief,' he said, motioning for his lieutenants to back off. 'I hear you. One of us. Ain't no thing.'

I pushed past him, heading back out to the yard. Furnace had looked like hell before, but now it was literally an inferno. Some of the inmates had stripped the sheets from the beds, building a huge pile in the middle of the prison floor which had somehow been set alight. It gave life to the walls, the red stone reflecting the flickering light and creating the illusion that we were all standing inside a living pyre. Although most of the smoke drifted upwards, joining forces with the shadows of the highest levels, black tendrils snaked around the room, making the cloying heat even more unbearable.

'Just our luck if we all end up burning to death,' coughed Simon, pulling his tattered overalls across his mouth. 'The warden would think Christmas had come early.'

Most of the inmates were still trashing their cells, the rooms and anything else they could get their hands on. I saw gym equipment being thrown onto the fire, and pickaxes too, their wooden handles causing the greedy flames to lick even higher. Somebody lobbed a bottle of cleaning fluid from the laundry and it vanished in a muffled explosion, a fountain of purple fire jetting upwards before fizzling out.

'You think you can stop them from burning everything useful?' I said as Bodie and his crew walked out behind me.

'If you wanna try calming them down then you go ahead,' he replied. 'But if I was you I'd let them get it out of their systems, else it'll be you burning up in there.'

'Thanks,' I muttered, trying to see past the exhaustion, past the smoke, past the fear to look for a plan. 'We should grab anything that we can use as a weapon. Pick-axes, shovels, and you must have shanks. If the suits do get in then we're going to need all the help we can get.'

Bodie leant towards a couple of Skulls and gave an order, watching them as they ran towards the chipping rooms. The rest of us headed for the elevator, steering well clear of the fire. There were inmates everywhere, some running wild, some cowering in empty cells as if hoping to be locked back in, others in brutal skirmishes – rivals finally getting a chance to beat on their enemies without risking a lockdown.

'Only thing worse than a prison with guards,' said Bodie, 'is a prison without 'em.'

I did my best to ignore the mayhem, trying to focus. We were under siege, and sooner or later the warden would figure out a way to get back in. When he did, we had to be ready. The thought of it caused a sudden rush of vertigo, the room spinning like a gyroscope. I felt like a tree that had been felled, suddenly toppling to my left. Luckily Simon was there, wrapping his arms around me before I could hit the floor.

'You okay?' asked Bodie.

'He's fine,' Simon answered for me. 'It's the nectar in his system, it's running out. Hang in there, Alex, you'll be okay in a minute.'

'I'm fine now,' I said, shrugging him off and easing myself up. 'I just tripped.'

I didn't need to see his face to know he didn't believe me, but there was no time to feel ill. I wiped a hand across my brow, feeling the heat radiating from my skin, then I set off again. The two Skulls by the elevator doors raised their guns when they saw me but Bodie was quick to wave them back down.

'Top priority is getting this open,' I said, looking at the elevator, the massive screen above it black and silent. The gap between the reinforced steel doors was thinner than a hair, the joint sealed tight to protect it from attack. It was going to take a hell of an effort to get through there. But if we could blow a hole in a rock floor to get to the river beneath then we could do anything. I smiled, the memory giving me an idea. 'Send some of your boys to the kitchen,' I said, turning to Bodie. 'Get them to unscrew the gas canisters from the oven. They're still there, right?'

'Yeah,' Bodie replied, nodding at two more Skulls, who sprinted back the way we'd come. 'Under some serious lock and key since you guys escaped, but they're there. You thinking of exploding your way out again?'

I shook my head. The gas in the gloves had demolished a rock floor, but steel was a different matter. It didn't shatter, and it didn't crumble. I doubted those canisters would even make a dent.

'We should be able to get in with the pickaxes,' I said, before looking to my side where the vault door stood closed and silent. 'But if the warden does poke his ugly mug through there then we can be sure he gets a warm welcome.'

Bodie laughed, clapping a hand down on my shoulder.

'I like the way you think, big man,' he said, and for a second I remembered Gary, the former head of the Skulls. He'd have killed me if I'd given him orders like I'd done to Bodie, even if I did know a way out. I had no doubt that Bodie was a nasty piece of work – he was a Skull, after all – but at least he wasn't a psychopath.

I saw the first two gang members racing back across the yard, each with a couple of pickaxes slung over their shoulders. They skidded to a halt by the elevator doors, passing one of the tools to me and another to Bodie.

'You want more?' wheezed one.

'Nah, this ought to do it,' I replied, gripping the wooden handle and remembering the countless blisters it had brought out on my hands. I'd have a few more by the time we got these doors open. 'Stand back.'

The Skulls obeyed, backing off as I swung the pick-axe round in an arc. It struck the elevator doors a good metre or so from where I'd intended, causing a clang that thundered through my eardrums as well as a jarring impact that almost separated my spine from my skull. I dropped the pickaxe to a round of whoops and cheers from the Skulls.

'Looks like someone needs some chipping practice,' laughed Bodie. 'You want another shot or you wanna let the professionals do it?'

I stood out of his way, nodding. My strike hadn't

even scratched the surface of the elevator, but it had almost torn me in two.

'Yeah, it's all yours,' I said, grimacing. 'I've got a bomb to make.'

UNDER SIEGE

Simon followed me back to the slop room to check on the gas canisters. The bedlam in Furnace was growing more out of hand with each passing second, the kids running out of things to rip from the walls and turning on each other. We kept to the edge of the huge room, willing ourselves to be invisible against the walls and the cell bars. But it was impossible when you were taller and broader than anyone else in the yard, and wearing a black pinstripe suit to boot.

We ducked in through the crack in the rock, both of us nervously eyeing the lifeless machine guns that jutted from the walls. The canteen was still pretty full, the benches occupied by quiet kids who didn't want any part in the madness outside. They retreated from us as we strode across the room, their skittish movements reminding me of stray cats.

'Any of you guys want to help?' I asked. 'We need weapons, we'll need slop too, if anyone feels like cooking.'

Nobody responded, even their breath locked behind tight lips until Simon and I had passed through the doors into the kitchen. Nothing had changed, the white walls and steel surfaces like a haven compared to the flesh and smoke tones of the prison. At least it was until I looked at the metal surfaces and realised how similar they were to the operating tables down below.

'Don't think about it,' said Simon, and I could almost see the same thoughts running through his mind.

'How are you getting on?' I asked the two Skulls who were crouching at the oven. They had pulled a leg from one of the counters and were using it as a crowbar to prise open a chain that had been looped around the base of the unit.

'Won't budge,' hissed one, the crowbar slipping out.

'Need a little extra muscle?' I said, squatting down beside them and taking the table leg. Slotting it into the gap between the chain and the oven I pulled on it with all my strength. I know I hadn't asked to become a monster, but it was satisfying to watch the steel links stretch like Play-Doh until the weakest one popped open. 'Now that's how you do it.'

The Skulls looked at the chain, then at each other, then at me.

'Remind me not to get on your bad side,' said one, his head disappearing behind the oven. I heard the creak of something being unscrewed and left him to it, looking up to see that Simon had vanished. I followed the sound of furious chomping and found him gorging on some cold leftovers in a pot of slop. He peered over the top and smiled.

'Man, I didn't think I was ever gonna taste anything

this good ever again,' he said. The sound of his stomach gurgled across the room, making me realise how hungry I was. I walked over, ready to scrape out a handful for myself, but Simon pulled the giant pot away. 'Not a good idea,' he said. 'You've had way too much nectar. You try eating this and you'll only spew it right up again.'

'You liar,' I said, raising an eyebrow. 'You just want it all to yourself. You had nectar and you're fine. Come on, share and share alike.'

He started to protest then obviously thought better of it, throwing his hands in the air.

'Don't say I didn't warn you,' he muttered.

I curled my hand round the edge of the pot, my taste buds almost gushing as I scooped the cold mush into my mouth. Simon was right, after so long without food it tasted like ambrosia, better than anything I'd had in my life, better even than the steak meal Monty had cooked up for us in this very room. I was grinning so hard I could barely keep my mouth closed as I swallowed.

I was pulling out my second handful when my body reacted. It felt like somebody had jammed two fingers down the back of my throat, my gag reflex so strong that I was barely even aware I was being sick before I saw the jet of slop explode back into the pot. I retched again, producing nothing but bile, then wiped the tears from my eyes to see Simon staring at the mess I'd made.

'Thanks,' he said. 'You think I want to eat your barf?'

'Jesus,' I replied, spitting a ball of acid. I walked to the tap, flushing my mouth out before tentatively swallowing some water. I felt it trickle down my pipe, cooling the fire that the slop had started. Fortunately the water at least seemed to stay down.

'Liquids is fine, the warden probably told you that,' Simon said, rooting around the pots for more leftovers. 'But the nectar won't let you eat. It gives you everything you need. Until it runs out, that is.'

'Then what?' I asked. Simon's only answer was a shrug.

Great! So when I got to the surface and the nectar finally ran out I'd starve to death. Another rosy possible future to look forward to thanks to Furnace and the warden.

If you get to the surface, another part of my brain chimed in. And it was right, we were a long way from freedom yet.

'If you two freaks have finished throwing your guts up, how about you take this,' said one of the Skulls. He held up one of the gas canisters, a squat metal cylinder with a valve on the top. It was obviously heavy because his whole body was trembling with the weight. I took it from him in one hand, studying the valve.

'Know what you're doing with that?' Simon asked.

'Nope,' I replied. 'Only thing I know about gas is that it goes kaboom. Reckon we'll be able to rig it up easily enough, though. Bring the others when you get them, I'm heading back out.'

'No worries,' he replied, his voice echoing from the pot his head was lost in. I was at the kitchen doors when the prison erupted with the sound of the siren, the klaxon even louder than before. I gripped the canister tight and legged it, barging my way through the canteen and back out into the yard.

Zee. It had to be Zee.

The prisoners were panicking, some running back to their cells like they'd been programmed to do, others heading to ground level armed with improvised weapons. As I ran round the fire I saw that the Skulls who had been clustered in front of the elevator were now standing by the vault door, shotguns levelled at the metal. I flew the last few metres.

'What is it?' I yelled over the siren.

'Not sure,' Bodie replied, pumping a shell into the chamber of his own shotgun. 'Heard something inside, though, banging or some such.'

Please let it be him, I prayed, slamming the gas canister to the floor in frustration. What if the banging was the blacksuits finally getting up from the floor below? What if it was them throwing Zee from wall to wall until . . .

'It might be Zee,' I said, trying to stay positive. 'He might have found a way.'

'If it is him then we'll let him through, but if it isn't –' Bodie's whisper suddenly became a shout as the siren stopped. It started again, the sound faint and flat for a second or so like it was running out of batteries, then fading into its own echo. 'What the . . .'

This time I heard the banging myself, although it was more of a grinding – like a distant elevator struggling up. Or a door opening.

'Get ready,' said Bodie. 'Anything that comes through that door which ain't one of us, it don't never get up again.'

The yard was flooded with sound as the klaxon booted back up, wavering high and low and reminding me of films when the cops turn their squad-car sirens on and off. There was a deep click inside the vault door, followed by a burst of sparks from the hinges which sent everybody jumping backwards. Something else thumped into place inside the mechanism, then with the grating squeal of metal on metal it began to swing open.

'Here we go,' yelled Bodie as the siren cut out again. 'Be ready. Be ready.'

With the alarm now off it was as though the entire prison was holding its breath to see what came through the door, even the roar of the fire dulling to a muted growl. A curtain of sparks exploded from the hinges as they swung out, parting to reveal the short corridor beyond and a single tiny figure bolting down it at full tilt.

Someone let off a shot, the gun flashing in the corner of my vision and a section of the tunnel wall blowing out in an explosion of rock and smoke. Zee collapsed, rolling awkwardly, and I screamed out to him.

'Zee!'

'Hold your fire!' yelled Bodie. 'It's our boy.'

I was in the tunnel before he'd finished speaking, heading for the bundle of bones and rags on the stone floor. I dropped to my knees beside him at the same time he was pushing himself up.

'You crazy?' he shouted, dragging me up with him.

'Sorry, they weren't trying to shoot you –'

'No, are you crazy? Run!'

I'd been so focused on Zee that I hadn't noticed the movement from the control room, the wave of black and silver that was pouring from the elevator.

'Run!' Zee yelled again, bolting towards the yard. I didn't need to be told a third time, keeping my head low as the blacksuits came after us. Then the world dissolved into noise and fire as everyone started shooting, neither side seeming to care that we were smack bang in the middle.

The war had begun.

FIRE IN THE HOLE

Momentum was the only thing that got us out of the tunnel alive. I didn't open my eyes to see where I was going, the walls of orange flame and smoke and noise on all sides so thick they could have been solid, the air shredded by thousands of lethal pellets – two fists that slammed towards each other. I didn't even breathe, I just ran, throwing myself back the way I'd come and hoping I'd reach the door before I was perforated.

I skidded out, tripping on a shape in front of me and tumbling to the rock, throwing my hands up to cover my head. I was vaguely aware of a stinging pain in my left leg, but I couldn't bring myself to look.

'Get that door closed!' I heard somebody screaming, probably Bodie.

I looked up, the entire prison punctuated by shotgun blasts. It was like watching a film with strobe lights, every juddering moment reduced to a snapshot by a burst of light and sound. One of the Skulls flew back as if struck by an invisible hand, his dead eyes questioning the distant ceiling. Somebody else grabbed his gun, struggling to pump a shell into the chamber.

'Come on!' yelled another voice, and I saw Zee above me, offering his hand. I grabbed it, scrambling to my feet and moving out of the doorway. Bodie and Simon plus a bunch of kids were round the other side of the door trying to push it closed and I ran in their direction, growling in pain as something stung my ear. I took a look inside the tunnel as I ran, seeing the blacksuits marching relentlessly forward, not slowing or falling despite the wounds that stained their jackets.

'They aren't going down!' somebody yelled.

'I'm out!' came another scream. 'We need more ammo.'

'Forget about it,' Bodie replied, the tendons in his neck like wires as he pushed the heavy door. 'If we don't get this thing closed then we're dead.'

It was too late for another kid, a Fifty-Niner this time. He rocked back, his chest opened up, the gun clattering to the stone. By the time he followed it he was gone. The other Skulls with guns were backing off, most furiously trying to reload from empty tube magazines and the rest firing their last rounds into the tunnel.

'Are you gonna help or what?' yelled Zee, who had joined the group behind the door, adding his skinny arms to the push. I ignored him, scanning the ground for the dropped canister. It had rolled just outside the tunnel entrance, visible between the legs of the retreating Skulls.

Throwing my hands up to protect my head I lurched back across the open door, the gunpowder burning my lungs.

'Hold your fire!' I bellowed above the shots, lifting up the canister and grabbing the valve.

'What?' yelled the Skull closest to me, letting off another round. 'You out of your mind.'

'Just wait,' I said. The kid dropped his gun to his side and dodged out of the doorway, watching me with terror in his eyes as I fiddled with the canister. The valve twisted round in a semi-circle, closed in one direction and open in the other. Even when it was turned fully it only released a whisper of gas.

Another kid fell, blood spraying from a wound in his leg. He screamed as he went down, a couple of Skulls dragging him out of the line of fire before the black-suits could finish him off. Bodie wasn't having much luck with the door, the huge slab of metal only scraping a couple of centimetres closer to the wall with each endless second.

It was this or nothing.

'Cover me,' I said, grabbing a pickaxe from where it had fallen, then running into the doorway. The guards were still advancing but their numbers had been thinned out, fewer shadowed forms visible through the smoke and the haze.

Praying that my plan wouldn't backfire, I placed the canister on the floor with the valve pointing back into the yard. Wedging it in place with my foot, I lifted the pickaxe and slammed the point down. The metal struck the stone a hair's width from the canister, causing a spark to dance over the valve. My heart almost stopped, but I raised the pickaxe and brought it down again before I could think too hard about what I was doing.

This time the blade landed right where I'd aimed, at the joint where the valve met the metal. It split and the canister came alive, blasting out from under my feet with so much force that I almost fell. I kept my balance, watching as the released gas propelled it through the door and into the tunnel.

'Fire in the hole!' I yelled. 'Shoot the canister!' But my orders weren't necessary. One of the suits must have done the job for me, hitting the missile at point blank range with his twelve bore.

There was a moment of absolute silence and stillness where the entire prison shone white, every detail embroidered with a golden thread like some heavenly tapestry.

Then a bubble of blue fire ripped from the mouth of the tunnel, bringing with it all the heat and horror of hell. The ground rocked so hard that I couldn't tell which way was up, the shock wave from the explosion sending me and everyone else nearby soaring through the boiling air.

Even with my head pummelled by noise I knew that the feeling of being in flight lasted too long. I peeled open one eye, saw that I was lying on the floor twenty metres or so from the vault door. The yard between me and it was like a lake of sapphire flames, vaguely human forms thrashing about in them like they were drowning.

What had I just done?

I picked myself up, the prison spinning around me as

though the explosion had knocked it into orbit. Staggering across the blistering rock I reached the tunnel, or what was left of it. It looked like it had been turned upside down, massive chunks of rock from the ceiling, along with the machine gun, strewn across the floor, and what could only be scraps of blackened suit pasted overhead.

There was too much smoke blocking my view of the control room, but I didn't need to see inside it to know that nothing could have survived the backlash of that explosion. Not even a blacksuit. In the yard, the fireball had enough space to fan out, limiting its power. But in the confined space of the tunnel and the room beyond it would have been like an atomic bomb going off.

The vault door was still intact, although a section of the rock surrounding it had crumbled, leaving it hanging limply from the wall.

I suddenly realised I could hear a voice past the ringing in my ears and turned to see Bodie by my side, his face the same but different. I couldn't quite make out what he was saying, but I could lip read well enough to know it wasn't pretty. Behind him I could see various kids getting to their feet, all rubbing their dirty faces and jamming fingers into their ears. Apart from the gang members who had fallen during the fire fight everybody else seemed to be moving, even if it was just squirming on the ground. To my relief I saw Zee amongst them, staggering in tight circles as he tried to recover his balance.

'. . . crazy . . . going through your head . . . buried us all . . .' I could make out snippets of what Bodie was saying. He saw my confusion and walked right up to me, his voice cutting through the chime. 'I said that was crazy. You could have got us all killed.'

'Few more seconds and the suits would have been through the door,' I replied in a voice so distant it sounded like someone else's. 'You saw how many there were, and that was just the first group. If they'd got the elevator working again then there would have been dozens of the bastards up here, dogs too. You think we had enough ammo to hold them off?'

'Yeah,' Bodie said, staring down the tunnel. 'I mean no. But that was a little drastic, don't you think?'

'And some warning would have been nice,' added Zee. 'You singed off my eyebrows.' He looked up at me and tried his best to smile. 'Looks like I'm not the only one.'

I raised my hand to my forehead, felt the smooth skin above my eyes, painful to the touch. A quick look at Bodie and I realised that's why he hadn't looked like himself.

'You both look like eggs,' I said. 'I could paint –'

'You think this is the right time for beauty tips?' snapped Bodie.

'We're alive, aren't we?' I replied, checking my leg to see a couple of tiny holes in my skin from the lead shot. They must have been ricochets, I'd been lucky. 'Come on, let's get this mess sorted, find out if everyone's okay.'

I ignored Bodie's muttered comments and turned to the first boy I could see, struggling to extract himself from a pile of dust and debris. Aside from a little bruising and a lot of shock – and the absence of his eyebrows – he seemed to be okay. I told him to head to the canteen, saying someone would be in there soon to give him a proper examination. The next kid was the same, traumatised but in one piece, and gradually there was a ragged line of Skulls and Fifty-Niners weaving unsteadily towards the slop room.

Minutes later everybody had migrated to the cooler air on the other side of the yard, leaving Zee and me alone with the remaining Skulls and two broken bodies by the door. Bodie had covered their faces with scraps of overalls and was kneeling beside them speaking under his breath. I stood there awkwardly until he had finished.

'They were good kids,' he said, standing up and wiping a tear from his eye. 'Good men, I mean. Knew them both from the street, soldiers then and always. They would have wanted to go fighting.'

Zee and I shared a look but Bodie didn't catch it. He tapped his fist over his chest twice, imitated by the small crowd, then turned back to the tunnel.

'We should check it,' he said. 'Make sure it's clear.'

'Need to barricade it too,' I added. 'There will be more suits where that lot came from, and the more we take out the madder they'll get.'

'No doubt,' said Bodie. 'After you.'

I stumbled over the twisted metal door frame, almost

slipping on a pile of loose rock as I walked into the tunnel. The only light was a bulb from the control room which blinked on and off like it was giving a secret signal, that and the tireless glow from the fire in the yard. Zee grabbed my arm, using it to keep his balance as he followed. Together we slipped and stumbled through the flickering darkness, half expecting a blacksuit to rise from the ashes to take revenge for his brothers.

'What the hell happened back there?' I asked, hoping my voice would keep the shadows at bay. 'How did you get the doors open?'

'I hotwired the master controls,' Zee said, stepping round a mound of what might have been shotgun barrels or splintered bones. 'The doors were on a fail-safe circuit, and once I'd rerouted the wires I managed to trick the main door into thinking the inner door was closed. Trouble was . . .'

Something moved up ahead, not seen but heard, and we stopped. The bulb winked on, the weak light struggling, and we saw more debris fall from the ceiling.

'Trouble was,' Zee continued as we started up again, 'I had to switch some of the electrical connections round as well. And the second I'd split the power to the door circuit I realised I'd diverted it back to the lower elevator as well.' He laughed, although I could tell it was strained. 'Man, you should have seen my face when I heard it coming up. Those doors swing so damn slow that by the time I'd got them both open the suits were almost on me. And you know the rest of the story.'

We stepped out of the tunnel into the control room.

The door at this end had fared less well, pulled completely from the wall and resting against the elevator. I could see that the cabin hadn't quite made it to the top, the layer of debris we'd thrown stopping its progress when its roof had reached knee height. But there had been enough space for the suits to crawl out.

'Jeez Louise,' whistled Zee. 'This place is messed up.'

He was right. The control room was completely black, as if quarried from coal. The bank of electronic equipment was nothing but a puddle of melted plastic and metal, only a handful of wires still visible. I turned to Zee, saw him chewing his lower lip, knew he was chewing on his thoughts as well.

'What?' I asked. He turned to see Bodie and the Skulls enter the room, then leant in towards me.

'You want the good news or the bad?' he whispered, not waiting for an answer. 'Good is that the warden can't control much of anything without a control room. Bad is that neither can we.'

I looked at him, shaking my head to show I didn't get what he meant. He flashed another look at the Skulls before directing more soft words into my ear.

'I'm saying that this was the only place we could have accessed the controls for the main elevator. And without them . . .' I felt my heart sink, turning to Zee as we finished his statement together:

'We're trapped.'

THE CALM BEFORE THE STORM

We stood in the middle of the control room for what seemed like forever, trying to collect our thoughts. Zee was kicking out at the surreal sculpture of melted equipment as though he could miraculously salvage something from the mess, but it was a lost cause.

'What this place used to be?' asked Bodie, staggering over a small hill of rubble and rock to get to the elevator. He bent down and tentatively stuck his head inside, squinting into the darkness beneath his feet.

'Just a room,' blurted Zee, looking at me uneasily. 'Nothing special like.'

'And this thing leads down to where the warden is?' Bodie asked, removing his head and rattling the charred remains of the elevator gates.

'Yeah,' Zee and I confirmed together. I finished: 'The only way up or down from the lower levels.'

Bodie grinned, his teeth a flash of diamonds against the dark room.

'Looks like the tables have turned,' he said. 'You blew this baby up good and true, Alex. It ain't going nowhere now.' He stuck his head back into the darkness of the shaft, which reminded me of a lion's mouth, and when he spoke next he was shouting. 'Hey, warden, you hear me down there? You hear what we's saying? You our prisoners now, we got the gates right here and you ain't never getting back up. You hear?'

We all held our breath to listen for a reply, but the underbelly of the prison was too far below. It was satisfying to imagine the warden hearing Bodie's words, though. I pictured him seething, foaming at the mouth as his frustration battled with his rage, taking it out on the poor suits who had suddenly found themselves fighting on the wrong side in a war that took no prisoners.

Ha, no prisoners, I thought to myself, my burned face stinging as my lips curled into a smile. *That's funny, Alex.*

For some reason the voice in my head made me think of Donovan, and the smile quickly vanished. I wished he was here, more than anything, more than I wished we could find a way out. He deserved to be here. And he'd have been so good in this fight, he'd have known exactly what to do. But he wasn't. He was dead. I had killed him.

I felt the lump rising in my throat, so big that it was like a living thing trying to claw its way out of my windpipe. I made for the tunnel, not caring that I was tripping and slipping on the broken floor, just wanting to get out of the darkness, away from the smell of death.

'Alex?' Zee shouted after me. 'You got a plan? Alex?'

I didn't stop, lurching over the debris like Franken-stein's monster as I struggled to get back into the yard. Only when I was out from the tunnel, the massive prison yard the closest thing I was going to get to fresh air, did I calm down.

I'm sorry, D, I thought, then I said the same words aloud.

'What?' said Zee, who had followed me. 'You say something? If you've gotta plan then you gotta tell me.'

'No plan,' I said.

'We just keep working at the main elevator,' came Bodie's voice, echoing from the tunnel. He appeared moments later. 'We get it open, and we find out how to make it work. You reckon we can blow the doors off with another can of gas?'

Both Zee and I shook our heads together.

'Did you not have your eyes open in there?' I said. 'We use gas on the elevator then it's stuck down here for good, and so are we.'

Bodie nodded, the cogs in his head practically visible through his eyes. After a moment or two he walked over to the elevator doors and scooped up a pickaxe that was leaning against them. Simon was standing there, nursing a burn on his giant arm from the explosion but other-wise fine. He was already holding his axe, examining several pale white marks on the steel doors, the only evi-dence that anyone had tried to break through.

'Okay,' Bodie said, resting the axe over his shoulder. The Skulls had gathered around him again, waiting for their orders, a few Fifty-Niners and other kids too. 'We'll carry on working on the doors. Pug, Clay, Omar, you take the ammo we've got left and set up in there,' he pointed back towards the tunnel. 'Make sure nothing comes up from below.'

The three Skulls started collecting shotguns, ejecting cartridges from breeches. I watched with growing dismay as the pile of red shells reached seven then stopped. They split the ammo between them, leaving one shotgun with a single shell for Bodie before heading back through the vault door.

'Alex, Zee, gonna need your help with the door,' Bodie said.

'Give me a minute or so,' I replied. 'Just got something I need to take care of.'

I walked off, Zee sticking to my side, the clang of picks on steel like a tuneless serenade marking our departure. Around us the inmates seemed to have calmed down, the explosion hammering home the fact that this had turned into something bad, something deadly. Most sat on the landings, legs dangling over the yard, watching the Skulls at work. Their attention turned to me as I passed beneath them, and every time I glanced up I saw firelight reflected in their eyes, like they were demons waiting to pounce.

'Got something in mind?' asked Zee. 'Or did you just fancy a stroll?'

I didn't answer, merely led the way around the outside of the huge yard towards the shower rooms. Ducking my head through the crack in the rock I saw

227

what I was looking for, a bundle of white against the red floor. I pulled off my jacket, wincing as my aching muscles protested.

'No point in washing,' commented Zee. 'Things are just gonna get messy again.'

I breathed a laugh through my nose, too soft for Zee to hear, then unbuttoned my shirt.

'Little privacy would be nice,' I said. Zee didn't move, his eyes on my chest as I threw the ruined uniform to the floor.

'Holy . . .' he started. 'Alex, how are you still even walking?'

I looked down, saw the claw marks that had gouged three huge trails across my chest. Around them was a patchwork of scars, some still with stitches from my surgery, the skin barely able to contain the bulging flesh beneath. There were bruises too, so many that I looked like I'd been swimming in grape juice. Most were already starting to heal, turning an ugly shade of mottled yellow.

'Nectar,' I answered, prodding a gash that had opened up in my side and wondering how I'd got it. The wound was already sealed with a layer of clotted black blood, the poison hard at work saving my life. There couldn't be much left in me now. 'Got to be grateful to the warden for something, I guess.'

'Yeah, that and your pecs, dude,' said Zee. 'Man, you look like a Mr Universe or something. Girls are gonna go wild for you when you get out of here.'

We both laughed softly. I flexed an arm, seeing my bicep swell to the size of a melon. It was impressive, yes, but the sight of it made me feel like I was going to hurl again. That wasn't my muscle under there, it was something age old and rotten stitched beneath my skin. Luckily Zee broke the tension by flexing his own arms. He looked like a rake holding two chopsticks.

'Reckon I can pull some fitties with these too,' he said, and this time our laughter surged across the room like running water. 'Seriously though, Alex, what did the warden do to you?'

'It's complicated,' I said, not even sure where to begin. 'I don't know what it is, I just know what it does. It makes me strong, Zee, gives me power I never ever imagined. But . . .' Zee didn't prompt me, waiting patiently for me to continue. 'But the price you pay for that power is, I don't know; you lose yourself, in anger, in hatred. The more it happens, the more of your personality is scratched away. If it happens too much then I'm going to end up an animal, like the rats, like Gary.'

Zee frowned, then started giggling. I looked up at him, not quite believing it.

'What?' I asked.

'Alex, what you're telling me is that the warden turned you into the Incredible Hulk.'

'What?' I repeated, my voice an octave higher.

'You no like me when I'm angry,' Zee growled, and this time I laughed alongside him. 'Hulk smash!' He stomped around the room for a few seconds banging his hands on his chest like a gorilla, then calmed down, wiping the tears from his eyes. 'You haven't even told me why we're standing in the showers.'

I turned away from Zee and removed my trousers, trying not to look at the scars that ran the length of my trunk-like legs.

'Okay,' said Zee. 'Now I'm really worried . . .'

'Just hang on a sec,' I said, groaning like an old man as I bent down and rummaged through the pile. Most of the prison overalls were way too small for me, but after a bit of a hunt I found some that had been stretched thin by time. I slowly slotted my feet in, pulling the upper half over my back. It was tight around the arms, and when I moved it tore under both of my pits, but other than that it seemed to be fine.

'Does my bum look big in this?' I asked, giving Zee a clumsy twirl.

'Your everything looks big in that,' he answered. 'You sure you want to trade that smart, comfortable suit for prison rags?'

'Yeah, I'm sure.' I picked up the suit, scrunching it into a ball. 'I'm one of you, Zee, I'm a prisoner, not a blacksuit. They may have dressed me in someone else's flesh, but they can't make me wear the suit, not now.'

'But what if you need it later on?' he said. 'Like a disguise or something.'

'They know who I am. There's no more pretending. And anyway, I'd rather die wearing the same uniform as you – as everyone – than spend another second in this.'

We stood for a moment, listening to droplets of water fall from the shower heads, suddenly aware of the immense blanket of quiet draped across the room.

'You think we will?' Zee said softly. 'Die, I mean.'

'I wouldn't give us great odds,' I replied. 'But we made it this far, right?'

'Right.'

'And now there's only a set of steel doors between us and freedom.'

'Well, the elevator doors, yeah, plus the blacksuits beneath us and the guards up in the Black Fort. And the electrified fence and the gates, not to mention Alfred Furnace and whatever he brings to the party. Oh, and the police as well, if we ever do make it as far as the streets.'

'Yeah, that too. But mainly just the doors.'

'Speaking of which,' Zee said, 'we should probably go give them a hand.'

We walked out without another word, leaving the silence and stillness of the shower rooms behind us. This time I didn't take the route around the outside of the yard but headed for the middle where the bonfire still blazed. I could feel its heat against my skin from thirty metres away, like invisible hands pushing me back. But I kept walking until the mound of burning sheets towered above me. It's not like I could lose my eyebrows again.

I tossed the suit onto the fire, watching tongues of flame lick around it as if they were tasting to see what it was. Then a mouth seemed to open up in the inferno, swallowing the suit with a roar of satisfaction. I watched until there was nothing left but smoke. If only there was a way to destroy all evidence of the warden's work so easily.

'Burn in hell,' I said, wishing I could have thought of something more original to say, and something more deserving to say it to. Then the heat became too much and I backed off, making for the elevator. It might have been my imagination but I thought the looks I got walking across the yard were softer – not so much friendlier as less hateful. I still looked like a blacksuit, but I'd chosen my colours. I was wearing prison stripes. I was one of them.

Simon was standing by the elevator talking to Zee, pickaxe in his giant hand and sweat pouring from him. He saw me coming and did a double take.

'Nice kit,' he said. 'Although it could do with some TLC.'

I was looking down at the holes in my uniform, at the threads which snaked out from every seam, when I heard something power up above my head. I staggered back instinctively, everyone else doing the same, eyes glued to the huge monitor mounted above the elevator doors. The screen flickered on, a white Furnace logo rotating lazily on a black background. Then the image parted to reveal a sight that forced screams and shouts of distress across the prison.

'It's over,' hissed the warden, his face immense, his eyes once again those lightless pits that promised an eternity of suffering, twin portals which seemed to bore right through me. 'Make your choice now. Surrender the traitors, or you will all die.'

ULTIMATUM

'Obedience is the difference between life, death and the other varieties of existence on offer here in Furnace,' said the warden from the screen, repeating the same line I'd heard so many times before.

I studied his face, saw the bruise that had begun to creep over the bridge of his nose, collecting in the deep bags beneath his eyes. Another blemish stretched from his ear down to his shirt collar, presumably where Zee had kicked him. He looked battered, but there was no sign of weakness in his remorseless gaze, which seemed to flood the prison with a cold, invisible darkness.

'Someone gave him a beating,' said Bodie, his hushed voice about the only sound in the yard apart from the fire. He turned to me. 'That you?'

'Team work,' I replied.

'Nice,' he said. 'Got what was coming to him.'

'Quiet!' said the warden, the word almost screamed, sending everyone flying back some more. I remembered the bank of television monitors in the warden's quarters, and the ones that had been mounted in the control room. I scanned the wall before me until I saw it – a black eye in the rock between the elevator doors and the warden's face, the camera he must have been watching us on.

'This is my house,' the warden went on. 'And in my house a riot like this is punishable by *death*.'

That last word was a snake's hiss, and it ushered in a wave of sobs and cries from the inmates around me. He seemed to smell their fear even through layers of rock, his nostrils flaring and his upper lip pulling back to reveal yellow teeth as big as tombstones on the monitor.

'For the most part, I would be willing to forgive this infraction. I have been watching you, and I know who is responsible. Those who return to their cells and wait for my men to lock you in will not be punished. I am even prepared to pardon those who took part in the fire fight, on one condition.'

'Here it comes,' said Simon. He had shuffled to my side, drawing ranks against the inevitable.

I stared into the warden's eyes, trying to remember how weak they had looked last time I'd met them – pale and watery and all too human. But all I could see now were black holes which caused the rest of the prison to disintegrate around them, sucking every trailing piece of matter into their soulless depths. As I watched, mesmerised, the warden's voice seemed to split in two, causing another rush of vertigo that almost had me on the floor.

'Bring me the three inmates who escaped from the

lower levels,' said one voice, the main one, which blasted from hidden speakers around the screen. The other had no physical source. It seemed to come from the gaping abyss of the warden's eyes, a sonic boom that ground itself into my brain.

How dare you, it said, the force of the words making my vision flicker. *I gave you strength that you never dreamed of possessing, power beyond your wildest dreams, and this is how you repay me?*

'Alex Sawyer, Zee Hatcher and Simon Rojo-Flores. Bring me those three and consider your debt to me wiped clean,' he went on. 'Life will go on just as it did, and this mess will be forgotten.'

The other voice spoke at the same time, softer than the real one yet at the same time a million times louder.

Never have I felt so much disappointment, so much shame. To throw everything I offered back in my face. I showed you secrets that would turn the world on its head, and I promised you a place in the fatherland to be unveiled.

'What choice do you have?' the warden's lips moved with these words. 'There is no way out of Furnace Penitentiary. Your attempts are futile, and if you persevere with them then I guarantee that you will all meet an agonising death.'

The crime you have committed here is unspeakable, and unforgivable, the voice was growing louder inside my skull, each syllable a knife edge. *There is no punishment fit enough for a traitor like you, but believe me when I say you will know all the pain of the world before you meet an agonising death.*

The warden's real words and those in my head were perfectly timed so that the final phrase – 'agonising death' – seemed to resonate *through* me. I felt the strength in my legs fade, tried and failed to stay standing.

'He cannot save you,' bellowed the warden as I thumped down onto my knees. 'Look at how weak he is. Neither one of you nor one of us. A coward, a traitor, a mutant, a *rat*, to be disposed of like trash.'

How does it feel when the power goes? How does it feel to be the pathetic boy you once were? How does it feel knowing that even when they trample you to death I will bring you back for more pain, more suffering? Oh yes, death will not find you here quickly.

Both Simon and Zee had their hands on my shoulders, their voices calling to me, but all I could feel was the warden's poisonous probing in my brain, and all I could hear was his real voice on screen.

'This will soon be over, and it is up to you to decide how it ends. Pick one path and all you will find is darkness. Choose the other and by lockdown tomorrow this will be but a distant memory.' The warden leant into the screen, his eyes expanding until there was nothing but a hurricane of lightless night. 'Leave their corpses by the elevator.'

The last few scraps of colour vanished from the monitor and it powered off. With it the pain from the warden's voice burst from my head like a startled bird, leaving me with nothing but nausea. I shook it off, letting Simon and Zee help me to my feet.

Every single eye was looking our way. Bodie and his

Skulls still brandished their pickaxes, but they were no longer facing the elevator shaft. Instead they moved as one towards us.

'Kill them!' yelled a voice from somewhere overhead. It was taken up by others, becoming a wave of sound that was almost powerful enough to crush me by itself. Bodie stared at the crowd then looked at the Skull to his left, who shrugged.

'Giving us immunity,' the boy said. 'Pretty generous, for the warden.'

'And all we gotta do is flatline these three,' added Bodie. 'Seem like a fair deal to yous?'

'Wait –' I started, cut off by another round of cries from the inmates. Even past my fear I thought that this must have been what it was like in the Coliseum, being condemned to death by a jeering crowd. 'Bodie,' I tried again. 'Come on.'

I imagined the warden watching events unfold on the screens in front of him, laughing as we were pounded into the rock. I was determined not to show fear, but I knew my expression was a mask of pure terror and there was nothing I could do to change it. Bodie was close enough now to strike, his knuckles almost white around the pickaxe handle. The Skulls and Fifty-Niners were moving around us, forming a ring of bodies, while others kids were trampling down the steps to get a closer view.

Or to join in when the slaughter started.

'You want me to kill them?' yelled Bodie, addressing the mob. There were a few more cries, but the inmates seemed uncertain now. There was a madness in his eyes, one that must have scared them as much as it did me. 'You want me to kill these three, the only ones who've had the guts to stand up to the warden? The ones who might just get us the hell out of here? You want me to kill them because he tells us to?'

This time the prison was silent.

'And for what? So he can lock us all up again? So we can go back to spending every waking hour terrified of our own shadows, and lie awake at night waiting for the wheezers?'

'The warden said –' came a voice from somewhere behind me.

'Yeah, the warden *said*,' interrupted Bodie, loud enough for everyone to hear. 'The warden *said* we'd die if we didn't obey. He *said* that we had to kill them. He *said* a lot of things just now, but the fact is he's saying stuff instead of doing stuff, and when have you ever known him to do that? He's locked beneath our feet, him and his suits. Alex, Zee, Simon, they put him there, in the ground, and he ain't getting back up anytime soon.'

This time the muttered words that emerged from the crowd were murmurs of agreement, and for the first time since the warden had vanished off screen I felt my body relax. Not much, but enough to let me breathe.

'Yous all know the rules of the street,' Bodie went on. 'Well, those of yous who're in here 'cos of the game, that is. Them that *say* are the ones who get ended by them that *play*. And the only ones who run their mouths off are them that don't have no power left but their own voice.'

That streak of insanity was still visible in Bodie's eyes, but now it reminded me of a preacher delivering a sermon, all fire and brimstone. And it was working. Those quiet chirrups of sound were growing into something more, a chorus of cheers building up around us.

'I can't promise that we'll all get out of here. Hell, I can't even promise that any of us will. But I know one thing for sure: we stand more of a chance staying alive by fighting to get outside than we do sitting in our cells waiting for the warden to pick us off one by one. So . . .'

He lifted his pick off his shoulder and held it up to my forehead.

'You want me to do them, then you just say,' he went on, and all of a sudden the prison fell quiet again. 'Or you want to tell the warden where to stick his pardons and then get the hell out of here?'

The inmates erupted, cheering Bodie on as he turned and threw the pickaxe at the screen. It struck the corner, a giant crack snaking out across the glass. Without pausing, Bodie grabbed the shotgun that had been leaning against the elevator doors and aimed it towards the camera.

'Screw you,' I heard him say as he pulled the trigger, the black eye exploding outwards in a geyser of shrapnel and sparks. He tossed the empty weapon to the floor and walked up to us.

'Thanks,' I said, picturing the warden fuming in his chair as the monitor blacked out. 'How the hell did you turn that round? I thought we were meat.'

'Gift of the gab,' he replied. ''Bout time I got to use my silver tongue for something in here.'

'The warden is gonna be pissed as hell,' said Zee. 'We better get that elevator open fast.'

'True that,' said Bodie. 'At least we know he's scared. He's shown his hand too early and it's empty. He knows we've got a chance of climbing the shaft – he must do.'

'Then let's do it,' said Zee.

I risked a quick look over my shoulder, wondering if there would still be inmates willing to shank me just to end the siege. There were hundreds of pairs of eyes looking my way but I didn't see any with murder in them. Bodie's speech had been good, the kind I wish I could have made. He'd united the boys of Furnace, they were with us now come victory or defeat, life or death.

Bodie, Zee and Simon were walking off but I raised a hand and stopped them in their tracks.

'Just a minute,' I said to Simon. 'Don't think you're off the hook. I've got a question I need you to answer and I don't want to hear any lies.'

Simon blanched, holding his hands up like he was frightened for his life. Zee and Bodie were both looking at me as if I'd gone mad, and I fixed Simon with a serious look for as long as I could hold it before bursting into laughter.

'Rojo-Flores?' I said. 'What the hell kind of name is that?'

CRACKING THE GATE

Bodie had been right. Five minutes after the warden vanished from the screen there was still no sign of him, no sign of the retribution he had promised. Ten minutes after that and the inmates of Furnace were starting to feel invincible, running round the prison looking for the hidden security cameras and shouting insults at the warden. Some were even flashing their backsides at him, or relieving themselves over the black eyes in the rock, and I couldn't help but laugh as I pictured him sitting in his quarters effectively getting pissed on.

And that was the least of his problems, from the sounds of it. Just as we were starting up on the elevator doors again one of Bodie's lieutenants came rushing from the tunnel, shotgun hanging by his side.

'Yo, boss, better take a listen to this,' he coughed, gesturing back with his weapon the way he'd come.

Zee and I followed Bodie down the tunnel back to the ruined control room, the crunch of loose rock beneath our feet masking the noises from below until we were right up against the gates of the lower elevator.

'Wait for it,' said the Skull who'd come to fetch us. 'Ain't loud but . . .'

We heard it, a muffled pop from somewhere deep under our feet. It was followed by several more, like a kid playing with bubble wrap. I thought I could hear something else too, a howling scream that sent shivers up my spine even though I didn't know if it had been real or in my imagination.

'What do you think's going on?' asked Zee, leaning on the skeletal remains of the elevator car. 'Sounds like gunfire.'

'What the hell they be shooting at down there?' Bodie said. 'Each other?'

'Gary,' I replied.

'Say what?' said one of the Skulls. 'You mean Gary Owens?'

'Thought he was dead,' said Bodie as I nodded.

'He was taken, yeah,' I explained. 'Taken the same time Zee and I were, out of the river. Warden was turning him into a blacksuit too, only . . . Only he became something else, something worse.' I tried to remember what the warden had called him. *A berserker.*

'Worse than what he was up in here?' said Bodie with a whistle. 'That *real* bad.'

I waited as a fresh round of gunfire exploded from below before telling them about Gary, the monster he'd become, and how I'd let him out of his cage to fight the suits. I'd seen him take down six or more armed guards without stopping for breath. If he was still down there rampaging through the tunnels then the warden would have his work cut out for a while.

And if Gary was loose there was nothing stopping him freeing the other prisoners, and releasing the rats. Hell, maybe the air of revolution had somehow found its way down to the prison underbelly. Even the rats weren't so far gone that they wouldn't recognise the smell of freedom if they caught it.

'Think he knows enough to find his way back here?' asked Bodie. I felt my blood run cold as I pictured Gary clawing his way up the elevator shaft, bursting into the prison. There'd be nothing to stop his killing spree.

'Let's hope not,' was all I could think of to say.

'And if he does,' Zee added, 'let's make sure we're well and truly vamoosed.'

By the time we were back out in the yard Simon and a large Fifty-Niner were pounding at the main elevator doors again, the sound of their pickaxes striking the steel making my ears hurt. Their aim was a lot better than mine had been, a cluster of pockmarks centred around the faint line where the doors met each other. As I got closer I could see that the metal was starting to weaken, each relentless strike parting it a little more.

'Good work,' said Bodie. 'Bit more and we might be able to wedge something between the doors, force 'em open.'

'A bit more and you're gonna have to pull my corpse out of the way first,' said Simon, panting hard. He held his pickaxe out to me. 'Here, your turn.'

'Yes sir, Mr Rojo-Flores,' I replied, snatching the tool

from him and ignoring his raised middle fingers. 'What does that name mean anyway?'

'Literally it means "Killer-of-those-who-take-the-piss",' he said. 'So watch it.'

'Means red flowers,' corrected Zee, making us all laugh – including Simon. He muttered playfully as he walked out of my way, leaving me a clear shot at the doors. Bodie took the other axe from the Skull and I waited for him to strike before bracing myself, squaring my shoulders and relaxing my muscles. This time I didn't put all my strength into it, focusing on my aim instead. My pickaxe made contact a couple of centimetres or so from the centre, the impact still jarring but not enough to dislocate my arms.

While Bodie struck again I looked out across the prison, watching the inmates mill around restlessly. Most were looking at us, others raiding the various rooms and cells in search of anything useful. At least they weren't still all trying to kill each other.

'In your own time, Alex,' said Bodie. 'It's not like we've got a deadline here or anything.'

I mumbled an apology, swinging my pickaxe again and grinning with satisfaction as it struck the line between the doors, opening up a lip in the metal. Bodie aimed for the same place and hit the bull's-eye with a whoop of triumph. I missed with my next two shots but he was bang on every time, the hole reluctantly parting a little more with each jarring impact.

It was my next strike which finally did it, however. With a grunt of effort I rammed the head of my axe square into the gap that was forming, the point sliding between the doors with so much force that it was jammed tight. I tried to pull it out but Bodie stopped me.

'Leave it,' he said, pushing me away and grabbing the handle. Instead of wrenching the pick free he braced a foot on the door and twisted, using it like a lever. There was an angry protest of gears from behind the wall as the doors began to part, sliding open a centimetre or two. Bodie grimaced, hissing out an order between his teeth as he struggled to hold the doors open. 'Get a prop in there.'

Zee was the first to react, grabbing another of the picks and wedging the handle in the crack at the bottom of the elevator. Bodie let go, panting hard but smiling at the shadowed slit that now separated the two doors. There was a round of cheers and high-fives from the cluster of kids by the lift.

'Who wants to do the honours?' he asked, stepping back. I walked to the doors, putting my face up to the crack between them and trying to focus on the muted light inside. It was impossible to make out any details through such a small space, but I was pretty sure that what I was looking at was the smooth metal walls of the elevator cab rather than the rough hewn rock of the shaft.

'It's down,' I said, eliciting another round of vocal celebrations. 'It's right there.'

'Then let's not keep it waiting any longer!' replied Simon, selecting a pick and taking up his post by the doors. He rammed the blade into the gap and levered it in the same way Bodie had, forcing the elevator doors open another centimetre or so. This time Zee was ready, holding a section of steel frame from one of the bunks that had been thrown onto the yard. As soon as the doors had parted far enough he slotted the bar between them, letting Simon pull out his pickaxe. The mechanism protested with a squeal, but the wedge held.

'Little more and we should be able to fit through,' said Bodie, nervously sliding his hand between the elevator doors as if making sure the gap wasn't an illusion. It was as he was pulling it out again that we heard it, a noise like a distant jet engine taking off, echoing down the elevator shaft. We all took a nervous step back.

'They must be pulling it back up,' somebody said, but I shook my head.

'No, that isn't the elevator,' Zee answered before I could open my mouth. 'It's something else.'

The sound came again, this time reminding me of the growls and screams we'd heard rising up from the levels below. Maybe the shafts were linked somehow, by air vents or something. Maybe it *was* the same noise we were hearing now.

Only this was louder, a roar that reminded me of dragons. And it was definitely coming from above us.

'Forget it,' said Bodie. 'Don't mean nothing. Black-suits up top are probably just trying to scare us, y'know.'

Zee moved to the crack between the doors, peering into the bruised light beyond.

'Has anyone not wondered why the elevator *hasn't* been pulled up?' he asked. 'Surely that's the first thing the warden would do, stop us getting inside and boosting out.'

'Maybe he can't operate it from down there,' I suggested. 'We did blow up his control room.'

'Say what?' exclaimed Bodie.

'Even if the warden can't,' Zee went on, ignoring him, 'whoever's posted in the Black Fort must still be able to work it. And I don't get why they haven't lifted it out of our reach.'

'Like I said,' Bodie interrupted, nudging Zee out of the way and lifting his pick again, 'forget it. Fact is the elevator's down here and the longer we spend talking crap then the more likely it is they *will* pull it up.'

He slotted the pick through the doors and leant against the handle, Simon adding his bulk to the effort. Their groans of exertion almost matched the grinding squeal of metal in volume as the gap widened another fraction. Somebody ran forward with a toilet seat, squeezing it between the doors and stamping on it until it was firmly wedged in place. When we all stood back we could see the interior of the lift, our ticket out of here, bathed in tremulous yellow light.

'Grab that side,' barked Bodie, taking hold of one elevator door and pulling hard, throwing all his body weight into it to try and jerk the metal open. Simon joined him, the two boys like a tug-of-war team in the last throes of battle. I moved to the other side, hooking my fingers around the cold metal. The big Fifty-Niner ducked under me, and together we gave it everything we had.

It was like trying to drag a truck up a hill, the stubborn doors refusing to budge more than a millimetre at a time. But there isn't much that can stand up to a group of inmates with freedom in their sights, and those millimetres soon started to add up. We pulled with every last ounce of strength we had, not stopping to wipe the sweat from our eyes or to rub the cramp from our backs.

When the doors had parted half a metre or so one of the Skulls wedged another broken piece of bunk frame between them. He hung from the bar, tugging it down from a diagonal to a horizontal and in doing so forcing the doors apart by another few centimetres.

'Sorted,' he said, turning to Bodie with his thumb raised.

There was a click from inside the cab, then the sound of something turning – like an electric drill. Too late I realised what it was.

The machine gun on the ceiling of the elevator spewed out a burst of fire and noise and I watched the Skull literally evaporate. An invisible stream of bullets punched what was left of his body across the yard, tearing chunks of stone from the floor before thumping into the bonfire like a giant fist. The blast cut through the metal bar holding the doors open, and with a grating crunch they slid shut. Only the upended toilet seat stopped them from closing completely, and through the sliver I could see the rotating barrel of the gun spin to a halt, lazy whispers of smoke curling out from the holes.

Bodie was the only one to move. He started off towards the fire, calling the Skull's name with such urgent, sobbing cries that I couldn't make out what it had been. He only stumbled a few steps before he realised how futile it was, the corpse now long buried in the hungry flames. Instead he looked down at the scar which had been clawed across the yard, blood pooling in the deepest parts of it like some nightmare canal.

I turned away, frightened that if I watched for much longer I might go mad. Instead I looked at Zee, slumped against the wall beside the doors, so grey I thought I could see right through him. He lifted his head, the flames reflected in his liquid eyes like an oil fire on water. He had to spit his words through a choked throat.

'Now we know why they left the elevator down.'

DAMNED

It felt like forever before anyone remembered how to move. The entire prison was a mausoleum, not even a whisper daring to break the silence. Eventually Bodie looked up from the ruined floor, gazing once at the bonfire, which had become a funeral pyre for his friend, then at us. His face twitched as it tried to find the right expression – morphing through such extremes of grief and fear and rage that it looked like there was something crawling beneath his skin. He lurched towards me, and for a moment I saw murder in his eyes, as though he thought I was responsible for what had happened, or he wanted to take it out on the nearest thing to a blacksuit he had. To my relief he barged past and slammed a fist against the elevator doors, seeming to swallow all his emotions in one stuttered gulp before turning to face the yard.

'Now what?' he asked, his voice shaky but his tone firm.

'That shouldn't have . . .' said Zee quietly. 'It . . . The armed response was switched off, and with the control room the way it is I don't see how they could have turned it back on.'

'Warden's quarters,' I said. 'He must have his own command system.'

'No,' Zee replied, shaking his head. 'If that's the case then why haven't all the guns been blazing? Don't make sense, not unless . . .' He paused for thought, ignoring the prompts from everyone around him. 'The gun in the elevator must operate on a different circuit. It must be programmed to fire automatically if the doors are opened with force.' He swore, banging his head against the wall.

'You can fix it, right?' asked Bodie. 'Same way you fixed the doors?'

'No way,' was Zee's blunt response. 'To do that I'd either have to get inside the cabin or, more likely, get to the controls at the top of the shaft. Christ, like we honestly thought it would be as simple as breaking through the doors.'

Bodie turned to me, everyone in the yard seeming to follow his line of sight until my skin crawled with the force of their expectation.

'I . . . I don't know,' I whispered. 'The elevator's the only way up. We have to find a way to get in.'

'Maybe you want to volunteer next time?' he snapped.

'We could make a shield or something,' said Simon. 'Out of metal. One of the surfaces from the kitchen maybe.'

'You saw the way that gun cut through the bar,' Zee said. 'And through the rock. Must be fifty calibre at least. It will tear any shield to shreds, along with who-ever's behind it.'

Bodie winced, that flash of anger appearing as a dark shadow behind his eyes. He started to pace, his entire body tensed like a spring. I tried to think of another plan, anything that would get us out of here, but my mind was locked up tighter than a cell door. There was nothing there but a growing sense of futility. Just to fill the silence I threw out a few meaningless words.

'Maybe it's worth a try. If we can hide behind some-thing until we get inside the elevator then maybe we can deactivate the gun. I don't know.'

'And watch someone else die?' Bodie said.

'Did you honestly think we'd get out without some sacrifices?' I spat back, my own temper fraying. 'You think I haven't lost friends? We all have. We just have to deal with it and move on. We can mourn them when we're out there.'

I pointed up, pulling back when Bodie came at me. He planted his hands on my chest and pushed hard before storming towards the centre of the yard. I watched him go, then turned to the Skulls.

'What?' I asked them. They looked nervously at each other before one found the courage to speak.

'That was his brother,' he said. I felt my heart drop from my chest, sinking all the way to my feet and leav-ing me hollow inside. Bodie was standing as close to the flames as he could, and even from this distance I could see his body shaking. I wanted to go to him, say something to make it better. I'd seen so many people die since coming to Furnace, boys who had become my brothers. But to lose actual flesh and blood, I couldn't even begin to imagine what that was like.

'Leave him to it,' said Simon, as if he was reading my mind. 'Nothing you can do. We just got to figure out a way past that turret.'

'How?' I spat. 'How the hell do we get inside?'

He didn't speak. Nobody did. But I had no idea that I was about to find out in one of the worst ways possible, no idea that our answer would come in the shape of the most terrifying nightmare Furnace Penitentiary had ever unleashed upon its inmates.

'Any luck?'

Ten minutes after Bodie's brother had died I was crouched down against the wall beside the elevator doors, studying the blueprint of the prison laid out before me as if I didn't know it was useless. The knotted white lines were like clumps of plant roots and I kept waiting for them to sprout out across the torn paper, a new escape route blossoming from nowhere. But there was just the single stalk of the elevator shaft leading to the surface. Everything else was buried deep beneath the ground, us alongside it.

'Alex, any luck?' Simon repeated, leaning over me and perusing the plans himself.

I shook my head, turning my bleary eyes out into the yard. The Skulls and the Fifty-Niners were holding court close by, talking in hushed tones. I hoped they were coming up with more than I was. A gargling from Zee's stomach a few minutes ago had reminded him of his hunger, sending him careening off towards the trough room in search of leftovers. Bodie hadn't moved from the fire, so motionless now that he looked like a graveyard carving silhouetted against the setting sun.

'I still say the shield idea is the best we've got,' Simon went on, running his large hand over the elevator doors but careful to stay away from the centre. 'We could use sheets to bind together three or four surfaces from the kitchen. That's bound to hold up for the few seconds we need to get inside.'

'The gun rotates,' I answered, not really listening to my own words. 'We can't get past it if it shoots us wherever we stand.'

'Then we blow it up,' he persisted.

'And risk sealing off our only way out? Come on, Simon.'

'All I'm saying is that we'd better think of something fast,' he said. I thought he was going to mention the warden and the blacksuits climbing up from below, but instead he nodded towards the gang members. I glanced up, suddenly nervous at the way they kept peering over at us.

'They wouldn't,' I said.

'Don't see what choice they have,' Simon muttered.

I used the wall to lever myself up, walking over to the huddle of whispering kids. They fell silent when they saw me approach, looking at me with a strange mix of anxiety and determination.

'Thought of a plan?' I asked.

'Yeah, we're putting a little something together,' replied one through a sneer. 'Why don't you and your buddy go and wait by the elevator. We'll be with you in a minute.'

'It won't do you any good,' I said, my hackles raised, my arms suddenly tensed by my side. 'You think the warden's going to let you go just like that if you kill us? You know what he's like, what he's capable of. He'll skin you alive for what you did to his blacksuits.'

'Oh, and you think sitting down here with our asses in our hands is gonna end us up any better?' said another of the Skulls. They began to fan out, the group opening up like a claw ready to snatch me. 'Ain't no way to the surface, man.'

'Better staying alive in here than dropping dead trying to skip,' said a Fifty-Niner. 'I ain't no martyr.'

I lifted my hands, ready for them. This wasn't what I wanted, but I knew I was more than a match for these guys, so long as the rest of the prison didn't decide to join in. The adrenaline began to pump through my veins again, carrying the nectar with it. The darkness inside me seemed to revel in the thought of combat, drawing a crimson veil over my vision and making me clench my fists so hard that I could feel nails piercing skin. The gang members eyed each other nervously but they didn't stop advancing.

'Go get the little one,' said the Skull who had spoken first, nodding towards the trough room. This time the wave of nectar that pulsed through my head made me growl, a deep throbbing roll of thunder which turned the boys to stone.

For what must have been a full minute we stood there, deadlocked, tensed, like two opposing dams ready to burst. It was only when the fizz of static filled the prison that we stepped off, the Skulls backing away as they watched the cracked video monitor above the elevator doors power on. The white Furnace logo floated lazily on its bed of black as if waiting for the entire prison to gather round, then parted to reveal a face.

At first I didn't recognise him, the warden so pale, so drawn that it looked like his mask of flesh was slipping away from the bone beneath. His eyes were still black pits that promised an eternity of suffering, but they seemed to flicker from dark to light and back again as though the power that fuelled them was running out. The bruises had spread across his nose and cheeks, and there was a thin trail of black blood winding its way down from one nostril. His tongue flashed across his upper lip, as if tasting the dark fluid, and when he smiled it was smeared across his teeth.

'We'll kill them,' yelled the Skull before the warden had a chance to speak. The camera beneath the screen was still smoking, but he must have had others trained on us because the words made him laugh – a dry hiss that sounded more like a dying breath. Somewhere behind him, broadcast into the yard through hidden speakers, we heard a gunshot. The noise seemed to startle the warden, his eyes becoming just eyes for a heartbeat before once again fading into endless shadows.

'Too late,' he said, more gunfire erupting out of sight. 'I asked you for one simple thing. I asked you to bring me the traitors, so that we could forget this whole sorry mess. I promised you leniency, mercy even.'

'Somebody do them,' said the Skull, but nobody in the yard was moving. The sight of the warden looking so weak had us all hypnotised, like rabbits caught in the headlights.

'I was willing to forgive your crimes, to let life go on without punishment,' he continued, wiping his hand across his face as the trickle of blood suddenly became a stream. 'But you have chosen another path.'

I thought I heard another noise from the screen, the sound of metal striking rock. As it grew louder, however, I realised it was something falling down the elevator shaft. There was a ringing clang as it thudded onto the roof of the cab, gradually ebbing into silence. I glanced at Simon, who was moving warily away from the doors. Above him, looming over us like a giant, the warden peeled open his lips again.

'You have made that choice,' he said through his soulless smile. 'It is too late to turn back. The time for forgiveness and redemption is over. Yes, you have made your choice and you now have to live with it. Not that any of you will live past tonight.'

A groan of fear shuddered across the yard, echoing off the walls. At least I thought it was an echo until the sound came again, that same grating roar that we had heard before. It was closer now, a bestial snarl punctuated only by the percussive clank of more metal falling onto the elevator roof. This time everyone took a stumbling step back.

'There is no way out of Furnace Penitentiary,' the warden said, emphasising every word. 'Because I would see you all die in here before you set foot outside of this prison. There will be more criminals to fill your cells, more children to take your place. Life will go on just as it did before. But you,' he paused as if he too could hear the raw, wet screams which dropped down the elevator shaft, 'your time is now over.'

There was a series of deafening crunches high above our heads, causing the very walls of the prison to tremble and sending curtains of dust spiralling down from the shadows. The sound was like explosives being detonated, the bangs muffled by thick rock. But deep inside me I knew the source of the noise was something far worse than dynamite. No, whatever the warden was sending would have none of the mercy of fire.

It was something big, something *living*, falling fast. I thought about the words I'd heard from the phone back in the warden's office, that impossible promise.

I am coming for you.

The warden seemed to read my mind, and like so many times before I felt his eyes boring into mine, dirty fingers in my brain.

'Alfred Furnace sends his regards,' he said, his eyes so dark, his lips curling back so much, that his face became a skull. 'Allow me to introduce you to the berserkers.'

There was another bone-shattering crunch from the shaft, powerful enough to rip a ragged gash down the rock. The screen shattered, the warden's grin splintered into a million shards of glass that sliced across the yard. The elevator doors ballooned outwards like they were made of rubber, a fountain of smoke and sparks concealing what lay beyond.

But past the haze, through the gap in the doors, I caught a glimpse of something surely too large, too fast to be alive, thrashing, pounding, howling.

Even though the screen had gone the speakers must have remained, because the warden's voice called out to us like a phantom's.

'May God have mercy on your souls,' it said. 'Because I won't.'

With a deafening crunch the yard went dark, the dull glow of the fire struggling to hold back the endless shadows. Then, with a burst of sparks, the bulbs of the blood watch came on, painting everything in thick red light. And over the sound of a thousand panicked screams came the warden's insane, howling laughter – a chilling battle cry which unleashed hell and damned us all.

BERSERKERS

I barely had time to move as the creature forced its way out, smashing through the elevator doors with such strength that they were torn from the wall, spinning over the yard like blades. I ducked to avoid one, seeing it plough through the fire and cartwheel into a cluster of cells.

I didn't want to look, didn't want to see what emerged from the guttering gloom inside the ruined elevator, but when a hellish bellow ripped through the hot air sheer terror wrenched my head round.

Even after everything I'd seen, all the horrors of Furnace Penitentiary, I couldn't believe my eyes.

The creature was so big that it had to unfold itself from the giant lift car, its long limbs as black and hard as a beetle's, its torso like an ancient tree gnarled and knotted by time. It seemed to wear a shroud of darkness, a cloud of poison that made my eyes sting just to look at it. But I couldn't blink, couldn't turn away, even when a vast maw opened in the stump of its head and it spewed that same awful shriek into the yard.

It wasn't that which filled me with fear, though. It was the two slits of blazing silver light perched unevenly above the mouth, surveying the prison with a cold, calculating intelligence that I knew right then and there had once been human.

The creature stood, every fibre in its ravaged body seeming to expand until it was easily half again as tall as me. Its spidery arms flexed, too many joints making them look like they had been broken in a dozen places. But there was no denying the power of the creature as it slammed its fists down onto the floor, gouging two ravines in the stone.

Then, using all four limbs, it began to run, tearing across the yard as fast and hard as a freight train. It bowled into a group of screaming inmates without mercy, its claws like giant scythes which cut through flesh and bone as easily as they sliced through thin air. The carnage was so swift, so relentless, that it didn't seem real, like I was watching a movie. Only when Simon ran over, grabbing my arm, did my brain snap out of its trance, the horror flooding back with such a sudden jolt of reality that my heart skipped a beat.

'Let's go,' he yelled, dragging me after him. A kid in a Skull bandana slammed into us, reeling as he bolted towards the far side of the yard and the entrance to the trough room. Almost every single inmate was heading the same way, a stampede of flailing bodies and stamping legs. All eyes were on the beast behind us and the route ahead, until another choked growl broke free of the elevator.

'Oh no,' I said, the words not even a whisper, like they were afraid to leave my mouth. Against every instinct I looked over my shoulder to see a second impossible form crawl from a hole in the lift ceiling. This one was as soft as its brother was hard, its pale, pink flesh like porridge, hanging in bags over its squat body. But it moved with the same speed, exploding into the yard on four huge legs and running right for us.

'You got a death wish?' screamed Simon, fingers still wrapped around my overalls. 'Come on!'

There was no way we could have outrun the creature, but luckily for us it was distracted. The three Skulls posted inside the vault door emerged, their faces dropping and their shotguns rising in unison. The first fired before he could even aim, the shot going wide and causing the beast to spin round, doubling back.

The Skull dropped his smoking weapon, retreating, but the other two fired together. The creature's baggy flesh rippled with the force of the impact, a bubble of inky blood bursting on its flank, but the shots didn't even slow it down. It barrelled into them, its mouth wide enough to engulf both boys. I turned away before I could see what happened, but it didn't stop the sound of tearing meat from filling my head.

There was a bottleneck outside the trough room, inmates practically climbing over each other as they fought to get through the narrow opening. I risked another look back as we joined the crowd, seeing the first beast still cleaving through inmates on the far side of the yard, and the second running a coarse, fat tongue across the wet floor, its corpulent body shuddering as if with delight.

'Come on!' shouted Simon, pushing through a cluster of smaller boys to try and get to the front. It was taking forever. There was no way we'd survive long enough if either of the beasts came our way.

'Go up,' I yelled, breaking off from Simon and making for the nearest staircase. The platforms above us were alive with movement, kids stumbling towards what they hoped was safety. We joined them, tearing up the metal steps as fast as we could until we'd reached the fourth level. From the narrow landing we had a bird's-eye view of the nightmare below, the two creatures momentarily distracted from their prey by the fire still blazing in the middle of the yard.

'What the hell are they?' Simon whispered. 'I've never seen anything like that down below. They look like . . .'

He faltered, unable to think of any comparisons. I couldn't either. Yeah the warden had made me a blacksuit, and he'd turned other kids into freaks, but even Gary with his misshapen body and his bloodstained claws hadn't looked anything like this.

'Berserkers,' I said, repeating the warden's name for them. 'They belong to Alfred Furnace.'

'How do you know that?' Simon asked.

'Gary,' was my reply. 'He's becoming one too. The warden told me, showed me. He doesn't know what they are, only what they are for. They're killing machines, Furnace's sick pets.' I suddenly realised what I was saying, why the beasts were here. 'You heard his voice on the phone same as me. He sent them because of what we did. This is our fault, Simon.'

The insect-like beast had grown bored of the flames. On two legs now it bounded across the yard in long, loping strides that reminded me of the wheezers. At first I couldn't make out where it was going, then I saw the two shapes huddled inside an open cell. The berserker uttered a high-pitched chirrup that sounded too much like laughter, grabbing the bars and wrenching them from the wall in a shower of rock and dust.

'We have to do something,' I said.

'No way,' said Simon, his voice laced with fear. 'No way, man. We lay low, wait for . . . wait until . . .'

I watched his face fall as he realised there was no help coming. He'd heard the warden as clearly as I had. Everyone in Furnace was paying the price for our attempt at freedom. Those creatures had their orders. They wouldn't leave until every last living thing in general population had stopped breathing, until we'd all been executed.

'Alex,' he said softly. 'If you go down there then you'll die. You're strong, yeah, but those things . . .' Events in the yard finished his sentence for him, the berserkers tormenting the inmates like cats playing with mice. I watched them for a while, the sight making my guts churn and my head pound, then looked back at Simon in time to see him toying with something in his pocket. He caught my eye, pulling his empty hand out and resting it on the railing.

'What is that?' I asked, remembering him stealing something from the warden's quarters. 'A blade?'

He shook his head, then, realising that I wasn't about to let it go, he slid the object from his overalls and held it up. Just seeing it seemed to make my blood boil, my body growing so hot that I had to check to make sure I wasn't burning. It was as if the nectar inside me was calling out for what Simon held in his hand, screaming for it.

'I didn't know what was going to happen to you,' he said, the dark syringe trembling in his unsteady grip, the flecks of golden light embedded inside seeming to spin like distant stars. 'Like I said, Alex, sometimes if you get pulled off the nectar too quickly then your body just decomposes. Figured if we had some then . . . y'know.'

Below us another chilling shriek exploded out across the yard, trailed by a chorus of weak, human screams that set my teeth on edge. The last of the crowd was squeezing into the trough room, but not fast enough. The fat freak was shuffling towards them too quickly, its rolls of loose skin dancing in the firelight. I saw its mouth open, lipless and grotesque but nonetheless still smiling.

I knew what I had to do.

'Give it to me,' I said, holding my arm out. Simon hesitated, gripping the needle as if it was a poisonous snake.

'If you take this then there's no telling what will happen to you,' he replied. 'Another dose of nectar and your body might not be able to find its way back. You might become a blacksuit for good.'

'It doesn't matter,' I said. 'If I don't take it then none of us are getting out of here.'

Simon flinched as another desperate wail drifted up from below, cut short by a gut-wrenching snap. Then he nodded, pulling the cap off the syringe and grabbing my wrist with his other hand. I drew up my sleeve, my mind too confused, too frightened to really make sense of what was going on. I knew this was a mistake – the warden's poison would do all it could to pull me back, to make me once more a Soldier of Furnace. I may as well have been handing myself back to him on a silver platter.

I felt the sting of metal in my flesh, looked down to see my veins pulse black, a creeping darkness that flooded my blood with cold heat.

'Just don't forget your name,' Simon said, waiting until the plunger was all the way down before sliding the needle free. 'Alex Sawyer, don't forget it. I'll be here for you when you come back.'

He carried on, but I wasn't listening. It was like I'd been thrown into a black lake, the world suddenly impossibly dark and quiet. All I could hear was my own breathing, and the thrashing beat of the nectar as it clawed its way through my system. My muscles tensed, my grip on the railing so tight that the metal buckled. But it wasn't enough; when I glanced into the yard that spectre of fear still loomed at the back of my mind.

'Slap me,' I said to Simon. The boy looked like he had suddenly shrunk, and his expression was one of terror – like I was another of the beasts below. I repeated my request, this time in a guttural growl better suited to some demon. Simon lifted his hand and brought his open palm hard across my cheek. The pain flared through me, carrying with it an anger so intense that it felt like my conscious mind was being buried in mud, locked away forever. I roared at the boy, raised my fist to return the blow, caught myself before it was too late. 'Again!'

He lifted his trembling hand and slapped me with even more force, hard enough to rock me back on my heels. This time the nectar poured into my brain like molten lead, snuffing out everything except for my fury. I opened my mouth and howled, the sound carrying so much force that it even blotted out the symphony of death from below.

I went to lash out at the boy, to punish him for striking me, but he had vanished. Instead I cast my eyes into the yard, looking for victims, looking for anything to take my anger out on. The prisoners were there, fear making them pathetic, and it was all I could do not to throw myself at them, tear them limb from limb as a punishment for their weakness.

Something stopped me, a quiet whisper from a place deep inside my head. It forced my eyes away from the swarming inmates to the two beasts which stamped and slithered across the yard. Then, as if that voice had been holding the reins of my rage and had now let them go, I felt the nectar take control.

And with a roar that turned every single head in the prison, I leapt over the railing and threw myself into battle.

ENDGAME

I was four floors up but I didn't even feel the impact as I landed on the yard, a web of cracks spreading across the rock beneath my feet. I was moving again before I even knew it, tearing through the thick crimson light so fast that I could feel the wind on my face, thick and heavy with the scent of blood.

The fat berserker had reached the dwindling crowd outside the trough room, scattering the kids like bowling pins. For an instant I thought I'd have the element of surprise, the monster too busy wrapping its dripping fingers around writhing bodies to notice me. But some instinct must have warned it because when I was a stone's throw away it suddenly swung round and reared.

Up close I saw the beast for what it was. Its body wasn't fat, as I'd assumed, but instead packed so densely with muscle that the skin had been pushed out in loose, useless folds. It towered above me, its quivering flesh suddenly solidifying into what looked like a pillar of solid rock. The vast cavern of its mouth opened wide, that hideous parody of a grin again, and I could see right down the red, raw gullet beyond. Perched above it like loose pebbles was a cluster of dark eyes, too many to count.

I didn't give the fear a chance to creep in, just lowered my head and let my anger do my thinking. I was on the beast in a heartbeat, dodging its obelisk-like fist and slamming into its torso. It was like running into a wall, the sheer density of it knocking the air from my lungs. But it worked, catching the berserker off balance and sending us both rolling across the yard.

We slammed into the wall, the creature on top of me, pinning me down like roadkill beneath a truck wheel. It raised its arm, its knotted hand the size of an anvil, slamming it down towards my head. I bucked to try and dislodge it, lurching to the side and feeling the explosion as the impact left a crater in the stone millimetres from my ear.

It raised its arms again before I could even catch my breath, but I didn't give it the chance to strike, ramming my fist into its throat, feeling the rigid cord of its windpipe lodged deep inside the muscle. I lashed out again, and again, each blow sending the creature reeling back until its bulk slipped off my legs. It staggered away, arms raised in defence, and I punched it hard in the gut only to feel a nerve-shredding blast of agony shoot up my wrist.

I pulled away, seeing the blood pour from between my knuckles. There was something lodged in the flesh, a long, twisted thorn that appeared to be made of bone. I stepped back, watching in horror as the creature's skin rippled, dozens of white spikes pushing outwards like hair. It shook itself like a wet dog, barbs sprouting from its shoulders and back, even the top of its head. Then, its tiny black eyes gleaming, it charged.

I ducked beneath its fist, splinters of rock detonating from the wall behind me, then made a break for the elevator. As I ran I noticed the first berserker, still feasting on something on the far side of the yard but gazing at me through slits of silver. It threw its meal to the floor and stretched up on its long legs, sniffing the air.

I didn't wait to see what it would do next, skidding to a halt and scanning the wreckage of the lift doors until I found what I was looking for. I had barely managed to lift the pickaxe before the fat berserker had caught up, its lethal knuckles cleaving the air in front of my face.

With a roar of defiance I swung the pick, aiming for its legs – the only place not covered in barbs. The blade caught it above the knee, sliding into the muscular flesh with a wet pop. The beast's entire body juddered, the vibration tearing the weapon from my fingers. It stumbled but didn't fall, its eyes blinking out of turn as they studied the object embedded in its leg.

I was lifting another pickaxe from the rubble by my feet when the world suddenly came apart. It was as if a black hole had suddenly opened in the middle of the prison, causing everything to spin into a disjointed orbit. It was only when I hit the floor, tumbling across the rough rock, that I realised what had happened. The beetle-black berserker had sped across the yard, striking me with enough force to send me flying.

I tried to get up, feeling something loose and broken inside me. Through my faltering vision I could make out the two freaks ploughing my way, cutting around either side of the bonfire before closing ranks.

Get up, I screamed at myself, disgusted by my own weakness. The nectar burned within, patching up internal injuries that would otherwise have been fatal. It seemed to react to my call, releasing a burst of energy that pulled me from the floor like I had puppet strings.

I realised I still had the pick, and hurled it with every ounce of strength I possessed. It was a lucky shot, the hooked blade striking the taller berserker in its metallic black skull. There was a crack like a firework and the creature crumpled, doing a clumsy forward roll, thrashing its long limbs as it tried to dislodge the weapon.

The spiked one didn't even slow down, careening across the stone so fast that its fleshy body was a pink blur. I looked around for something else to defend myself with but there was nothing, the yard almost completely deserted of people and objects.

I ran, the floor trembling beneath me as the berserker gained ground. There was nowhere to go but up, and with a grunt of effort I propelled myself towards the platform of the second level. The sheer power of the jump made my head spin, vertigo almost causing me to miss my target. But just as I felt gravity grip me I reached out and grabbed the railing, vaulting onto the landing.

A glance over my shoulder revealed the beast in mid-jump, its loose skin fluttering like bat wings. I crouched, then launched myself into the air, clutching the bottom of the third-level platform. Beneath me the berserker burst through the railing, the metal framework groaning with its weight. It came after me again, its spiked hands gouging chunks from the wall as it clawed its way up.

I swung myself up onto the landing, then legged it past a dozen empty cells until I reached the stairs. The berserker wasn't giving up the chase, the platform bouncing like a funhouse walkway as it advanced. I leapt up a single flight in two bounds, spinning round and taking the next lot just as effortlessly. The creature's bulk was giving it problems on the narrow stairways but it was winning the battle, its spikes shearing through the steel each time they made contact.

I kept running, rising, up past the fifth level, then the sixth, then the seventh. The nectar was like nitro, turning my heart and lungs and muscles into an engine that didn't once protest, not even when I'd climbed to the twelfth level and run halfway down the landing. The air up here was stale, never used, the yard below as small as a playground. There was no sign of the inmates, but the other berserker was still down there, its gunmetal body more like a beetle than ever as it squirmed and thrashed in a growing puddle of dark blood.

There was a snarl from the stairwell, the bolts almost ripping from the walls as the fat freak pulled itself onto the landing. Keeping all four limbs on the floor it crashed towards me, its gaping maw even darker than the blood-red shadows draped over the higher levels.

I searched the closest cell, not even a bunk to use as a weapon. Then I looked at the door, the steel bars, remembered the way the blacksuits used to bend them like they were rubber. I gripped the top of one and pulled hard, the metal squealing in protest. The berserker saw what I was doing and increased its speed, a tornado of pink muscle blasting right for me.

The door screeched but it was a cry of surrender, the metal bending down and out. I tugged, flexing the bar back and forth until it snapped loose from the frame. I held the two-metre length of solid steel like a baseball bat, standing my ground as the berserker hurtled down the platform.

When it was within reach I swung, aiming right for its head. The creature was quick, lifting a hand to protect itself, but the momentum of the bar was too great, the crack of a breaking bone reverberating out across the prison. It roared, spraying me with hot spittle, then lunged forward with its mouth open. I fell back, its jaws snapping shut around the bar and biting off the tip as though it was candy. Its other hand slammed down, hooked barbs ripping into my side.

Even with the nectar the pain flared, my vision turning white. I ignored it, ramming the bar into the back of its throat like I was skewering a fish. The berserker retreated, choking on blood, and I pulled the bar out, thrusting it forward again into its nest of black eyes.

It panicked, swaying clumsily away and swiping its

good arm blindly in front of it. Using the bar as a crutch, I hauled myself to my feet, then swung my makeshift club at its head. It hit with enough power to bend the metal, but the berserker still wouldn't go down. Instead it flailed wildly, stamping its legs as it struggled to get away.

Something popped from the wall, the stone cracking and the platform lurching. I dropped the bar, grabbing the handrail and watching my weapon spiral gracefully down to the yard twelve storeys below. The berserker staggered, broke through the railing, then managed to grab the landing with a barbed fist, trying to haul itself back up.

Another bolt gave up under the pressure, tearing loose from the rock. Then the platform was falling, taking me and the berserker with it. My stomach flipped, my guts almost blasting from the top of my head as I watched two levels fly past, then five, then seven, all the time falling faster and faster.

The platforms were close enough to reach but I was plummeting too fast, my arm almost ripped from my shoulder as I tried to grab a landing. The jarring impact must have slowed me, though, as I spun once and reached out again, somehow managing to hook my elbow round a railing. My body slammed into the metal, almost pulling another set of bolts from the wall. But it held.

Looking down I saw the loose platform strike the yard only two or three levels below, the berserker imitating it a millisecond later. It was as if it had C4 packed into its legs, the flesh exploding into a river of black blood which hissed angrily as it sprinkled over the fire. I let go of the railing, dropping to the floor, feeling like every joint in my body had been dislocated or broken.

Both berserkers were down, but I could almost see the nectar inside them repairing their broken bodies. The beetle-black freak was still trying to pull the pick-axe from its head, too busy to even know I was there. The other one was already starting to push itself back up. I could see its bones moving beneath the skin, resetting themselves, and knew it was only a matter of time before it was back in the fight.

'Alex!' I heard a voice, half-recognised the boy who was sprinting from the trough room struggling to hold something. Aside from me he was the only living person in the entire yard. 'Use this!'

I ran to meet him, hearing the sound of shearing flesh behind me as the berserker finally managed to wrench the blade from its twisted skull. The kid's eyes widened as he looked past my shoulder, stumbling to a halt. He must have seen something demonic in my eyes too, as he threw the object to the floor before I reached him, legging it back towards the canteen. The cylinder rolled in a half-circle, packed tight with the same gas that had wrought so much damage earlier.

I snatched it up, turning to see the tall berserker bound towards me on its two long legs. Half of its head had been torn away, but the one silver eye which remained stared at me with unrestrained fury. Its claws caught the firelight like shards of obsidian, raised and ready to strike.

I never gave it the chance.

Grabbing the canister by its narrow valve, I ran at the berserker, waiting until the last possible moment to swing. The heavy cylinder caught the creature on the good side of its head, causing an eruption of dark matter from the pickaxe wound. Its legs turned to string and the beast flopped to the ground, twitching.

I didn't stop, momentum carrying me towards the other freak. It only had stumps of legs to stand on, but it showed no sign of weakness – its arms tensing and its barbs bristling as it watched me approach. Somehow it managed to pounce, its dripping maw growing impossibly large, ready to swallow me whole.

I rammed the canister down its throat with everything I had. The creature choked, retching as it tried to disgorge the metal tank. Ignoring the barbs, I tackled the beast, lifting it off the ground and charging towards the fire. I couldn't see where I was going but I could feel the heat singeing my skin. I waited until the last possible moment before hurling the berserker at the flames.

The flailing creature vanished into the pyre, its screams soon becoming a pitiful whimper. I staggered back, holding my hands up to protect my face from the sheer intensity of the blaze. I had retreated only a few steps before the canister exploded, the shock wave blasting across the prison in a tsunami of heat and blood and tattered flesh.

I peered through the smoke, waiting for the other berserker to attack. But it was retreating towards the elevator. It curled its body through the doors, looking back once with a sliver of pure silver hatred, then vanished through the hole in the ceiling.

Like frightened rabbits in their burrows, inmates began to emerge from the rooms around the yard. One – the same kid who had given me the canister – ran right towards me, but the nectar in my blood was still raging and I stopped him dead with a guttural snarl. He watched me, they all watched me, with wide eyes and open mouths.

I could feel the warden's poison urging me to attack, calling on me to finish the job that the berserkers had started. I was a Soldier of Furnace too, after all. It was my duty to obey the warden, to obey the nectar. And it would be so easy, the figures before me nothing but insects in the face of my wrath. The thought brought down that crimson cloud again and I was charging forward before I even knew it.

Then the voice began to speak, a whisper from the deepest recesses of my brain – *You are Alex Sawyer. You are one of them. You are Alex Sawyer. You are one of them* – the mantra barely audible but repeated again and again and again until it filled my head.

I clamped my hands over my ears and howled to try and mute the voice, but it didn't give up, cutting through the nectar, cutting through my anger, cutting through the darkness.

You are Alex Sawyer. You are one of them. You are Alex Sawyer. You are one of them.

The two sides of my mind were waging a war just as

ferocious as the one that I had been fighting seconds ago, the conflict threatening to tear my soul in half. I was Alex Sawyer and yet at the same time I wasn't, I could never be that kid again. I wasn't him, and I wasn't a blacksuit. I wasn't human, and I wasn't strong enough to be anything else either. I was nothing. I was *nothing*.

I ran for the stairs, heading for the upper levels, for the only thing that would end the madness in my head once and for all.

THE ONLY WAY OUT

I barely even looked where I was walking, focusing just enough to stop myself tripping up the stairs. Behind me, from the yard, I could hear people calling out a name, *my name*, telling me to wait, but I wasn't listening. The pain in my head was too much to bear, the nectar and the voice like artillery shells pounding seven shades out of each other in the battlefield of my brain.

I knew now how to escape it, how to escape Furnace. A few seconds of free fall, then oblivion, freedom. If I didn't end it here then there was no telling what I would become, what I would do.

I don't know what made me stop. I reached the top of a set of stairs and peered along the landing, the view the same as every other level in Furnace but somehow different. I glanced down into the yard, now swarming with bodies in white overalls, and realised I was six floors up. Something made me let go of the banister, walk down the platform, until I came to a halt outside a cell.

There was nothing inside but a set of bunks and a toilet, and with the war still raging in my head I entered and sat on the lower mattress, the frame bending under my weight. My eyes roved around the tiny room, seeing the fingernail marks on the wall, smelling the residue of gas that seeped up through the sheet, peering out of the bars at a view which was somehow so familiar.

This had been my cell, so long ago that it seemed like a different life.

The nectar did its best to blot out the memories, coating them in coiled tendrils of smoke. But being here gave the voice strength, and each time it spoke – *You are Alex Sawyer. You are one of them* – the warden's poison seemed to ease its grip a little more.

I saw a face drop down from the mattress above, blossoming into a smile so big that it seemed to fill the cell with light.

You still here? said Donovan, the hallucination flickering like film from a damaged projector. The nectar surged up my throat, carrying with it another animal growl, but it possessed none of the strength it had before. I closed my eyes, Donovan's smile imprinted on my retinas like the sun. Past its glow I could still see the cell, filled with boys – D, Zee, Toby and me – laughing as we smuggled our gas-filled gloves beneath the mattress, as we planned our escape, as we talked about our plans for the outside.

I haven't forgotten about that burger, said Donovan's voice. *You better eat that thing for me, kid.*

'I will,' I said, my words chasing the last of the poison from my system. 'I promise.'

I opened my eyes. Donovan's face had dissipated into

thin air, but there were two boys standing nervously in the doorway of the cell, drenched in red light. Zee took a step forward but Simon held him back, his wary eyes never leaving mine. I smiled at them, doing my best not to make it a blacksuit's grimace.

'It's okay,' I said. 'I won't bite.'

This time both boys burst in, Simon sitting on the mattress next to me and gently poking the gaping wounds in my side, already sealed with clotted blood. Zee stood by the wall, wiping a tear from his eye. He opened his mouth, but it was like a million different things were trying to come out at once, the tangled words more sobs than sentence. He stopped, took a deep breath, tried again.

'You okay?' he waited for me to nod, then, 'Man, that was awesome, you totally owned those things.'

'When you made that fat one explode,' said Simon. 'Hell, that was just genius.'

'Yeah, thanks for the gas,' I said to Zee.

'Any time,' he replied. 'I thought you were gonna kill me, though. Your eyes, they looked just like a blacksuit's. You looked seriously pissed.'

'It was the nectar,' I explained. 'Simon injected me with another dose. It was the only thing we could do.'

Zee started to say something but he was cut off by a chorus of shouts from the yard below. I eased myself off the bed, walking out of the cell to the railing, praying that the berserker hadn't reappeared. The inmates were gathered around the elevator doors, their cries more of excitement than of fear.

'We should go see what they're doing,' said Zee, walking towards the stairs.

'I thought you were going to jump,' Simon said before I could follow. 'How did you fight the nectar? What brought you back?'

I looked into the cell, at the top bunk. It was empty, the sheets stripped, but I could still see Donovan there, legs dangling over the side, watching us go with a sad smile.

'Come on,' I said, turning away before the lump in my throat dissolved into tears. 'We're not out yet.'

I thought it would take a while to fight through the crowd, but as soon as the prisoners saw me in their midst they backed off without question, parting like the Red Sea all the way to the elevator doors. I assumed it was fear which sent them skittering away, then I saw that most were smiling, their eyes awe-filled, some even murmuring their thanks in quiet tones.

From outside, the elevator looked like a write-off, the doors gone, the floor dented, a gaping hole in the ceiling. The berserkers had punched through one corner of the cabin like it was aluminium foil. They had ripped the machine gun from its mount, bending it into the barely recognisable hunk of metal that now lay forgotten against the rear wall.

Through the splintered gap I saw the elevator shaft stretching upwards to infinity, no sign of life other than the handful of inmates who stood on the roof. Bodie was one of them, and when he saw me enter he stuck his head down through the hole.

'What do you think?' he said. 'Looks like Furnace's pets have given us a clear route to freedom.'

'No way,' said Zee, following me in. 'You kidding me?'

Simon pushed past us, using his bigger arm to haul himself up through the hole. Bodie made way for him, ushering for us to follow. I grabbed the broken ceiling, doing my best to forget about my aches and pains as I hefted my weight onto the roof. It was as black as solitary up here, but my eyes picked out every detail in silver light – the metal scaffold that held the counterweights, the power cords, and the massive steel traction cables which connected the elevator to the surface.

'Don't forget about little old me,' yelled Zee, his voice tinny. I ducked back in, offered him my hand, surprised at how little effort it took to pull him up. He snatched a startled breath as he found his balance. 'Jesus it's cold in here.'

It was, and we all knew why. Dropping down the shaft from a mile above our heads was a current of cool, fresh air. We stood in silence for a minute or so, all of us breathing it in and grinning as though we could see up past the rock, past the Black Fort, to the rain-drenched world outside.

'Man, that feels good,' said Bodie. 'Think we can all climb it?'

'We might not need to,' said Simon. He was standing over the reinforced bolts which connected the cables to the car. From what I could see everything looked intact, the berserkers having broken through close to the edge of the roof. Not that I knew the first thing about elevators. 'Don't see no damage.'

Before anyone could answer we heard a thump from way over our heads, panic driving us back through the hole so rapidly that we almost crushed each other. We peered up from the relative safety of the cabin, the source of the noise invisible.

'Like I said,' repeated Simon, his pulse so hard that I could hear it in his voice. 'Those cables look like they're all intact. Elevator might still run.'

'Yeah, but the doors are screwed,' said Bodie. 'You think this thing will go without 'em?'

'Not to mention the controls are up top,' Zee added. 'Someone's gotta get up there first.'

'I'll do it.'

Both Simon and I had spoken the same words at exactly the same time. We laughed at each other, the sound filtering through the hole and echoing up the lift shaft like it was making a break for freedom without us.

'The hell you will,' said Zee. 'You think you get to be the heroes again 'cos you've got the muscles? I can climb just as well as you.'

'With those twigs you call arms?' Simon replied. 'You can't even see where you're going. You'd make it five metres, maybe ten.'

'First round of fries up top says I beat you,' he said. 'Not that I've got any money on me.'

This time we all giggled, the oxygen blasting down the shaft like a drug, making us giddy. We didn't care about the tang of dust and oil, or the reek of the berserker which had pulled itself back up to the surface. All we could smell was freedom.

'We all go,' I said, turning to Bodie. 'When we get to the top –'

'*If*,' interrupted Simon.

'*When* we get to the top, we'll pull up the elevator. Make sure you clear the wreckage from around the doors, and fill it with as many kids as you can. With any luck we can bring everyone up in a few trips.'

'No doubt,' he said, nodding. 'We don't hear from you in a few hours, then we'll send up another group.'

'How you gonna know when a few hours is over?' asked Simon. Bodie shrugged.

'Just be safe,' he said. 'And don't get so carried away by escape that you forget to press the call button, you hear me? We all counting on you down here.'

I nodded, and moved to climb back through the hole before turning instead to stare out of the elevator doors. The sea of faces gathered outside reminded me of the day I'd arrived here, the first time I'd stepped from these very doors into the yard. The memory rushed back, bitter-sweet – the fear and the anger, then the hope when I saw Donovan's smile. He'd been the only reason I didn't jump on my first day, and the only reason I didn't jump on my last. He'd once told me that he wasn't my guardian angel, but he was, and once again I found myself missing him like a part of myself.

Stop being such a wuss. I heard his voice, knew it was my imagination but at the same time hoped that if there was anything left of him he was making this break with us. *Get your ass up to the surface!*

'Yes, sir,' I said under my breath. I took one last look at Furnace Penitentiary, still lit by the blood lights and the dying embers of the fire, like it was being bled dry. I guess it was, the inmates that kept its dark heart beating about to flood from its main artery, reducing the prison to a husk.

My eyes glided across the yard, over the doors to the trough room, the showers, the chipping halls, up the stairs and past the cells. Every scrap of stone, every rusted knot of iron, every bruised shadow, carried with it a charge of memory and emotion so powerful that it knocked the air from my lungs. I knew without doubt that I would never see this place again. Even if I was caught, I would die before I came back.

'We beat you,' I said, addressing the walls, the cells, the air, and the warden, who was probably still watching us through his cameras. 'We beat you good, you bastard.'

Then, with Bodie and the Skulls wishing us luck, telling us again not to forget them, I followed Simon and Zee through the roof into the cool, dark shaft.

OUTSIDE

It was a hard climb, but it was the easiest thing I've ever done in my life.

The steel cable dug into my hands, soon slick with blood from Simon and Zee above me. Our feet slipped, the growing abyss like the mouth of some vast creature, waiting for us to fall so that it could finish the job it started so long ago. Our wheezed breaths echoed back at us from the walls, reminding us of our exhaustion, of the impossibility of what we were doing.

But that cold air never stopped blowing, giving us the strength to keep putting one hand above the next, to keep climbing. Even though the pain in my muscles was greater than anything I've experienced in my life I never once thought about giving up, because that draught was the breath of the outside world, a ceaseless whisper that became more powerful with every step, and whose promises of freedom made us smile through our agony.

We didn't say a word to each other, focusing on the cable like Indian rope climbers, pinching the thick metal with our feet and pulling ourselves up a metre at a time. I tried to keep track of how far we'd come, but it was a futile attempt, the shaft narrowing to a point in both directions like some endless Möbius strip. Only the illusion had no power because I knew the end was just ahead of us, almost within reach. It was ours for the taking.

Simon saw it first, so drained by the climb that his words dropped down in unintelligible clumps. I looked up, the tendons razors in my neck, saw a glimmer of soft light like daybreak. The excitement that gripped my gut was almost enough to make me lose my footing, before settling into one last burst of pure adrenaline which propelled us up the final stretch of cable whooping like madmen.

I was terrified that we'd get to the top and find another set of armoured doors that were impossible to break through. But Furnace knew it was beaten. When we were close enough we saw the hole that the retreating berserker had punched in the metal. A finger of white light stretched through it, wavering back and forth like it was beckoning us on. In that second we became as weightless as the motes of dust we saw dancing in the glow, our laughter like wings which drew us effortlessly into the light.

The worst part was the short jump from the cable to the broken doors. My heart was in my mouth as I watched Simon pounce, almost losing his grip on the torn steel and plummeting into the darkness. He recovered, pulling himself through the hole then reappearing, arms stretched out to catch a screaming, flailing Zee.

By the time they had vanished through the gap I was in mid-air, the bottomless pit like a black tongue which reached out to pull me in. I hit the doors, almost bouncing off but managing to hook my fingers into the edge of the hole. Then Simon's hands were around my wrists, hoisting me into the Black Fort.

For what seemed like an eternity we lay there on the polished stone floor, our breaths coming in deranged fits of giggles as we stared at the ceiling. There were no sirens, no cries of alarm, only the soft hum of the electric lights – blindingly bright after so long in Furnace.

Eventually I sat up, several muscles cramping in protest. We were in the windowless room where we'd first put on our prison uniforms, the shower cubicles shut tight and silent against each wall. The gate at the other end stood ajar, and through the bars I thought I could see bloodstains spattered across the corridor beyond. Something out there sparked, making us all jump, a weak firework show falling from the ceiling.

'What the hell happened up here?' said Zee, his voice fluttering high and low like a badly tuned radio.

'Must have been that thing,' Simon answered, hobbling to his feet like an old man and wiping his bloody hands on his overalls. 'You obviously scared the crap out of it, Alex, 'cos it sure as hell tore through here in a hurry.'

'Come on,' I said. 'Before Furnace sends any more surprises.'

'Somehow I think he might have his work cut out for him,' replied Simon, offering a hand each to Zee and me and hauling us to our feet.

He was right, if that berserker had made a break for it then Furnace would have bigger problems than escaping inmates. I pictured the beast charging off into the city, the damage it would wreak out there, and found myself smiling despite the horror. At least the world would know about his experiments, know the truth about the prison and what they did to us here.

Even though there was no sign of life in the Black Fort we took our time, glancing nervously at the cameras embedded in the ceiling and listening out for guns being cocked, the booming laughter of the blacksuits. I led the way across the room, through the gate, trying not to look at the corpse of the guard propped up like a rag doll in a puddle of his own blood. Glistening black footprints, too big to be anything but the berserker's, pointed us in the direction of the exit. The wind on our faces was now an arctic gale, urging us forward.

On one side of the room lay the window where I'd been handed my Furnace overalls, now as dark and empty as the rest of the Fort. We passed by it breathlessly, entering another corridor featureless except for a gate to one side and a door at the far end. It was open, and through it lay the outside world, visible only as a pale light too pure, too beautiful to be artificial. I couldn't stop myself staggering towards it, only Zee's hand on my arm pulling me back.

'We've got to get that elevator up,' he said. I didn't move, every instinct in my body and mind screaming at me to make a run for the exit now, before the blacksuits came, before we were thrown back into the pit. But there was no way we could leave everybody else to rot. I nodded, and the three of us uttered a shuddering sigh in unison as we turned away and walked through the gate.

The passageway beyond was lined with barred doors, but it didn't take us long to find the control room. It too was deserted, the gun rack empty of weapons and the smell of gunpowder still lingering in the air. I didn't know exactly what had happened, but I figured that the remaining guards had been sent in pursuit of the rene-gade berserker.

I scanned the screens that lined the wall, seeing on one marked 'Deliveries' a black truck parked in a load-ing bay. The logo on the side made it clear that the vehicle belonged to Alfred Furnace, and I guessed that it had been used to transport the berserkers here. It would be going back empty. I couldn't make out a single living blacksuit anywhere.

I swept my gaze across the monitors until I found the one I wanted. The elevator was packed to bursting point, hundreds more inmates thronging around the doors.

'This must be it,' said Zee, running his finger across a set of buttons embedded in the control panel.

'Main elevator,' said Simon, reading the stencilled letters on the console. 'Wow, Zee, you really are smart.'

Zee flicked him the bird, then pressed his finger onto the button marked with an up arrow. A tremor ran through the stone beneath our feet, and on one of the screens I saw the crowd buck away from the elevator. The image was small, but I could make out sparks flying from the doors as the lift struggled to rise.

'Come on,' I hummed under my breath. 'Come on, you can do it.'

The elevator lurched up, hard enough to send a couple of inmates spilling from the doors onto the yard. Then the cabin was suddenly sucked out of view, the vibration in the rock around us letting us know it was on its way. Zee whooped, turning to give us a high-five that both Simon and I ignored in our excitement. We looked at each other, grinning so hard that all we saw was teeth.

'You ready for this?' Zee asked.

'I ain't never been more ready for anything in my life,' Simon replied. 'Come on, before the Skulls beat us to it.'

I swear we almost floated out of that room, down the corridor, through the gate, our bodies as light as air, as dreams. We didn't so much as breathe as we entered the main hall, not until we saw the heavy doors buckled outwards, and beyond them the electrified cage torn to shreds. Then we each exhaled as one, our breath becoming soft, uncontrollable cries as we walked towards freedom.

I faltered when I reached the threshold, staring at the line that separated the polished stone of Furnace from the rough ground outside, too afraid to look up, to take that last step, in case it was an illusion. But the cool breeze wrapped itself around me and drew me from the door, pulling me out into the night.

I stumbled forward, caressed by the gentle rain which fell from the moon-drenched sky. The strength had all but gone from my legs, but there was enough to carry me out of the ruined cage before I fell to my knees in the mud.

I was out. I was free. *I was free.*

I looked up, hearing my own relentless sobbing, seeing the boundless heavens through my tears. Past a weave of clouds I could make out the moon, watching us from a bed of stars, so crisp, so far away that I was gripped by vertigo. Flecks of rain fell like diamonds, coating the landscape in molten silver, bringing life to every blade of grass, every flower, every pebble.

I shifted my eyes to the horizon, the skyline of the city burnished by a copper glow as dawn prepared to roll out over the world. Somewhere a bird was singing, the sound so alien to me that I didn't understand what I was hearing.

It was all too much – the sights, the sounds, the smell of the rain, the wet earth beneath my fingers – too much to be real. It *couldn't* be real. I clamped my eyes closed, feeling the universe spin. Then I felt a hand on my shoulder, anchoring me, and risked looking again to see the world that I thought I had lost forever, still laid out in platinum and bronze before me.

'We made it,' sobbed Zee, helping me to my feet.

'We're free. I don't believe it, Alex, we're free.'

'Free, but not safe,' said Simon. 'You hear that?'

I cocked my head, rivers of rainwater running down my throat, parching my thirst. It took me a while to recognise the sound of sirens, the slow whump of helicopter blades, still distant but growing louder.

'Now that we're out there's no hiding it,' Simon went on. 'Can't ignore a prison break when the inmates are on the street.'

The noise was lost beneath more sounds, screaming voices and the clatter of scores of feet on stone. We turned to see an ocean of kids breaking from the main gate, surging towards us, the whites of their eyes like sunlight flecking the tips of waves. Some crashed to the ground, overwhelmed by the existence of a forgotten world, others flew past us, cheering as they streamed out onto the street, flowing towards the safety of the shadows. I saw a number of Skull bandanas amongst them, but no Bodie. I called out his name.

'He's in the control room,' explained a Fifty-Niner, stopping for long enough to suck in some air. 'Sending the elevator down for the next lot. We sorted out a rota so nobody would get left behind.' He looked nervously through the door, back into Furnace. 'I hope they make it in time. Something's trying to come up from below, we heard it. You guys had better scram 'fore it gets loose.' He started to run, then whipped round, grinning. 'Oh, and thanks.' Then he was gone, lost in the sea of bodies.

'He's right,' said Zee. 'We should get out of here. We've done enough.'

'Got that right,' said Simon. 'Anyone know where to go?'

Zee and I shook our heads. With a prison break like this the whole city would soon be in lockdown, every stone turned over by the police, every hiding place probed. Not to mention the fact that the berserker was out there, that the warden and his blacksuits would soon join the hunt, that the rats were probably heading for the surface too.

And I didn't even know what would happen when the nectar inside me ran out. I might already be dead, living on borrowed time.

But none of that mattered. Right now we had made it. We had beaten Furnace. We were free. I cast one final look behind me, at the broken gates of the Black Fort, the dark tunnels that led back underground. It was a fleeting image, but one I will never forget.

I started to turn, laughing so hard it hurt, but I didn't get far before catching a glimpse of the sculptures that decorated the sides of the prison – monstrosities of stone depicting boys like me being punished for their crimes. I screwed my eyes shut, my mind back inside the warden's office, seeing the same figures carved into his desk, hearing that voice on the end of the phone.

I am coming for you.

And suddenly I was on my knees again, Alfred Furnace in my head, his words no longer a whisper but a raging storm that forced blood from my nose, my ears, my eyes.

Do you hear me? it screamed. *I am coming for you.*

I forced my eyes open, the prison now a hulking behemoth that seemed to pull itself from the earth like a giant leech in pursuit of its prey. Against the backdrop of that hallucination I saw another: a fleet of trucks, each carrying a creature that howled with bloodlust, all heading this way. And ushering them forth was a man who was nothing but shadow against the night, but whose skin seemed to crawl as though he had just stepped forth from a maggot-infested grave.

'Alex!' Hands on my collar, trying to pull me up. I blinked, the prison once more just a prison, the vision of Furnace's army nothing more than bile in my throat. I looked at Zee, saw his confusion, and for a second I thought the whole thing had been a waking nightmare brought about by exhaustion. Then I turned to Simon, saw my own expression mirrored in his red-rimmed eyes, knew he'd seen it as well. Of course he had, there was nectar in his blood too, Furnace's poison running through his veins, channelling that inhuman voice.

'Alex,' Zee repeated. 'Jesus, get up. Are you blind?'

He pointed, and I followed his arm to see the first of the police cars speeding down the road, skidding to a halt before the tide of inmates spilling towards it. Zee tugged on my overalls again and this time I responded, getting unsteadily to my feet.

Then we were running, bolting into the rain-slicked streets of the city. And even though we had the prison at our backs, even though the blacksuits were far behind us, even though the loving arms of the rising sun welcomed us into a long-forgotten embrace, I couldn't shake the image of Alfred Furnace from my head.

He was coming for us. He would find us.

And when he did, there would be all hell to pay.

DARE YOU ENTER
FURNACE?

www.escapefromfurnace.com